The Book of Library Secrets

The Secret Books of Gabendoor
Book Four

J. Michael Blumer

Quails Run Publishing
Stillwater, Minnesota

The Book of Library Secrets:
The Secret Books of Gabendoor, Book four.

ISBN 978-0-9900095-3-5

9 8 7 6 5 4 3 2

First Edition May 2012

Second Edition November 2013

Quails Run Publishing

www.quailsrunpublishing.com

To Jane, as always,
and to you readers who keep me motivated.

Acknowledgements

Jennifer, Cris, Maxwell and Faith, you kept the press running through some tough times. I thank you for that and for giving me the opportunity to tell my stories. I wish all of you cold hear more of the great comments I get from readers. They appreciate you. I appreciate you.

The Book of Library Secrets

The Secret Books of Gabendoor
Book Four

J. Michael Blumer

I: Crash

The beeping from Windslow's alarm clock woke him. He looked at the ceiling where the clock, a birthday gift from his stepsister, projected the time in red digits. After a good yawn and stretch, he flipped a switch his dad had installed on his headboard. The beeping stopped. He flipped a second switch. His room lights turned on. "Weird dreams," he mumbled and grabbed the trapeze bar hanging above him. After maneuvering into his wheelchair, he headed for the bathroom.

"Windslow, are you up?" Trish, his stepmother, called from the direction of the kitchen. "We don't want to be late for the first day of school."

"Yes! I'm up," Windslow yelled back. "I don't know about Hillary. Her door's still shut!"

"She beat us all up," Trish answered. "She's helping me make lunches. Get a move on, kiddo."

Because he didn't need to share the bathroom with Hillary this morning, it didn't take him long to get dressed. Back in his room, Windslow grabbed his backpack and magic book bag. He carried most of his things in the magic bag because everything he put in it shrunk down somehow. Just like Hillary's magic pouch, it had almost infinite volume. His bag always stayed the same size. Hillary could stretch or shrink her pouch. Windslow had to be careful though. If he pulled out too many things in a place where others might notice, it could raise suspicion. After stuffing the magic bag inside his backpack, he slung the pack over the handles of his wheelchair. Although things shrunk inside the magic bag, they didn't change weight and the bag felt heavy.

"Whoa, what's this doing in here?" Windslow pulled out the magic *Book of Library Secrets,* which had appeared at the end of Hillary's and his last adventure in Gabendoor. "I thought Hillary had this." He put the book on the floor and used a yardstick from his desk to shove it under his bed. Rolling out to the garage, he let Hillary push his chair up the ramps to the family van. He didn't use his electric wheelchair much anymore, preferring to keep himself in better shape by using his regular chair. Besides, he had met many new friends last year when someone would offer to push him down a hallway at school. This year he was hoping, almost planning, to meet many gorgeous female helpers.

"Wow," Trish said from the driver's seat, "High school. I can't believe I have two kids in high school. You're growing up so--" Trish slammed on the brakes. Both Hillary and Windslow lurched forward, their seat belts tight across their chests. Hillary's backpack slid off the seat next to her and landed on the van floor. A horn honked and tires squealed as the red car, which had darted from a side street, sped away. "Idiot!" Trish yelled out her window.

"Talking about fast," Hillary said. "You're driving a little crazy, mom. And nice example of driver courtesy."

"Ignore her, mom," Windslow said. "She's been studying all that driver training stuff she got."

"You should be studying it too," Trish said. "Bill has already checked into what it will take to equip the van with hand controls."

"Really?" Windslow said. "So cool. Hey, Hillary. I bet I get my permit before you do."

"No chance," she said to him as she grabbed her backpack from the floor and lifted it back to the seat. "Remember, my little stepbrother, I'm two months older than you. You can't beat me unless you find some kind of a time warp to jump through. What's the book doing here?" Hillary bit her lip and winced. "Um... I mean, how dumb of me. I packed... I ah..."

Trish adjusted the rearview mirror. "What's the matter, honey?"

Windslow rescued his sister. "Real smart, Hillary. What other dumb stuff did you pack besides that big dictionary?"

Trish turned the mirror back the way it had been. "Just leave it in the van, Hillary. I'll stick it back in your room."

"Actually, I might need it." Windslow said. "Give it to me. That's one advantage of being in a wheelchair. I don't have to worry about hauling extra stuff around. Here, stick it in my book bag."

Hillary looked at her brother. Silently she mouthed the word, "Thanks." She grabbed the magic *Book of Library Secrets* from the floor. She shrugged when she handed it to him.

Trish had stumbled into their last adventure in Gabendoor. Less than a week after it had ended, she had no memory of being there. Hillary and Windslow were certain the magic, that had blocked their mother's memory once before, had come back. They decided that it would be best to keep their nightly Gabendoor travels secret again.

Windslow looked at the rear view mirror. He couldn't see his stepmother's eyes. Taking a chance that meant she couldn't see him, he pressed the brass latch on the leather strap holding the magic book closed. A soft click sounded. He glanced at the mirror then back to the book. The other magic books of Gabendoor had started out blank as this one had been the last time Hillary and he had checked it. Now there were sketches and words on the pages. When Windslow reached the first blank page, new words formed in a rhythm that matched the beating of his heart.

Wizards' spell at Shimmer-dawn
The time they have is nearly gone.

Bring them now to meet the rest
When they join, there will be death.

Windslow closed the book and shoved it inside his book bag.

There will be death, he said to himself.

Trish screamed. Everything blurred. The van's horn sounded along with two others. Tires screeched. The van lurched as metal crunched and glass broke. The impact threw Windslow forward in his seat. Two more crashes sounded. Both he and Hillary screamed. The van spun nearly all the way around, teetered up on two wheels and crashed back down.

"Mom!" Hillary yelled. Windslow glanced at his sister. Blood ran down her forehead and she clutched her arm. He looked at the front seat. His stepmother lay slumped over the deflated airbag covering the steering wheel. Pieces of glass, shaped like tiny thin ice cubes, covered her hair and the dashboard. He realized the horn still blared.

Windslow undid his seatbelt, but couldn't reach the clamps that held his wheelchair in position. In the background, he heard sirens.

"Help her, Windslow. Help her," his sister cried.

Windslow tried to reach the clamps again. Voices shouted outside and smoke curled up from the van's hood, now a wrinkled sheet of metal twisted and bent to one side. Someone opened the driver's door. Windslow saw a man. "Help my mom!" he yelled.

Someone else pounded on the van's side door. With scrapes and moans, it opened.

"There are two kids inside," someone yelled.

"Mom!" Hillary called again between her sobs.

Windslow looked at a woman and man who climbed into the van.

"Are you hurt?" The woman asked. "Are you hurt?" she asked again.

Windslow shook his head. "No, I don't think so. My sister is. Help our mom first. Please, help our mom!"

"We'll take care of all of you," the man said. "The fire station is right over there. We're with the first responder team. We were outside washing our truck. If you're going to have an accident, this is a good place to have it. Tim, grab something to pry with," the man called over his shoulder to someone. "The wheel chair brackets are jammed."

Another man reached in with a metal bar. Windslow heard something snap and the sound of metal rolling across the floor. Both men grabbed Windslow's wheel chair and lifted him to the ground. The man named Tim, rolled Windslow to the curb and up on the sidewalk. Windslow strained to turn around. He saw the firefighter and woman helping Hillary from the van. He couldn't see what was happening to his mother.

Near the back of the ambulance, a woman asked Windslow some questions about his back, unbuttoned his shirt, and pulled up his pant legs. Two men lifted him onto a stretcher and put him in the ambulance. "What about my mom!" he yelled, but no one answered him.

The same two men lifted another stretcher into the ambulance. Windslow tried to sit up but straps on the stretcher held him down and his chest hurt. He could see it was Hillary.

Blood soaked through a gauze bandage wrapped around her head. Windslow could see what looked like a splint on her arm. "Hillary, what happened to mom?" he said almost yelling. She didn't answer.

A woman climbed inside and the doors shut. The siren sounded. Windslow tried to say something, but his words wouldn't come out. His head pounded and it hurt to take a deep breath. He closed his eyes so the woman wouldn't see him cry. Tears ran down both sides of his face.

ཐཐ

The ride to the hospital was short. People rushed in and out of Windslow's room without saying much that was useful to him. Two cars and a truck had been in the accident, including the van he, his sister, and stepmother had been in. Someone ran a red light while talking on a cell phone. Somebody else swerved and hit another car or something. Windslow wasn't sure and didn't care.

A nurse drew his blood and checked him all over. A doctor poked and prodded Windslow and asked lots of questions. They sent him to another room for x-rays and talked about some sort of scan. Bill, his dad, arrived at the hospital not too long after Windslow and Hillary had. Bill didn't have much information for Windslow. Apparently, Hillary was all right. She had a cut and a bruised shoulder. All his dad would tell him about Trish was what the doctor had said. They were running more tests. Bill said the doctors didn't have much more to say. That's what worried Windslow most; the things no one would say.

After the initial flurry of nurses, doctors and technicians, things settled down. Bill kept moving back and forth between Windslow's room and Hillary's room. Whenever Windslow asked about Trish, Bill just shrugged, shook his head and said he didn't know anything new. He told Windslow not to worry, that she was safe and would be all right.

Windslow had only seen one nurse in the last half hour and figured it was about time for his dad to visit again. The curtain that closed the entrance to the examination room drew back. The metal rings made a scraping sound as the white cloth moved across the pole the curtain hung from.

His dad stood behind a wheelchair. In the chair sat his stepsister.

"Hey, bro. We're twins," Hillary said. "Like my wheels? I hear you're okay except for a cracked rib and a couple bumps."

Windslow smiled. It felt good to see his sister. "So how many stitches?"

"None," Hillary said. "The doctor used some stuff like super glue. I guess scalp wounds bleed a lot, but the cut wasn't very big or deep. Good thing is I won't have much of a scar. My shoulder is really sore. But nothing's broken." Hillary looked up at her step-dad and back at Windslow. "We know some more about mom," she said. "We get to see her in a few minutes."

Windslow leaned forward in his chair. Before he could say anything or ask a question, his father spoke.

"Your mom's doing fine, all things considered. The air bags saved her life. When the van slammed sideways, she took a pretty good blow to her head. That's what all the worry and testing is about. She's been unconscious since the accident. They did a brain scan. Nothing is bleeding, and nothing is blocking blood flow. Those are the two main worries. Now they are treating her for a severe concussion and she's in a coma."

"What? A coma. But... I mean...Why is she..." Windslow stammered. His eyes filled with water.

Hillary put a hand on his leg. "It could be just for a couple hours or a couple days. One of the doctors said that sometimes the body heals itself that way. Let's go see her."

Windslow wiped his eyes and nodded. He took a deep breath and winced. His rib didn't bother him too much unless he breathed in deep or moved his left arm a certain way. "Hey dad..." Windslow hesitated. He had a question he had been afraid to ask all day. "Dad, whose fault was the accident?"

"Not your mom's," Bill said and ruffled Windslow's hair.

Normally it annoyed Windslow when his dad did that, but this time for some reason it felt good.

"Your mom's a hero, or heroine, I guess would be the right word. The whole thing was a chain reaction. It started with someone talking on a cell phone and not paying attention to his driving. He ran a red light and would have hit a couple of kids on bicycles. Your mom swerved to block his truck. She positioned the van to protect the kids and take the brunt of the collision where she sat. The police are talking about giving her some sort of commendation when she's better."

Windslow felt relieved and proud of his mother. That's just the kind of thing she always did. He still had to blink back tears. He had lost his birth mother and grandparents to a drunk driver. He'd dealt with those feelings long ago, but they were trying to push back out.

Bill pulled Windslow back from his thoughts. "I guess you could say that on the bright side, we'll be getting a new van. The old one burned to a crisp. Oh, that reminds me. The doctors said you can go to school tomorrow, but both your backpacks burned in the fire. All you can do is peek in on your mom. She looks like she's sleeping. After we see her, we'll get something to eat. If you two are up to it, we'll stop and replace what you need for school."

2: Library Secrets

In another dimension in time and past the constellation Cassiopeia, D.J, Librarian and Keeper of the Secret Library of Gabendoor, sighed. His large frame barely fit in the chair he sat in. It matched the other chairs spaced neatly around the long trestle table in the library. His sides bulged over the chair arms. His thick legs barely fit under table. He leaned back, sliding his hands across the polished wood. "I'll miss this place," he said and glanced around at the rows and stacks of leather-bound books.

Overhead, a domed, stain glass window, tinted the sunlight that painted the large three-story room with dappled pastel colors. All the books sat neatly in their places, organized by the type of magic they held secrets to. D.J hadn't read many of them. The pages held no words unless someone who knew their secrets, or someone who the book had selected, opened them. When a book wanted to reveal itself to D.J, he would find it sitting open on the table. A name and a spell would be visible on the first page. It was D.J's duty, as keeper of the library, to recite the name and spell. When he did, the words would fade away; the book would close, and then disappear. D.J would make a note in his ledger. After days, weeks, or even years, the book would reappear. D.J would mark the book "returned" in his ledger and put the book back in its proper place, on the proper shelf, in the proper section.

"I won't miss the boredom," D.J said. As he pushed back from the table and stood, the sound of the chair legs scraping on the floor seemed loud in the otherwise silent room.

He looked at the large grandfather clock at the far end of the library. He knew it was time. He had known by the stars. He had checked the stars last night. The clock only confirmed what he had read in the changed night sky. The clock had no numbers on its dial, only magical symbols for seasons and centuries, events and people. The four clock hands held round discs for planets and stars. You could watch them and never see them move. They didn't mark minutes and hours. They measured magic. They measured progress. They measured whatever one of the magic books wanted to judge.

D.J walked to the middle of the room and reached up to the third shelf. The two books he needed sat together. He ran his finger along the gold lettered names embossed in the spines, *Windslow Summerfield* and *Hillary Windgate-Summerfield.* He took the books off the shelf and placed them in the center of the table.

For his next task, he had to use the open staircase at the end of the room and move across the second level catwalk to reach the shelf he needed. He removed the books, *Haggerwolf the Elder, Fernbark the Benevolent* and *Larkstone the Compassionate.*

D.J climbed to the third level. The catwalk creaked with each step D.J took. He rarely climbed to the top level. Rather than shelves, wide bookcases held the volumes. The bookcase he needed was different from the others. This case glowed. A soft brown light came from the wood, almost making the case look out of focus. This bookcase held the original magic books of Gabendoor. He needed the second, third, and fourth books.

D.J gave another sigh as he fondly stroked his fingers down the spines of each book. Removing these three books would be the hardest thing he had ever done as Keeper of the Secret Library. Slowly he slid the books from where they had sat for hundreds of years, *The Book of Molly Folly Sallyforth*, *The Book of Tillie Truly Sallyforth* and *The Book of Nelly Never Sallyforth*.

Back at the table, D.J sat each of the eight books on its end with the front facing outward. Carefully he moved them together to form an octagon. He looked over his shoulder at the clock to make certain he had the books in the proper order. With a nod and another sigh, he stepped back.

The glowing colors from the skylight swirled. The individual colored pieces of glass turned soft and blended together, like paint stirred by an artist's brush.

D.J felt a rush of outside air when the swirl of light opened like the iris of an eye, the eye of the Secret Library, the eye of Gabendoor. Soft, gentle, blue wisps of magic flowed from the shelved books, bathing the room in their glow. The eight books on the table shook and rattled as if the soul of Gabendoor awoke. The books lifted from the table and spun, blurring together. The whirl of leather and pages shrank, condensed and turned to amber. The shaking stopped. The whirling stilled. Where the circle of books had been, now sat a large jewel, five fingers in diameter, cut and faceted like an amber diamond.

D.J lifted the jewel. It was lighter than he had expected but looked exactly as the picture that had appeared in his book of instructions. He admired its beauty and sparkle, wondering why it was named the "ratStone?" It wasn't his job to understand the riddles of the books, but to carry out their bidding. With an underhand throw, he tossed the jewel upward, toward the open skylight. His throw wasn't hard. It didn't need to be. The magic in the stone launched it out of the library. D.J knew from the book's instructions, the stone would arch over Gabendoor, selecting a landing spot at random. Fate and chance would determine if it were ever found. That worried him. One fate could lead to death, yet the other could lead to the end of the Sallyforth Triplets.

Nearly finished with his part, D.J removed a book that had sat on a stone pedestal for three hundred years. He placed it on the floor and stepped back. The book opened. Pages tore free, filling the air with parchment and the sounds of ripping and rustling paper. Magic tore the sheets into round and oval shapes of different sizes. The torn paper began stacking, one sheet atop the other, quickly forming an odd shaped column. A second column formed close to the first. As the stacks grew higher, they leaned toward each other and touched. D.J recognized the shape as the merged column rose higher. When the book was empty, the shape was complete. The paper had created a man, and clearly mimicked every detail of both the person and his clothes.

D.J approached and whispered in the paper man's ear. "Run! Your magic isn't strong enough. The magic will trap you again. Flee to the east. Run now!" Not sure what role the parchment man would play, D.J gave it one last look.

It was now time for his final task. A shelf near the doorway held a thick book with worn edges. It was his book, *The Book of Derrick Jones.* D.J placed it on the floor and watched it open. He checked the clock one last time. The hands showed that an "event" had happened on Earth, the planet linked to the Children of the Summer Wind. Not only were their lives at stake in Gabendoor, another life was at risk on Earth. Mixed feelings of sadness, adventure and pride, tumbled in his stomach. He took a breath, blew it out and stepped onto the open book.

With a whoosh, D.J's form became a cloud of blue magic the book drew into itself. Pages fanned and bold letters burst forth on the once blank pages. Filled with the legend of D.J, the covers snapped shut. The book floated out the library door and hovered briefly. Accelerating as it shot into the sky, the book cleared the treetops. Even in daylight, the book left a trail of light like a meteor flying upward. With a final burst of light, it disappeared from sight on its journey to the stars. That evening, changes in the ancient constellations would fuel more talk and speculation of the legend. Next to the three constellations that had appeared the previous night would be the "Keeper of Knowledge." Gone would be the "Beguiler."

With everything in place, the Secret Library's doors flung open with a boom of wood against stone. Nearby trees shook and swayed. The blue light of Gabendoor's magic bathed the parchment man. The tall form moved an arm as paper turned to flesh and bone. It took a small step forward to keep balance. The light blinked out. No longer paper, Dreadlore breathed in deeply and stretched; weary and still groggy from his long magic sleep. He turned, eyes blinking against the sunlight. Memories of the struggle that had turned him to parchment gripped him. His next thought was the one planted in his mind by D.J's words. Dreadlore ran from the library and headed east.

ഗ്ര

The residents of Wartville, Eldervale, and other villages of Gabendoor stepped from their cottages to gaze at the night sky. At the edge of Lake Shimmerdawn, Haggerwolf, Fernbark and Larkstone, the three last wizards of Gabendoor, stood silently. Moonlight shimmered on the water like silver butterfly wings rippled by the slight breeze.

"The stars are faint, but they're back," Haggerwolf, the elder of the last three wizards of Gabendoor said. The gentle wind puffed at his long white beard. He pulled his dark blue robe closer around his chest. As the cloth moved, the outlines of forest animals embroidered into the fine linen seemed almost real.

Fernbark and Larkstone, both stout and shorter than Haggerwolf, nodded in unison. Fernbark stood with both hands hidden in the pockets of his robe, similar in shape to Haggerwolf's, but green with embroidered plants and trees.

Larkstone pointed at the sky. The broad sleeve of his light blue robe and its embroidered fish and seashell patterns slid down his arm and bunched at his elbow. "Daughter of Secrets," he said. "She would be the constellation on the right. The Maiden of Truth is in the center if I remember correctly."

"That's the right order," Fernbark said. "The Child of Intuition is on the left."

Haggerwolf turned away from the lake. "This isn't good. I didn't expect the stars to appear during our lifetime. I knew someone would need to deal with them eventually. I didn't think it would be us. I don't want it to be us." In the dark, he headed up the beach for the path to Larkstone's cottage. Larkstone and Fernbark followed.

At the path into the woods, the torch they had propped in the sand flickered, casting a mix of yellow light and black shadows across the trees bordering the trail. Larkstone grabbed the torch and held it high to light the way as he and the other two wizards walked. "By morning everyone on Gabendoor will know the time has come," he said.

"True," Fernbark said. "People will invent even more versions of the legend than there are now."

"That's part of the challenge," Haggerwolf said. "Chaos, doom and death are in all the versions. It's too close to harvesting season for this to be happening now. People will be going hungry. The legend points at many futures and countless paths. Only one route leads to hope. The burden of finding that route now falls on us whether we want it or not." He shook his head and continued up the path.

The giant pepperwort fronds hung in peaceful slumber, not bothered by the passing wizards and their light or conversation. The stout and age-wrinkled limbs of the flute-bean trees arched down as if curious about the somber conversation drifting to them in the still night air. Torch-cast shadows of the branches scampered and danced as if playing between the wizards' steps.

"I don't want that burden," Haggerwolf continued. "And I don't want the burden of putting Hillary's and Windslow's lives in jeopardy."

"None of us want that," Larkstone said. He stopped at the door to his cottage and turned to face the others. "All the versions of the legend hint at choices. We could choose to leave the Children of the Wind out of this."

Fernbark folded his arms and pursed his lips. He gave a sigh. "That choice is part of the path, isn't it?"

"I believe so," Haggerwolf said. "Hillary and Windslow are the Children of the Summer Wind. We've needed them for every crisis we've faced so far. We probably need them this time."

Larkstone snuffed out the torch and opened his cottage door, letting light from the doorway join the warm glow peeking through the two windows. He paused at the entrance and softly recited a verse from one version of the legend.

Fright town
Night town
Things that aren't right town.

Night death
Right death
Choice becomes plight death.

"I was thinking the same thing," Haggerwolf said. "It's connected to the Three Guardians. I don't think we are those guardians. No one would name three constellations after wizards. It can't be Windslow and Hillary. There are only two Children of the Wind."

"I agree," Fernbark said. "But that doesn't change what we must decide tonight. Only one spell will work to bring them here at night and tonight is the only time we can use it. I'm afraid Windslow and Hillary could face death if we do cast it. Gabendoor will be in even greater danger if we don't'."

Chapter 3: Night Spell

After missing the first day of school, starting on the second day made Windslow more than a little nervous. Bill put Windslow's collapsible wheelchair in the car trunk for the drive to school. Bill planned to stay at the hospital all day and promised to let both Hillary and Windslow know if he learned anything new about Trish. Windslow noticed his dad took a different route to school, avoiding the accident scene. Part of Windslow wanted to see it. Another part of him was glad about his father's decision.

When his father dropped them off, Windslow felt strange with his new backpack and how light it felt compared to the one that burned in the fire. He would miss his magic book bag, but had to admit he didn't feel very bad about its contents. Right now, dream-slipping and Gabendoor were the last things on his mind.

The second day of school hadn't gone as Windslow had hoped. There were lots of pretty girls who hurried past him. He didn't know them from last year and none offered to help or even said, "Hi." When someone he knew offered to give him a push, he declined. Everyone seemed to know about the accident and said nice things about his mom.

Some of his new teachers he knew by reputation. In every class, there were students he knew from last year. One person he hadn't expected to be in his science class was Molly Folly Sallyforth.

"Hi, Windso," she said and took a seat next to him at the lab desk. "I sorry about your mommy. This not a time to worry. This going to be pretty fun class. I be your partner." The small triplet sister from Gabendoor, who never seemed to change or get older, gave him a big smile.

"Molly, what are you doing here? I thought you were still a year behind us."

"Nope. We take extra catsup classes this summer. Nelly and Tillie catsup too."

Windslow smiled. "It's catch up, not catsup. Catsup is that red stuff you put on a hamburger."

Magic had saved the three Sallyforth triplets from death in Gabendoor and transported them to Earth at the end of his and Hillary's first adventure in Gabendoor. Molly was probably his best friend now. Sometimes other students made fun of the way the sisters spoke or dressed. Identical triplets, except for hair color, they all wore the same outfits nearly every day. Whenever someone did tease them, somehow the girls would turn things around and either make a new friend or embarrass the person who had picked on them. In Gabendoor, the girls always had been, and probably always would be, a mystery. They were somehow linked to the Secret Library of Gabendoor. The library was the source of each magic book that had taken Hillary and him to Gabendoor.

"We have lots a-fun in this class. I gonna make biggie experiments," Molly said, interrupting his thoughts. "We need a have fun here because bad things starting in Gabendoor again."

Windslow looked at her. "I don't think I want to go to Gabendoor for awhile. Can you keep me from dream-slipping somehow? And besides, the *Book of Library Secrets* burned up in the van."

The bell rang, signaling the start of class. He and Molly sat at the front desk so Windslow didn't have a chance to get an answer. During class, Molly seemed strangely quiet. When class ended, she gave him a hug and said, "Don't worry. I take care of you. You still my best-ist boyfriend." She rushed out of the room without saying anything else. Windslow opened his backpack to stuff his science book inside. "This can't be," he muttered. Inside was his magic book bag. Inside that was the *Book of Library Secrets.*

He didn't see Molly or her sisters the rest of the day. After his last class, he stopped at the office and used the phone to call his father. There was no news about his stepmother and Bill said he'd be at school after soccer practice to pick up Windslow and his sister. Windslow headed for the athletic department. He had signed up to assist with the girls' soccer team. Hillary had made the tryouts and Windslow figured that helping would be more fun than just waiting for his stepsister to finish the school day. Before his stepmother's accident, he had thought it would be another chance to find a girlfriend.

After soccer practice ended, he finally had a chance to tell Hillary what Bill had said. Hillary told Windslow she had talked to Bill too and got the same information. She was surprised to learn about Windslow's magic book bag and the *Book of Library Secrets.* She checked her own backpack and found her magic zipper pouch inside.

Bill picked Hillary and Windslow up in the gymnasium parking lot. He didn't have much to say on the drive to the hospital. In Trish's room, she lay on her back in bed. A tube ran from a hanging plastic bottle to a needle in her arm. A monitor sounded a soft beep each time her heart beat. Both Windslow and Hillary spoke to her and held her hand. She offered no response. Windslow found it hard to look at her and stared at the window. The sound of the beep seemed louder and louder. He tried to ignore it. The pitch and volume rose even higher, echoing in his head. He pushed his wheelchair away from his mother's bed and clamped both hands over his ears. "Stop it," he yelled and rolled into the hallway.

Both Hillary and Bill ran after him. In the hallway, Windslow sat with his knees pushed against the wall to his mother's room.

"Let me do this, Dad," Windslow heard Hillary say. Windslow started to cry when she knelt down beside him.

"Reminds you of your real mom, doesn't it," Hillary said softly.

Windslow nodded.

"All we can do is hope and pray. Sitting here doesn't do anything to help her. We need to take dad home so he gets some sleep. Until mom is back on duty, we need to take care of dad and take care of each other."

On the ride home, Bill stopped at a drive-through restaurant. They all ate as he drove. No one said much of anything. Windslow and Hillary went to bed early. This night neither hoped they would dream-slip.

ꟷ

Moonlight filtered through Windslow's bedroom window. He lay deep in sleep, blankets pulled up tight against his chin. Parts of his wheelchair blocked the soft glowing light, casting faint shadows across the carpet to mimic the chair's wheels, backrest and handgrips. No shadow formed around the magic book bag lying on the wheelchair's seat. The bag added its own glow to that from the midnight moon.

The bag twisted and slid until it rested flat on the wheelchair seat. Windslow stirred, but did not wake. He mumbled the word, "Cassiopeia."

Something inside the bag moved and grew, its rough shape hinted at by the cloth draped over it. The magic fabric outlined a cube shape, the size of a child's wooden alphabet block. The bag puffed and draped again. More forms grew beneath the first. The bag stilled, now hiding a pyramid shape with stepped sides.

Clouds raced the night wind and dashed across the moon, temporarily blocking its light. Inside Windslow's room, the glow around his book bag did not fade. The glow detached itself from the cloth to swirl into a soft transparent shape that floated above Windslow.

Windslow's head twisted one-way then the other. His red hair lay at odd angles from his restless troubled sleep. His eyelids twitched. "Dreadlore," he said, his voice a whisper. His breaths came fast. He licked his lips. His arms twitched. He muttered the name again.

The magic light brushed gently across Windslow's forehead. He stilled. His breathing slowed, settling into a long steady rhythm of deeper sleep. Moonlight once more spread through his window. The magic glow joined it, changing the light from cold white to a warm peaceful glow. On Windslow's wheelchair, his magic book bag now lay flat and empty.

In the next room, his sister slept, her room dark with curtains pulled across her windows. A drawer in her desk slid open. Inside floated her magic zipper pouch, it too a gift from the wizards of Gabendoor. The brass zipper-pull moved slowly, opening the blue cloth pouch. A burst of sparkling, silver, pearl-sized lights launched upward to float in the darkness of her room. Arranged in a pattern, they twinkled like tiny stars.

"Cassiopeia," Hillary mumbled in her sleep.

The silver lights doubled and rearranged themselves. Hillary moaned softly and rolled to her side. "Maiden of Truth," she said, the words barely audible.

Again, the lights changed. Hillary whispered, "Daughter of Secrets." She wiggled closer to the edge of her bed.

The lights moved. "Child of Intuition," Hillary said. She wiggled, twisted to her stomach, and let her arm dangle over the edge of her mattress. The leather bound *Book of Library Secrets* floated out from under her bed. Hillary's fingertips dragged across the leather cover as the book moved. "Dreadlore," she said, her whisper a bit louder. She jerked her arm away and shoved it under her pillow.

Clear of her bed, the book floated upward and settled on Hillary's desk. The brass clasp on the binding strap clicked. The cover opened. A page turned. Six sliver lights streaked from the ceiling of her room to the aged yellow paper. Another page turned, more lights merged with the book. When the last of the lights had made their marks on a page, the book's cover closed. Hillary's bedroom returned to darkness. Her breathing calmed. Her long red hair settled softly across her flushed and freckled face. The zipper pouch closed. The desk drawer softly shut.

ꕥ

In center of the table, a candle illuminated the kitchen in Larkstone's cottage. It cast faint shadows and moving patterns of yellow light across the three wizards.

Haggerwolf lowered his arms as he finished the complicated third part to the spell that would summon Hillary and Windslow and would remove the constraints of celestial time from the magic of dream-slipping. "Well, it's done," he said. Joining the other two wizards, he sat down and placed his wand on the checkered tablecloth.

Fernbark sat with his head down and stared at his hands while he ran his wrinkled thumb back and forth across the smooth wood of his magic wand. "I don't like this. We've put them in great danger."

A burst of air pushed the candle flame on its side as wood from the cottage door splintered and glass shattered.

The three wizards jumped from their chairs. Haggerwolf instinctively grabbed for his wand. His fingers touched it. At the same time, a rush of bodies pushed into the kitchen, knocking the table over and pushing him backward. He toppled over in his chair. He struggled to stand but a shoulder slammed into him and he fell back to the floor, his attacker on top of him. With no wand, Haggerwolf used his fists but only struck one blow before hands grabbed his wrists and twisted his arms. He stopped struggling when a cloth bag was yanked over his head and a cord tightened around his neck. A bristly rope replaced the hands holding his wrists. Haggerwolf winced as another layer of rope wrapped around the first and cinched tighter.

The sounds of other struggles ended. Someone grabbed Haggerwolf under the arms and sat him upright on the floor.

"Slide back against the wall," a voice ordered.

Haggerwolf scooted backward until he felt his shoulders hit something solid. He felt something else. Long and slim, at first he thought it might be a piece of wood from the shattered door. He twisted just a bit and felt between his bottom and the floor. He tried not to show any reaction when he recognized the feel of his magic wand. Haggerwolf had no way to conceal it and trying to cast a spell now would be risky and foolish. He broke a small piece off the thick end, coughing loud to mask the *snap*. He kept the wand in one hand, just in case he had an opportunity to use it. He held the broken piece in his tightly closed fist. The inch length of wand would only be capable of powering several small spells.

Someone yanked the bag from Haggerwolf's head. The cord tangled in his gray-white beard and pulled out a tuft of hair. Haggerwolf made a face but kept silent. A lantern hung from a broken piece of window shutter. Fernbark and Larkstone sat tied sitting against the wall on either side of him. Two men stood watching. Two others lifted the table up and righted the overturned chairs. All four men wore purple hoods that looked like pillowcases with holes torn out for their eyes and noses. The hoods had wet spots where they covered each man's mouth. The wet cloth fluttered when the man in front of Haggerwolf unrolled a scroll and read from it.

"Under edict of Dreadlore your use of magic is hereby suspended. There is no right of appeal. This decision is final. If you violate this edict, you will be severely punished. Such punishment may include death."

"You're insane," Larkstone said. "Dreadlore doesn't exist. He died hundreds of years ago. If you're some half-baked, overzealous, fruitcake follower of his who dusted off his moth eaten purple hood of loyalty and think you can come in here and--"

A kick to his stomach silenced Larkstone. He slumped to his side, took a moment to recover and wiggled to straighten himself.

"Dreadlore, the Beguiler, has returned," the hooded man answered. "You know how to read the stars. So do we." He turned to the man next to him. "Find their wands. Search the cottage. Take anything that looks like it could be used for magic."

Two of the men tore apart the cottage, dumping drawers, flipping rugs and overturning pots. Anything movable, they searched and tossed into one corner. The man who searched the wizards didn't comment on the shortened state of one wand and handed the three to the man giving orders. When the search finished, the leader took a small box out of his pocket and opened its lid. He removed a large seedpod that looked like a fuzzy brown clove of garlic. A small puff of fine orange powder rose from the pinched bud at its top. He turned to the wizards. "Tell us where the Children of the Wind will appear when they dream-slip into your cottage."

"I'll show you," Haggerwolf said. He tried to get up but couldn't.

The hooded leader helped him stand.

"You're in my way," Haggerwolf said and the man stepped back. Haggerwolf stepped sideways until he was in front of Larkstone and Fernbark. He opened his palm, hoping the other two wizards would see the broken piece of wand. He clenched his fist and walked over near the steps leading to the second level. "Use your spellpod there," he said and pointed with his foot.

The leader bent and squeezed the seedpod several times. Each squeeze puffed a small dusting of orange powder into the air. The powder settled to the wood floor outlining the shapes of where Windslow and Hillary would wake from their dream-slip.

One of the men stepped outside and returned with a large canvas bag. The contents clinked with the sound of metal. He dumped the bag, revealing four sets of shackles and chains. Kneeling, he pried open each metal shackle until a click sounded. When they were open, he positioned one set carefully on the outlines of both pairs of ankles. He positioned the other sets on the wrist outlines. With one finger, he lightly touched one of the shackles. It snapped closed like a sprung bear trap. He took a key from his pocket, reset the lock and put the metal cuff back into position.

"Ha!" Haggerwolf said, "Feel stick. Unclick."

"What did you just say?" the leader asked and grabbed Haggerwolf's arm.

Larkstone answered. "He slurs his words when he's scared. He said, unlock those and he's feeling sick. I'd let him sit down before he upchucks his dinner all over that fancy hood."

"Shut up," one of the men said and gave Larkstone a kick.

Haggerwolf jerked his arm away from the leader. "Closed eyes. Ropes tie."

The leader punched Haggerwolf in the stomach doubling him over. "I said no magic and no tricks either!" he yelled.

Haggerwolf gasped for air and fell to his side. Pulling his knees up to his chest, he rolled slightly until his hands touched one of the cuffs. He tucked the small piece of wand against it and rolled back to his other side.

"Idiot!" Fernbark shouted out. "He said you've messed up our cottage and Hillary and Windslow will be suspicious. They'll know something's wrong."

The leader spun around. "Who's the idiot? You may as will leave them a note. As soon as the Children of the Wind dream-slip here, they'll be under arrest, just like you three. They'll be shackled and you're the ones who helped us do it. If this fool hadn't helped," he said, pulling Haggerwolf to his feet, "I might have run out of spellpod spores before finding where they'd appear."

"Old fools," one of the other men said. "That's why Dreadlore needs to take control of wizardry. You three may be the only wizards left, but you're ineffective, you're useless. He should strip you of the few abilities you have left. He has the power to turn his true followers into wizards. We'll be his first group. Maybe Dreadlore will give us this cottage. It's a mess but we can use you three as servants to clean it up."

The four men laughed.

"Get them up and take them to Eldervale," the leader said, nodding his head toward the bound wizards. "I'll wait for the wind children and bring them after they materialize."

Haggerwolf moved to the other wizards. “All I can say is suspicion grows. Hillary knows.”

Quickly Fernbark said, “He means Hillary will be suspicious when she wakes up in shackles. You don’t need to hit him again.”

The men laughed again, grabbed their lantern and pushed the wizards toward the doorway. The leader relit the candle, placed it back on the table and settled into one of the chairs to wait for the Children of the Wind.

4: ratStone

Windslow and Hillary began their dream-slips nearly at the same time. Neither one had prepared their backpacks, but both bags traveled with them as always. Hillary was the first to open her eyes to see herself soaring through the universe, watching planets and suns pass by as she raced to the distant planet of Gabendoor. She looked back and could see her stepbrother not far behind. He waved at her and pointed at a distant comet. Hillary nodded and looked back ahead. She spotted the constellation Cassiopeia at the edge of the Milky Way and closed her eyes. Once she passed the W shaped group of stars, she would awake in Gabendoor.

It barely seemed an instant when she felt herself lying on a hard floor. Gravity replaced the calm weightless feeling of dream-slipping. She opened her eyes and heard several soft *clicks*. "What the..." she said when she sat up. " Windslow!" she yelled. "Watch out!"

Her warning didn't help. Windslow sat beside her, bound by metal cuffs and chains as she was. The sound of a chair scraping across the floor grabbed her attention. A man wearing a strange purple hood stood by the kitchen table. He unrolled a sheet of parchment and read.

"By declaration of Dreadlore, you are deemed insurgents. Your presence on Gabendoor is considered a contamination. You will be detained until your trial, after which you will be purified." He rolled up the scroll and stuffed it inside his shirt.

"What's going on?" Windslow asked. "Get these chains off of us and who trashed Larkstone's cottage?"

"Answer my brother," Hillary said, her voice sharp and loud. "Who's Dreadlore? What do you mean we'll be purified after a trial? We're not guilty of anything and it sounds like you already have a verdict."

The man picked up a six-foot long pole from the floor. He used one end to prod Hillary. "Dreadlore wouldn't charge you if you weren't guilty. The trial is a fair way to determine how he'll purify you. The usual way is with fire. Any more questions will cost you a bit of pain. The more questions, the more anguish." He rapped the end of his pole against Hillary's shin.

"Ouch!" she snapped. "You'll regret this."

The man rapped her on the shin again.

"That wasn't a question," Windslow said. "It was a promise. Where are the wizards?"

The man jabbed the pole into Windslow's stomach. "Two questions cost twice the pain. I suggest you both keep quiet."

Hillary felt her cheeks burn as adrenalin fueled her growing anger. She moved her hand and felt something that made her look down. She saw a small piece of somber-wood. From the small animals carved into the stick, she recognized it as a piece of Haggerwolf's wand. His voice sounded in her mind. The metal cuffs around her and Windslow's ankles and wrists clicked and fell away.

"Closed eyes. Ropes tie," she said. The hooded man stumbled backward, shut his eyes and slumped to the floor. Near the food pantry, a cabinet door sprang open. A coil of rope snaked out, wrapped itself around the man's legs and wrists, and tied itself into a triple loop knot.

"What's going on?" Windslow asked and tried to stand. His legs wouldn't cooperate and he stayed sitting.

Hillary held up the piece of wand. "Haggerwolf left this for us with some dormant spells. They started to activate when I touched it. I heard him say a bunch of stuff in my head. I know what to do. Roll over."

Windslow twisted until he lay on his stomach. Hillary touched the wand to the lower part of his back. "There," she said. "That should do it. Your crutches are by the fireplace. We need to get out of here."

Windslow staggered to the fireplace where his magic crutches sat. Shrunk to a few inches in length, he pulled on the ends to stretch them back to full size. Both he and Hillary grabbed their backpacks and hurried out of Larkstone's cottage.

"What's the deal," Windslow said. "It's dark out. We've never dream-slipped here in the dark before, except that one time you did. And that time it took some special magic."

"All I got from Haggerwolf's message was something about everything in Gabendoor being out of order. Let's get going," Hillary said and started walking.

Windslow moved after her. "Where to, and who is Dreadlore, and who's the guy in the purple pillowcase?"

"I don't know," Hillary said. "I mean about Dreadlore, the purple guy and that stuff. Haggerwolf's message said we were in great danger. We're supposed to run and hide and absolutely stay away from Eldervale."

"Okay," Windslow said. "So like I asked. Where too?"

"Eldervale, of course," Hillary answered and looked back at her brother.

"Cool," he said and grinned.

ꕥ

Hillary and Windslow had decided to stay off the main path that would take them to Eldervale. They stayed ten to fifteen feet off the road and in the woods. That way they could parallel the route and be quick to hide should someone happen along that they didn't want to meet. The moon was bright and lit up the road, but did little help to let Hillary and Windslow move through the trees and brush. Hillary chanced a small spell to cast narrow lights from the toes of her tennis shoes. She felt quite proud of herself for including words in the spell that would only make the light visible to her and her brother. Although the spell seemed to work fine, Windslow, walking behind Hillary, grumbled and complained about not seeing sticks or roots that nearly tripped him up several times. Hillary had her own complaints about Windslow constantly stumbling into her from behind. They tried to keep their comments soft but several times "watch it," "be careful," "that was my foot," and "do you have to keep doing that," filtered out through the trees in slightly louder voices.

The night air seemed unsettled. Several times the wind came up, blowing strongly through the trees, bending branches and making eerie whispering sounds. As suddenly as it started, the wind would stop and the sounds of crickets and other night insects would break the silence. Windslow noticed the moon first looked full, then half, then full again. He decided it was just clouds and tricks of light and shadow. Hillary reminded him of Haggerwolf's voice saying that Gabendoor was out of order. Twice it seemed dawn was coming. The sky turned orange-blue and they could see without Hillary's shoe lights. After five minutes of dawn, the sky turned dark again. The third time, the light stayed and grew. The air warmed and dew formed on the grass and plants.

"It looks like it might stay morning this time," Windslow said. "How close do you think we are to Eldervale?"

"I have no idea," Hillary answered. "Maybe we should have some sort of plan for when we get there. I still have no clue what's going on."

"Why do you think Haggerwolf doesn't want us to go there?"

Hillary shrugged her shoulders. "Beats me. I'd guess because that's where the danger is. You know how protective all three of the wizards are, especially Haggerwolf. I wish we knew if that's where he, Larkstone and Fernbark are. I wish Molly and her sisters were here too."

"Yah," Windslow said and bumped into his sister's back again.

"Stop doing that. Watch where you're going."

"Sorry. So many things aren't making sense. Usually the Sallyforth girls show up here right away. They always have a plan if the wizards don't. Why are we even here? I think we could use some help. Those stupid books are never very useful until after everything's happened. That's about the only time you can figure out what they mean."

"The book," both Hillary and Windslow said at the same time.

Windslow un-shouldered his backpack, pulled out his magic book bag, and from that, the magic *Book of Library Secrets.* Hillary knelt on the ground beside him. Together they looked for new writing.

"There is more stuff," Hillary said and pushed closer to her brother. "Look." She read the words aloud.

A special stone moves time and space.
Each of eight must find their place.
Three will go and three will stay.
The other two will find the way.

"There's more on the next page," Windslow said and read the words.

Start from the middle and read to both ends
ratStone begins where will it end?
Strength from a sister and love from a brother
Should they survive could bring hope for a mother.

He finished reading and flipped several more blank pages before shutting the book. "Well like usual, it's not much help, but it's saying something about us and mom I think. If it is, then this is going to be our most dangerous and important test in Gabendoor."

"Well," Hillary said, "at least we know it's something about a stone, but there are a lot of stones in Gabendoor. This one is obviously important for lots of reasons. We have to figure this out and find that stone as fast as we can.

Windslow flipped the book back open. "Hillary, look at how *ratStone* is spelled. It starts with a small letter and has a capital S in the middle. Usually those kinds of things aren't mistakes. They mean something. Maybe there are some more words." Windslow fanned through the pages.

"That's enough, Windslow," Hillary said and grabbed the book from him. "We'll have to figure it out later. I know you're upset. You know she's my mother more than she is yours. Don't you think I'm worried about her too?"

Windslow yanked the book out of her hands. "What do you mean, she's more your mother? Just because my mother... Just because she's..." Windslow squeezed his eyes shut.

"Oh, crud-o," Hillary said. "That was really a stupid thing for me to say. Windslow, I know about your real mom. I know she died when you were little. I thought I knew how you must have felt and still feel. I was wrong. But, I'm beginning to understand now. I'm trying to stay strong," Hillary said, her own eyes welling up with tears. "But I'm really having a hard time. I don't want to think about mom. When I do, it starts to hurt inside really bad. That kind of hurt is new to me. Now I know you've been hurt the same way before and even worse. Feeling it again must be horrible."

"Hillary," Windslow said, now both eyes streaming with tears. "I don't think I can handle it again. I don't think Dad can either. She is your mom, but I love her too. You're lucky. You're part of her. And you're like her too," he said and managed a small smile. "You're as stubborn as she is and just as smart. Well, maybe almost as smart."

Hillary wiped her eyes and gave a big sigh. "If she were here, she'd want to know why we are wasting our time feeling dopey. She was a princess of Gabendoor at one time. Somehow, she's still linked to this place, like it or not. Too many things are happening all at once. I think they're related. And like you said, we need to figure things out in a hurry. We won't get that done sitting here. We need to find the Wizards. I think we need them more than ever before."

ᘓᘐ

Heart-Thorn forest held many secrets. Brave travelers found no paths. Trees and plants grew as near to each other as they could tolerate. Some plants freely intertwined their sprouts or branches. Others simply crowded tight to fill in gaps. Vines, unwanted in other forests, found willing hosts to twist and tangle with; creeping from one plant to another, trailing a web of rope-like stems and leaves. Few secrets stay forever hidden. On this night, one secret now stirred, awakening, and ready to reveal itself.

This secret lay deep within Heart-Thorn in a place trees had never found a grip to grow and tower up to cast gray shadows back to earth. Giant ferns, moss, and tangled vines draped to hide a form beneath them that rose from all sides to peak at the center. Atop the peak stood four stone rectangles, each ten feet tall, narrower than a man, and thicker than a child. Thrust up and clear of vegetation they monitored the stars. Three of the stone watchers stood close together facing the north sky. The fourth stood, its back turned the other way. It watched the south.

A hole bored through each slab's top cradled a rough-cut colored jewel; black for the first watcher, green for the second, orange for the third and blood red for the fourth. The jewels pulsed faint light, a greeting to changes each stone saw in the night sky. The black jewel timed its pulses to match the faint twinkling from stars that formed the Child of Intuition. The green stone glowed steady, mimicking the Maiden of Truth. The orange stone kept its light soft to match the stars of the Daughter of Secrets. Behind them, the bloodstone pulsed, its light growing and dimming like a slow beating heart. Like the others, it linked to a constellation, its name the Beguiler. Tonight the time had come for Heart-Thorn forest to reveal more secrets. For centuries a name lay hidden, incised in a block of stone forming the temple that lay beneath the four watchers, obscured beneath the carpet of moss, sheltered under the tangled vines.

The ground rumbled. Trees shook. The single tier of blocks that formed the pyramid of watchers stayed steady. Slowly the blocks rose. Stretched tight, the tangled vines strained and snapped. A second tier of blocks pushed up to form a new base, wider and broader than the first. The ground rumbled again. A third layer of the hidden temple rose from the ground, ripping away the last of the vines. More layers rose. Long dormant magic awakened. Black flames burst from ancient spells, licking at the moss, burning away all traces of nature. Flames gnawed at the trees and undergrowth, burning clear a field surrounding the temple. Winds fanned the flames, then snuffed them out and dusted away the ash. The temple of

Aberratia gleamed, restored to its glory and awaiting the name carved in the stone, *Dreadlore,* its master.

ꕥ

Dreadlore ran from the Secret Library. He looked back and saw its image waver like heat waves on a summer day. Blurring more, the image vanished in a blue flash. More forest was all he saw. He slowed, stopped and listened for any sound that might be a telltale sign of danger. All he heard were normal woodland sounds. He rested, leaning against a tree and sorted through his memories. The last he remembered was the battle on the day he found the Secret Library. Many wizards had died that day. That didn't matter to Dreadlore. What mattered was control of volumes of magic books that were almost his. Somehow, the library sensed the danger it was in. Dreadlore remembered the magic freezing him. He remembered the spell beginning its work, turning him to paper.

Dreadlore shook his head, as if it would clear the fog still shrouding his memory. "It was magic," he muttered and smashed his hand against a tree. "Someone put those words in my head."

Dreadlore turned and retraced his steps. After only a few yards, the grass tramped by his feet, and small broken twigs that had marked his trail, disappeared. Brush thickened as he watched, blocking his way. "It's that cursed library!" he yelled, not caring if anyone heard him. He fumbled in his cloak and was relieved to find his wand still in an inside pocket. He pointed it at a large tree. Flames leapt from the trunk as magic burned a large letter X, marking it as if branded. Dreadlore walked another ten feet and branded a second tree to mark his path. He looked back for the first X. He didn't see it. He looked for the X he had just burned and saw the last of it fade as fresh bark covered the burn. "I'll still find you!" he screamed. "I found you once. I'll find you again. I'll clear this whole forest if I have to!"

Frustrated, he looked up at the sun to get his bearings, and headed south for Aberratia. His immediate plan was simple. He'd find what was left of his followers. It would be easy enough to find the Sallyforth Sisters. They always showed up where there was trouble, and he *was* trouble. He was trouble for them, and for anyone who dared to get in his way.

5: Cheers and Fears

Hillary and Windslow stayed parallel to the road to Eldervale. As they had hoped, the sun stayed this time and it wasn't long before Hillary shut off the magic lights on her tennis shoes. She kept the small piece of magic wand in her hand, hoping it would absorb magic faster than if she put it in her pocket.

"Finally," Windslow said. The forest ended where fields of planted crops began. Across the rows of cabbages, potato plants, and other vegetables he saw the whitewashed single story homes and their steep thatched roofs that formed the village of Eldervale. "Now maybe we can find the wizards and get some help."

"Hold on," Hillary said. She grabbed her brother's arm. "Let's think this through. Do we really want to go barging into town? Haggerwolf's warning did tell us to stay away. It's probably dangerous. And who knows when we'll dream-slip back home. Time is all out of whack here."

"Good idea," Windslow said. "Hey, look." He pointed to the far end of one of the fields. "There are some people working in the field. Maybe we could talk to them without anyone seeing us from town. Do you think there's enough magic in that chunk of wand to make us some clothes like they're wearing?"

"Shouldn't be too hard. It looks like they're wearing gunnysacks. How do you feel about wearing a skirt, little brother?" Hillary didn't wait for an answer. She held out the piece of wand and muttered something. Windslow held out his arms and looked down at himself. He wore a brown rough woven sack for a shirt with holes cut out for his head and arms. Tied by a length of twine, a long skirt draped from his waist to the tops of his tennis shoes.

Hillary muttered again, and in the wink of an eye, she stood dressed just like her brother except for a piece of darker brown cloth tied with a bow that formed her belt.

"Glad to see you gave yourself a little bit of style," Windslow said and pointed at the ribbon.

Hillary shrugged. "Come on. We'll stay along the edge of the woods and get as close as we can before we walk out into the open."

She led the way, weaving through the sparse trees until it was time to walk out into the field. They didn't walk far through the tilled soil and straight rows of turnips, before one of the two workers looked up.

Hillary grinned and broke into a run. "Granny Gilderbun! Grandpa Dimbleshoot!"

"Land oh gosh-ins," Granny Gilderbun exclaimed and stopped hoeing the ground.

Dimbleshoot spun around, nearly hitting his wife with his shovel. "Hillary. Windslow. Quick get down on your hands and knees. Pretend you're weeding. Gilderbun, get over here and help me block the view from the village. Dreadlore's men could be watching."

Hillary and Windslow knelt down. They both pretended to weed. There weren't any real ones to pull. "What's going on?" Hillary asked.

"Oh, children," Granny said and sighed. "Everything is changing. The stars have changed and everyone says it signals the start of an old legend. I'm afraid we're in for a hard time."

"Humph," Dimbleshoot said. "Dreadlore thinks he can outsmart it. I think the whole thing is a bunch of hogwash."

"The legend is real," Granny Gilderbun said and shook her finger at her husband. "You're an old fool and it's an old legend. It's not hogwash." She leaned against her hoe and put one hand on Hillary's shoulder. "The stars have moved and changed. The legend said they did that once before, very long ago. That's what brought magic to Gabendoor. The legend said that someday the stars would change again. Well low and behold, they did, just last night."

"Everybody move down the row a ways," Dimbleshoot said. "We should look like we're working." He glanced over his shoulder before pushing some dirt around with his shovel. "The legend hints that there is one way to put everything back in order. It has to do with some sort of magic stone. Dreadlore figures he's going to find the stone and fix everything."

"Slow down," Windslow said. "My crutches keep sticking in the dirt. You still haven't told us who Dreadlore is."

Granny Gilderbun answered. "He's bad. Dreadlore will kill you quick and outright or make you suffer. He's an idiot who thinks he's a genius. If we have to follow his notions, then we will likely starve to death. Things will be messed up enough without him meddling with everything."

Windslow gave a long yawn. "Oh-oh," he said. "I think we're getting close to dream-slipping." He yawned again. "We really need the wizards."

"If you mean Haggerwolf, Fernbark and Larkstone," Dimbleshoot said, "Dreadlore's men have them locked up in that building over there." Dimbleshoot turned and pointed to a small building on the edge of town. "The new prison is close to our cottage. I can hardly get any sleep the way the guards keep snoring all night."

"Balderdash," Gilderbun said. "Your snoring blends in with theirs. I have to sleep with cotton in my ears."

Hillary started to talk, but her yawn stopped her. She pinched her cheeks, hoping it would keep her from falling asleep and dream-slipping in the middle of the field. "We need to talk to the wizards," she said. "Can we get to your cottage without raising suspicion?"

"Don't know," Dimbleshoot said. "Only one way to find out. Windslow, grab a handle on that basket of turnips. Hillary you grab it too. We'll start walking and see what happens. If anyone speaks to us, let me and Granny do the talking."

Dimbleshoot and Gilderbun walked just in front of Windslow and Hillary. Four or five times Dimbleshoot halted the group and dug a bit with his shovel. Twice he stopped, pulled a turnip from the ground and tossed it into the basket. Both Hillary and Windslow fought back yawns as they neared the cottage. Once inside, Gilderbun hurried them into the back room. "Quick, one of you slide under each bed. At least when you dream-slip back, you won't be out in plain sight."

Windslow slid under a bed and pressed back against the wall. He heard a knocking sound at the front door.

"Coming!" Gilderbun yelled. "Go stall whoever's there," she said softly. Windslow assumed she was speaking to her husband. Windslow listened and yawned, staring up at the bedsprings. They shifted out of focus as he yawned again. He could hear voices arguing. Someone yelled. "They're under the beds!"

Windslow felt hands around his ankles. He closed his eyes and began his dream-slip.

ℬ☙

Hillary opened her eyes, expecting to see the bottom of Dimbleshoot's bed. Tossing off her covers, she grabbed her robe, pulled it on and wiggled her feet into her slippers. She almost ran as she hurried upstairs to her father's bedroom. She glanced inside the empty room and headed back down for the kitchen. Bill sat at the table and cradled a cup of coffee in his hands. He hadn't shaved and he wore the same clothes he had worn yesterday. His eyes looked puffy.

"Any news?" She asked.

Bill shook his head.

"Have you slept at all?"

Bill looked up. "A little," he said and took a sip of coffee.

Hillary leaned over and stuck her finger in his cup.

"Hey!" Bill protested and pulled his cup away.

"Cold," Hillary said and wiped her finger on her bathrobe. "I thought so. You've been sitting here all night, haven't you."

"Is your brother up?" Bill asked. "I'll take you both to school and then I'm heading over to the hospital. I'll give you some money for lunches and we can go through a drive-through for breakfast."

Hillary put her hands on her hips and stood straight, trying to look taller. "First, you're taking a shower. Then you're going to shave. Mom will have a fit if you show up looking and smelling like this. Now, get moving." She turned to the doorway. "Windslow," she called, seeing her brother wheel himself into the living room. "We're going to be late for school if we don't all hurry. I'm making dad some coffee while he gets cleaned up. Have you got time to make us some lunches?"

"No problem," Windslow said and rolled into the kitchen. "Hey, what stinks?"

Bill stood.

"Geeze, dad," Windslow said. "You really need a bath. Phew."

"So I've been informed," Bill said. He gave them both a small smile. "You guys aren't kids anymore, are you?"

Both Hillary and Windslow looked at Bill as he ran his hand over the stubble on his cheeks and chin.

"I was worried about you two needing me. I sat up all night trying to convince myself I had to be strong for my kids. I lost a night's sleep for nothing. I just figured it all out. Right now, you two don't need me as much as I need you. I'm so worried about Trish. I'm having a tough time holding myself together. I... I... I'm so glad I... We... your mother and I are so glad we have you two. I..." Bill put his arm across his face.

"We're all going to be all right," Windslow said, "but only if you get in the shower. I'll bring a cup of coffee into the bathroom as soon as it's ready. You know, maybe we could call a taxi to take us to school and then you could get a couple hours of sleep before you go to the hospital."

"Hey, we-a taxi," a voice said from the living room.

"We not much-a hurry, so ever-body take-a time," a second voice said.

"An we charge-a fair fare," said a third voice. "What stink?"

Molly Folly Sallyforth pushed past Windslow and Hillary. Pinching her nose with her fingers, she walked up to Bill and stood in front of him. "Muffy Chris-fif-shun bring-our-fan. Windso and Hillre ride wif us-a fhool. You geff shum sleef."

"Hello," Mrs. Christensen called from the living room. "We let ourselves in. We thought maybe it would help you out if the girls and I gave you kids a ride to school. Is everyone decent? Is it all right if I come into the kitchen?"

"Ever-body all right, but I not come in if I you," Molly said.

"Hi, Jane," Bill called out. "We're decent, but I've been told a couple different ways that I need a shower. That would be so great if you could give Hillary and Windslow a ride to school."

Mrs. Christensen poked her head around the doorway.

"Ok, everyone out," Hillary said. "Dad, that means you especially."

Molly, Nelly and Tillie scurried past their mother.

"This really is nice of you," Bill said and hurried out behind the girls.

"You too, Windslow," Hillary said looking at the clock. She held up her thumb and finger with about half an inch between them. "We're this close to being late."

"I'm gone," her brother said and gave his wheels a push.

Mrs. Christensen took the coffee pot from Hillary. "You too, dear. I'll take care of the coffee. The girls and I made lunches for you and Windslow. I do hope you like peanut butter, banana and chocolate sandwiches. The girls all swore that was your favorite." She held out her hand. "If not, here's some money for lunch."

Hillary bit her lip. She looked at Mrs. Christensen's hand. She started to say, "Thanks," but her lips wouldn't form the words. Hillary's face tightened up and she squeezed her eyes shut. When she felt Mrs. Christensen's hand on her shoulder, the strength Hillary had been able to scrape together fled. Tears shoved their way through closed eyes. Her lips quivered and released the waves of sobs she had tried to hold back. She returned Mrs. Christensen's hug, holding tight to her mother's friend.

Hillary sniffed. Mrs. Christensen released her hug and handed Hillary a fist full of tissues. Hillary sniffed again and blew her nose. She tried to say something to Mrs. Christensen, but couldn't. Hillary was afraid if she opened her mouth, she'd start crying again.

"Go get ready for school," Mrs. Christensen said softly. "We'll wait for you out in the van so you can have some privacy. Everything will be fine."

ജ്ര

All the way to school, the Sallyforth triplets sang songs, made jokes and teased each other. Windslow wondered how Mrs. Christensen could concentrate on driving. At first, he felt nervous, but the laughter and antics of the girls took his mind off his mother.

At school, many students asked about his mom. Windslow thought it was nice they asked, but didn't like telling everyone over and over that he didn't know anything about how she was doing. He kept hoping the nurse or someone from the office would page him. That would probably mean his dad had left a message or had news. A "ding-dong" note would sound through the loudspeakers alerting everyone before an announcement or page. Whenever the notes sounded, Windslow would stiffen up in his chair and listen intently, then slump as he heard about the day's lunch menu, reminders about events that week, and other announcements.

Science was his last class for the day and still, there had been no messages from his father. Windslow sat at his lab bench and pulled his homework assignment from his backpack.

Until last night, Windslow always had done his homework. For the first time he had left his homework unfinished.

"Hi, Windso," Molly said and sat down beside him. "You got all-a answers right on your homework again. I not so sure about mine."

"Not this time. I didn't finish it. Hey," He looked at the pages. "What the... all the answers are filled in. Molly, did you do something?"

Molly smiled.

"All right, let's get started," Ms. DiMarco, his science teacher said from the front of the classroom.

Windslow listened and watched as his teacher wrote formulas on the board and spoke about precipitates and particles. After a short lecture, she handed out worksheets.

"Oh, oh," Windslow heard Molly say and looked at her. She seemed blurry and out of focus, except for her hair. She blinked.

"Whoa," she said softly. She came back into sharp focus. Her hair turned from black to green to black again.

"Hi, Windso," she whispered. "It me, Tillie. Something not right."

She blurred. Her hair color shifted from black to orange to black. She put her lips close to Windslow's ear. "This very good thing. I not Nelly." Her eyes widened. She hiccupped and blurred.

Windslow glanced around the room. Everyone was busy working on the assignment.

Nelly's hair color shifted from black to orange to black.

"I back, I think."

"Molly?" Windslow whispered.

She nodded her head.

The bell rang signaling the end of class. Most students stuffed things into their backpacks and headed for the door. Others sat and talked.

"What's going on?" Windslow asked Molly.

"Things not working right in Gabendoor. All-a stuff getting messed up." She shouldered her backpack and headed for the hallway. Windslow shoved hard on his wheels and rolled after her. Leaning against the lockers, she waited for him. Before Windslow could say anything, Marcy Sisedeli, captain of the cheerleading squad came up behind Molly.

"Hi, Windslow," Marcy said. "Sorry about your mom."

Windslow shrugged his shoulders. Marcy was probably the most popular girl in school, and one of the meanest. Three grades back she had teased Windslow about being in a wheelchair. She rarely had anything nice to say about anyone but herself. He glanced past her and saw the group of girls that constantly followed Marcy around.

"Do you ever wear anything else?" Marcy asked Molly. "I suppose you like wearing the same outfit every day, but you'll need to upgrade your style for tryouts. There is a lot more you'll need to change too, but why bother. You don't have a chance of making the squad."

The girls behind Marcy giggled. Marcy glanced back, gave them an acknowledging smile, and looked back at Windslow. "You're blocking my locker. Can't you find someplace else to hang out with your friend?"

Molly moved behind Windslow's chair and grabbed the handles. "I need-a buy some really nice leggings like yours, Marshy. Where you get them with big lump in back. It make it look like your leg have-a biggie muscle."

Marcy twisted and used one hand to sweep her skirt to the side.

The girls behind her started laughing. A fabric softener sheet from the laundry formed the lump at the back of Marcy's ankle. She gave a short scream and pushed through her crowd of admirers. "Why didn't one of you say something?" she said as she hurried away.

"It wasn't there before," one of her friends said. "Suddenly it was just there."

"Hey, Marcy," Windslow hollered. "Now I know why you smell so fresh today. Normally you're spoiled." He wasn't sure if she heard him or not. He really didn't care. "You did that, didn't you," he asked Molly.

"Shush," she said and pushed him down the hall. "We need-a go to the office. Dingy thing going to announce you got message."

Before Windslow could say anything, the announcement tone sounded, followed by a voice that said, "Windslow and Hillary Summerfield, please report to the office."

Windslow didn't ask how Molly knew his sister and he would be paged. The Sallyforth triplets were always a mystery and Windslow was almost certain they could work magic, although they always denied it when he asked.

In the office, Mrs. Christensen waited along with Hillary, Nelly and Tillie. "I spoke with your father," she told Windslow and Hillary. "Physically your mom is doing fine. She's out of danger."

Windslow sniffed and wiped his face. Hillary hugged Mrs. Christensen. "Whoopee," the Sallyforth Sisters shouted together.

"We give her a cheer," Molly said. The three sisters lined up in front of the reception desk.

The girls held their arms out straight to the side and touched fingertips to space themselves. They bent down, hands on knees. Molly began their cheer. All three girls stood straight, bent, twisted and moved their arms in wild motions, timed with the cheer.

We got hope and Marcy is a dope.
She no smarter than a jumping rope.
Mommy get well. We think that swell.
Let's get started. We not wait for a bell.

The girls ended their cheer by jumping up and down.

Mrs. Christensen clapped her hands. Hillary stared. Windslow laughed.

"Oh, dear," Ms. Donner, the receptionist said. "The P.A. system was on somehow. The whole school heard that. Well, ladies," she said looking at the Sallyforth sisters. "I think your cheer is about to make you famous." She used her hand to cover an obvious smile.

"Well," Windslow said. "We aren't waiting for the bell to ring, so let's get to the hospital. I want to see mom."

Hillary grabbed Windslow's wheelchair handles and pushed, almost running as they headed for the parking lot.

6: Wind-Climber

Hillary and the Sallyforth sisters darted out of the elevator as soon as it opened. Mrs. Christensen pushed Windslow in his wheelchair, but couldn't keep up with the girls. Not far down the hallway, Bill greeted them at the door to Trish's room.

"Dad, how is she?" Hillary was the first to ask.

Bill waited until Windslow and Mrs. Christensen caught up. "Physically your mom's doing great." Bill said. He put one arm around Hillary and the other around Windslow. He hugged them both. "She came out of the coma around noon."

"I'm so relieved," Hillary said and jumped up and down. "I want to see her. Is she awake?"

"Yes," Bill said. "There's a nurse checking her right now. As soon as the nurse is finished, we can go in."

"What's with the suit and tie, dad?" Windslow asked.

"Ya," Hillary added. She unbuttoned his jacket and held the sides apart. "Dad, you didn't iron your shirt."

Bill shrugged his shoulders while Hillary buttoned his suit coat. He mumbled back his answer. "I wanted to look nice for your mom when she woke up."

"You look fab-a-lis and handsome too, daddy Summerfield," Molly said.

Mrs. Christensen moved closer to Bill. "Any change with the other thing?" she asked.

"No," Bill said.

"What other thing," both Hillary and Windslow asked together.

"Well, you see..." Bill said and loosened his tie. "Your mom has amnesia. The doctors say her memory could come back at any time by itself. They're going to run more tests and... and check things."

"Check what?" Windslow asked.

They all turned to the door when a click sounded. A nurse stood in the doorway. "Tests to make sure there isn't anything in the way of your mother's recovery," the nurse said. "We're monitoring her medications to refine each dosage. We're checking her blood chemistry. The doctors are doing all they can to help your mother heal as quickly as possible."

Windslow twisted his chair, expecting the nurse to move out of his way. She remained blocking the doorway.

"One, two, three, four, five, six, seven," the nurse counted. "That's a few more visitors than we normally allow at one time."

"Oh," Mrs. Christensen said. "I'll wait out here."

The nurse glanced at everyone else, looking each person in the eye. No one moved or spoke. "Well, all right. Just this once, but don't stay too long; five minutes max. Your mother is more than a little confused. She may not recognize you. If she doesn't, don't let it worry you and don't say or do anything to upset her. Mr. Summerfield," the nurse said, "Remember what the doctor told you. You're in charge of this visit."

Bill nodded. The nurse smiled as Bill took her place at the doorway. "Okay," he said. "Not everyone at once."

"Girls," Mrs. Christensen said to her adopted daughters, "You three wait here for a minute."

Bill stepped into the room. Hillary walked behind him. Windslow muttered something and shoved on his wheels.

Trish lay in bed, the upper end raised to let her sit up. Hillary leaned over the bed and put her arms around her mother. Windslow noticed his mom kept her arms across her chest and turned her cheek away when Hillary kissed her.

"Mom, we were so worried," Hillary said. She straightened up and sat on the edge of the bed.

"Hi, Steve," Trish said. "I'm sorry. It's Bill. Yes, Bill. And you're Hillary, and you're Windslow. Oh, you're still in a wheelchair. How long will you be in it?"

Hillary looked up at her dad.

Windslow looked at the wall across from Trish's bed. Mounted below a television set was a white marker board. On the board, someone had written the names Bill, Windslow, and Hillary. "I'll be in this chair forever, mom," Windslow said. "I'm paralyzed. It happened a couple years ago. Don't worry about it. I'm used to it. Um... you don't recognize us do you?"

"Oh, children. I'm so sorry," Trish said. Tears formed in her eyes. "I don't even remember who I am. But, you're such beautiful children. I can tell you're mine. I see it in your faces."

Bill interrupted. "They are fantastic children. I was kind of hoping they'd jog some memories. Doesn't matter. You're the best mother... you're the best wife... you're..."

"Hi, mommy Summerfield," three voices chimed together when the Sallyforth girls walked into the room. They rushed around the other side of the bed and jumped up to sit on it.

Trish opened her mouth but didn't say anything. She looked at Bill. She looked at the marker board and back to Bill.

"No," he said and gave a small laugh. "We just have two. These are Mrs. Christensen's daughters. She's one of your best friends."

Trish tilted her head a bit and looked at the girls. She bit her lower lip and wrinkle lines formed on her brow as she stared intently. "The Maiden, the Daughter, and the Child," she said. "I know you three, but I don't know how. My memory is so fuzzy." Her eyes opened wide and her brow smoothed. "Your time has come." Trish held one finger to her lips. "Shush. Beware the Beguiler. He's back." She looked around the room, her eyes searching.

Tillie reached out and touched Trish's hand.

"Thank you, Tillie," Trish said and smiled at the young girl. "I think I will go to sleep for awhile." Trish's eyes shut and her breathing settled into a slow rhythm. The three Sallyforth girls gave each other quick glances and slipped off the bed.

The door opened. The nurse stepped in, looked at the monitor, and motioned them out of the room. Out in the hallway, she gave them all a smile. "Well that must have gone well. I was just coming in to give her a sleeping pill. This is the first time she's fallen asleep without one. Her pulse looks great too. It was a bit elevated. These are great signs." She looked at Bill. "Did she recognize anyone?"

Bill shook his head. "Not really."

Windslow looked at Hillary. Together they looked at the Sallyforth girls.

"Time-a go home," Molly said. "Don't worry. Have lots-a hope. That good thing a do." She turned away and she and her two sisters skipped down the hall toward the elevator.

Bill gave a large sigh and ran his fingers through his hair. "We need some sleep too," he said. "How's the homework situation? How about some deli chicken?"

"Sounds good," Windslow said. "We can use leftovers for lunch tomorrow."

Not saying a word, they headed for the car. Conversation during the ride home was full of questions with few answers. Most of Bill's questions and comments were about the Sallyforth sisters and the strange comments Trish had made. Hillary and Windslow did have homework and both rushed through it. Hillary ironed a couple shirts for her dad and told him not to wear a suit. She told him he looked too geeky wearing it in the hospital. Windslow made some sandwiches for his sister and him to take to school the next day. It wasn't very late, but everyone was tired and anxious to get some sleep. Windslow didn't have much time alone to talk to his sister. He hoped the Sallyforth girls would be in Gabendoor that night. He had a *lot* of questions for them.

ꕥ

Before Hillary had gone to bed, she had taped the small piece of wand to her hand. She wanted it to be there when she woke in Gabendoor and didn't want to take the chance of dropping it in her normal sleep.

She didn't remember falling asleep, but now soared through the stars and knew she would soon wake in her dream-slip. She checked the piece of wand. The tape held it against her skin. She closed her eyes, feeling the tingling sensation she always felt when she was about to materialize. Her thoughts blanked. The pull at her ankles woke her and she looked up at the bedsprings in Gilderbun's cottage.

"Got her!" someone yelled.

"Got him too," called another voice.

Hillary waited until she was free of the bed. "Amnesia socks!" she said, her voice loud and firm.

The hands released her ankles. Hillary rolled to her side. A man wearing a purple hood held her brother's legs. "Ditto," she said.

The man let go of her brother's legs and stood. "Um...," he said and looked at the other man who stood near Hillary. "Um... what were... what was?"

He sat down on the bed. The man near Hillary scrunched up his face and looked around. Almost stumbling, he walked out of the bedroom.

"Hey," Windslow said to the man sitting on the bed. "You're with him. You're supposed to get out of here. You and he were headed for the woods to pick a basket of thorns. Better get going."

The man looked at Windslow. Without saying anything, he walked out.

"That was creative," Hillary said. She got to her feet and shouldered the backpack she had prepared for her dream-slip. Windslow grabbed his pack and expanded his crutches. With them firmly under his arms, he moved to the bedroom door and peeked out. "Gilderbun," he said and moved through the door. Hillary rushed after him.

Gilderbun and Dimbleshoot each sat tied to a kitchen chair.

"I should ah known not to have worried about you children," Gilderbun said.

"Leave us tied," Dimbleshoot said when Windslow approached him. "It will look better that way. Dreadlore won't suspect us of helping you that way."

"But we can't just leave you," Hillary said.

Windslow pulled aside the curtain covering one of the kitchen windows. "Dimbleshoot is right. But what do we do now?" He turned his Eldervale friends. "How many guards do they usually have watching the wizards?"

"Not many," Gilderbun said. "Sometimes none. The problem is, Dreadlore himself showed up last night. He and his men are staying in the building next to where the wizards are. Dreadlore's men are in and out all the time."

Windslow turned to his sister. "Got any magic left in that stick?"

"We'll find out," Hillary said. "Let's go."

She hurried out the door and ducked around behind the cottage. She was certain no one saw her and her brother. Watching, waiting, and then moving as fast as they could, they moved from building to building, ducking under laundry hung out on ropes to dry. It didn't take them long to reach the back of the building that Gilderbun had pointed out to them yesterday.

"Any ideas?" Hillary asked her brother.

"Ya," he said. Windslow grabbed several bed sheets drying from a line. He tossed one around his back and pulled two corners up over his head and down under his chin. He tied the ends in a knot. Her grabbed more laundry and wadded it up in his arms. "We're here to change the bedding," he said and grinned at Hillary.

"You look dopy," Hillary said. She grabbed another sheet and wrapped it over her shoulders and head like her brother. She held out her hands, palms up and open. "Nap time," she said. A basket formed on top of her hands. Warm muffins appeared, giving off the sweet aroma of blueberries.

"Too bad you can't cook for real," Windslow said and grinned.

Hillary stuck her tongue out at him. "You can't even butter bread, brother dear. Let's go," she said and marched around the building.

"Hey, what's this?" a man with a purple hood asked. He sat on a stool next to the building's door. The door opened. Two more men wearing purple hoods stepped out.

Hillary held out the basket. "Food for you. Linen for the prisoners."

"Let 'em stink," one of the men said. He grabbed a muffin and took a large bite. The other men nearly knocked the basket out of Hillary's hands in their greediness. *Plop, plop, plop.* The men slumped to the ground.

Hillary pushed the door open and stepped inside. Windslow backed in, closing the door behind him.

A row of metal bars divided the room into two spaces. Behind the bars sat Haggerwolf, Fernbark and Larkstone. Hillary looked at the lock on the cell door and saw the words, *Forge Twiddler.* She dug in her backpack and found the key she wanted. The lock *clicked* and opened when she turned the key.

"You shouldn't be here," Fernbark said.

Larkstone grabbed the cell bars. "You're not safe anywhere."

"Where's the wand?" Haggerwolf asked.

Hillary held the small piece of wand out to him.

"You keep it," Haggerwolf said to her. "I just need to use it for a second." He touched the piece of wood with one finger and chanted a spell.

Magic door above the floor.
When we're gone, it's there no more.

A small opening formed in the back wall of the cell. Larkstone and Fernbark ducked through it. Windslow went next.

"Go," Haggerwolf said to Hillary.

"In a second," she said. Hillary closed the cell door and locked it. "Let them figure this one out," she said.

"Smart girl. Now go," Haggerwolf said.

Hillary hurried through the opening. She turned to help Haggerwolf. He was already through and motioned silence by holding a finger to his lips. He took Windslow's bed sheet and held it out. Hillary could see Haggerwolf's lips move but heard nothing. Realistic images of trees, grass and sky appeared on the sheet.

Larkstone grabbed her arm and led her around behind it where the others stood. From this side, it simply looked like a sheet. Haggerwolf no longer held it. It floated by itself, forming a camouflage shield for them to hide behind.

Larkstone began walking. Hillary moved up to her brother in case he needed help with his crutches. Haggerwolf moved next to them and tapped Hillary's hand. She held out the piece of wand. Haggerwolf touched it and whispered something. He put his fingers on Windslow's back.

Windslow turned around and mouthed the words, "Thank you." As they walked, he shrunk his crutches and tucked them away in his backpack.

When they reached the woods, the sheet tangled in the trees.

"Let's get away from here," Haggerwolf said and picked up the pace.

"What's going on?" Hillary asked. "Dimbleshoot and Gilderbun couldn't tell us much. They said something about Dreadlore."

"Dreadlore ruled the wizard's centuries back," Fernbark said. "He went crazy with power and turned evil. He still has a group of followers. Gabendoor almost ripped apart the last time he wielded his power. It's happening again. We need to find something called the ratStone before he does. We need that stone and we need to figure out how to use it."

Windslow ducked under a branch and had to stop when it tangled in his backpack. He snapped the dead wood and hurried ahead. "What can you tell us about the--"

"It's them!" a voice yelled from somewhere ahead. "Forget about the village. Those are the ones Dreadlore wants. Take the wizards alive. It doesn't matter about the kids!"

"I see them!" a different voice yelled from behind.

Hillary looked back and saw men wearing purple hoods, running from between the buildings.

"They've spotted us," Haggerwolf yelled after looking behind. "All right. We're going east. You two run west," he said. "We'll meet up at Biffendear's old cottage in Gristly-Grim Swamp if we make it. Hillary and Windslow, if we don't show up, find that stone. Now run!"

ꕥ

The chestnut brown Wind-Climber sat on a high branch and watched the people below. Most wore purple hoods. Another smaller group looked different from the rest. Wind-Climbers didn't care much for people. Sometimes people offered food. Sometimes they were mean and threw stones or sticks. The Wind-Climber shook its squirrel like tail and gripped the branch tighter with its hind feet. Three oddly dressed men ran to the west. A girl and a boy ran east. An image flashed in the Wind-Climber's head. The image from the stone matched the girl running away.

Days ago, a stone dropped from the sky and nearly

hit the Wind-Climber. Like all Wind-Climbers, it liked pretty things. It had emptied its front pouch of glitter-specked stones and water polished rocks to make room for this new stone. The sun made the eight-sided stone sparkle with amber light. The stone was all the Wind-Climber could fit in its pouch. Ever since it had found the stone, images had formed in its mind, urging it to do strange things. An image formed now.

The Wind-Climber gulped in air and spread out its front arms. The air chambers in the furry loose skin connecting its front and hind legs formed perfect airfoils. With a powerful push from its hind legs the Wind-Climber leaped and glided to another treetop to follow the fleeing girl.

7: Tracked

Windslow and Hillary ran, weaving through the ganternut trees. Fallen orange colored needles from the trees kept ground brush from growing thick. The terrain dipped, forming a shallow ravine. They followed the slope down, and back up the other side where it rose even higher. The steep incline slowed them down. They both stumbled after every few steps. Soon they climbed nearly on hands and knees and grabbed branches and roots to keep from sliding back into the ravine. They reached the ridge and stopped to catch their breath.

"We need to keep going," Windslow said. He started moving in a fast walk. Hillary nodded and followed.

"We need to angle south if we're going to meet back up with the wizards," Hillary said. "It's going to take us at least two days to get to Gristly-Grim Swamp."

"Longer than that," Windslow said and slowed to a walk. "Look ahead. We'll be climbing again. We're getting into the mountains. I think they're the Charm-Mist Range."

"Haggerwolf told me about them once," Hillary said. "They're not far from Lake Shimmerdawn. They got their name because no one knows much about them. There are lots myths about strange creatures and mysterious people. Supposedly, anybody who is stupid enough to explore them either never comes back or comes out completely loony."

Windslow stopped and craned his neck to look up the slope. "Ha," he said. "We're already crazy, so we don't need to worry about that." Windslow stumbled again. "This one is going to be a climb. At least the trees will help."

They climbed for an hour before resting at a spot where the slope leveled out for a short stretch. Ahead, it rose even steeper. The trees thinned. The ground became more rock and boulders than soil. Hillary climbed onto a stone outcrop and let her legs dangle over the edge. "It's getting dark, but I don't think it's night yet."

A sudden wind pushed up from the way they had come. Gusts kicked up sand, and small pieces of sticks.

"Whoa," Windslow said. "I bet the temperature just dropped ten degrees."

Hillary fastened the top button of her flannel shirt. "That usually means a storm is coming."

Another strong gust pushed against the few trees clinging to the slope. The trunks bent and strained upright. The sky darkened.

"Come on," Windslow said. "I think we're going to need some shelter." Instead of climbing, he moved parallel to the slope. "Duck in here," he called against the wind.

Hillary squeezed into the space where a dislodged boulder had been. Only four feet high and barely three feet deep, the depression was barely large enough to hold them. Huddled together on their knees, they both held their backpacks in front of their faces to shield them from the wind.

Windslow moved his pack when he heard a muffled *clunk*, then another, then more. "Look at the size of that hail," he said.

Larger than golf balls, the round chunks of ice plummeted the trees, stripping off leaves and breaking small branches. A shower of small stones and loose sand rolled down the slope and across the opening of their shelter.

"I don't like this," Hillary said. "What if the hail starts a landslide? I don't know if this is a good place to be."

"You want to be out there? Those hail stones are big enough to crack our skulls."

More rocks, larger than the first, rattled down, adding to the pile in front of them. The wind blew stronger, pushing the falling hail at an angle. Small thuds sounded against both backpacks.

"We have to chance it," Hillary said. She leaned forward and held her backpack on top of her head. "Come on!"

She ran toward one of the trees. She screamed when a hailstone smashed into her knee. She screamed again, when another hit the back of her calf. It felt like someone hit her with a small hammer.

Windslow stayed behind her. When they reached the tree, the hail stopped. The wind died. The sky lightened.

"Really, great," Windslow said and rubbed his arm. "Because you get a little spooked I nearly get my arm busted by a hailstone."

They both turned when they heard the rumble behind them. Piles of dirt and boulders, the size of large pumpkins, rumbled down the slope. In seconds, the landslide covered the spot where they had taken shelter. The ground shook. Trees swayed back and forth. Both Hillary and Windslow lost their balance. Overhead, lightning crackled and booms of thunder sounded so loud Windslow could feel the shock waves. As quickly as it began, the lightning, thunder, and earthquake ended. A few more stones rolled down, sounding loud *clacks* as they added to the pile of rubble.

"Let's get out of here," Windslow said. "The weather is getting weird around here."

They decided not to attempt a climb from where they were, and moved farther along the bottom of the cliff. After half an hour, they found a rift in the rocks, which formed a natural upward path. Windslow took the lead and often had to reach back and offer a hand to Hillary to pull her up. After another half hour of climbing, they reached a large plateau or valley. Windslow wasn't sure which. The forest grew thick around the edges of a large open meadow with knee-high grass and scattered patches of pink and lavender wildflowers. At the far edge of the meadow, the slope changed to another cliff wall.

"This is better," Windslow said. He dropped his pack and sank to his knees to rest.

Hillary used her pack as a backrest. She leaned back and stuck out her legs after taking a long drink from her plastic water bottle. Windslow drank from his own bottle and offered his sister a piece of jerky. Hillary shook her head and unwrapped a granola bar from her pack.

Windslow yawned. "We better find another place to hide. I think we'll be dream-slipping soon. At least this time nothing's chasing us or trying to pound us to death."

Hillary yawned. She plucked one of the lavender flowers and held it to her nose. "You're right. Maybe we can find somewhere over in the trees. I don't like the idea of being out in the—Eew, what stinks? Something smells like wet dog, only worse."

"Um," Windslow said. "Get up really slow and be ready to run. I think the stink is coming from them."

Across the meadow stood four beasts the size of Great Danes. Long black matted hair covered their bodies. Flies buzzed around them in circles. Each beast snarled with lips curled back to reveal rows of white shark-like teeth.

"Let's head back the way we came," Hillary said. "We can block them from following us down the rift."

She and Windslow ran. The beasts broke into a loping run, making sharp "yipping" sounds as they split into two groups.

Two beasts ran in a broad arc to the left of Windslow and Hillary, forcing them to change direction and angle to the west away from the nearest trees and closer to where the mountains rose again. When Hillary and Windslow neared the rocky outcrops, the other two beasts sprinted ahead to cut them off.

"They're herding us," Hillary said. "Maybe we can make it to that tree." She changed direction, running toward a massive tree standing alone near the meadow's edge. The beasts ran a course parallel to Hillary and Windslow then drew in tighter to cut them off.

Hillary yanked the piece of wand from her pocket. "Raspberries," she yelled. A long tangled row of wild raspberry plants, with needle sharp thorns, sprang up in front of the dogs. Hillary kept running. The beasts turned, heading for the end of the berry row.

"Start climbing when we get to the tree," Windslow yelled from behind his sister. "If those things catch up to us, I'll try to hold them off until you figure out another spell. We can't let them herd us into a corner and trap us where they can rip us apart."

"There's nothing around the tree," Hillary yelled back. "We'll be trapped."

"At least we might be safe enough to dream-slip." Windslow said. "Look way up the trunk. There's a big nest or something."

With a trunk too big for a person to circle their arms around, the tree stood not far from the cliff. The lower limbs reached out like strong arms that welcomed climbing. Higher up the trunk tapered and split into five final branches covered with wrinkled bark that gave a look of age and strength. They curved up and outward like fingers of a hand. The wooden palm cradled a large nest made of sticks and twigs.

Hillary reached the tree first and jumped, grabbing a stout limb. Her hands slipped. She fell. Windslow grabbed her under the arms and pulled her up. "Jump," he yelled.

Hillary's hands gripped the limb. She felt her brother push up on her feet. She struggled and pulled herself higher.

"Swing your legs up."

Hillary swung and kicked up with her legs, managing to hook one over the branch.

The ground shuddered. The sky turned dark. The tree shook. Hillary's leg slipped from the branch.

"Try again," Windslow yelled.

Hillary took a breath and kicked her legs. She got one ankle over the branch.

A rush of cold air wove up the valley and stormed across the meadow. Sleet, pushed by wind, stung Hillary's face and made the branch slippery. She pulled and squirmed until she straddled the limb. While she shimmied to the trunk, Windslow pulled himself up behind her.

"Climb to the nest," Windslow hollered. He looked back. The four beasts ran together, their backs covered with a light dusting of snow. They lowered their heads. Their loping gate turned to a full run.

"What's the matter?" Windslow asked. "Start climbing."

Hillary knew what to do. She just wasn't sure how to do it. She looked at her brother. "I'm not good at this."

"I'll boost you," Windslow slipped around her, braced his back against the trunk and folded his hands together.

Hillary grabbed his shoulders to steady herself and put one foot in Windslow's hands. He hoisted. She stretched and grabbed a higher branch.

The beasts circled the tree. The largest one stood on its hind legs, its front paws pushed against the trunk. It sniffed the air and let out a long mournful howl. The others circled the tree and sniffed the ground, yelping as they ran.

The snow stopped. The wind stilled. Sunlight flooded the meadow with the heat of a blistering summer day. As quickly as it had grown hot, the air cooled.

"Something weird is going on," Windslow said as he helped his sister climb the next tier of branches. "It's hot. It's cold. It snows. It melts. It's light. It's dark."

"And what about the earthquakes," Hillary said as she flopped into the nest.

"I wish the Sallyforth Sisters or the wizards were here," Windslow said. He clambered over the nest's lip and crawled to its center.

Nearly six feet in diameter, the nest provided ample room for the Children of the Wind. Downy feathers, dead grass, and shredded bark, cemented together with dried animal droppings made the nest both sturdy and fairly comfortable to sit in.

"Oh, gross," Hillary said and looked at her hands. "It's filthy in here." She took a bottle of hand sanitizer out of her backpack, squeezed the pale colored jell onto her hands and rubbed them together.

"Would you rather be down with them?" Windslow asked. He peered over the nest's rim. "Look at those teeth." Windslow gave a long yawn. "I hope those things find something else to eat while we're gone."

Hillary rubbed her forehead with the back of her hand.

She yawned twice, the second longer than the first. "It's going to be creepy dream-slipping from here. I hope whatever bird made this nest abandoned it. It must be huge. At least there aren't any bones strewn around. Maybe it's a vegetarian."

Windslow didn't answer. He settled back, yawned and closed his eyes. Hillary yawned again and took a large plastic trash bag from her pack. She split it open and spread it out on the nest as something to lie on. She too closed her eyes and began her dream-slip.

ꙮ

The Wind-Climber tucked in its arms to speed its descent. At a treetop by the edge of the mountain meadow, it thrust its arms back out to spread the airfoil formed by the fur covered skin between its front and hind feet. Flapping its arms, it landed on a branch. It closed its large brown eyes to protect them from the stinging frozen rain. The rain turned to snow that melted. The air became warm, then cool. The ground growled and shook all the trees.

The Wind-Climber had followed the girl and boy up the mountain. Keeping out of sight, it waited for a chance to approach the girl. She and the boy had run from large black beasts, climbed into a tree with a sturdy nest and then disappeared. The Wind-Climber reached into the pouch in front of her belly and touched the amber stone. An image formed in her mind. She wrapped her loose furry skin around herself and closed her eyes. The stone showed the girl returning in the next day.

ꙮ

Hillary woke early, took a fast shower and changed the linen on her bed. She put the clothes she had worn on her dream-slip into the washing machine and dumped in a double amount of detergent. She used a soapy rag to wipe the bottom of her backpack. She thought for a moment, grabbed her tennis shoes and checked the soles. Even though she didn't see anything they might have picked up in the bird's nest, she wiped the bottoms anyway. By the time her brother and father woke, Hillary had made lunches for Windslow and herself, and pancakes for everyone.

"Whoa, what's with you?" Windslow asked his sister. He sat down, smeared butter over a stack of pancakes and drenched them with syrup. "Umm... ary goof," he said with his mouth full.

Hillary ignored her brother's manners and handed her dad a cup of coffee when he walked into the kitchen.

Her father sat, took a sip, grabbed a fork and helped himself to a bite of Windslow's pancakes.

"Hey," Windslow protested.

Bill grinned and took the plate of pancakes Hillary handed him. "Thanks, Hillary," he said. "This is a real treat. So how's my shirt look? Ironing isn't so hard."

"Did you do the sleeves and back or just the parts that show through your sport coat?" Hillary asked.

Bill shifted in his chair and buttoned the front of his coat. "I did enough," he said. "I'll get the car ready. I'll stop and see your mom after I drop you two off at school. I need to check in at work for an hour or so and then go look at new vans. I'll see your mom again and then pick you two up so you can see her." He looked at Hillary. "You've got soccer practice, don't you?"

"Yah," Hillary said. "But I can skip it so we can spend more time with mom."

"You know she wouldn't like that," Bill said. "She's

really excited about you playing this year." Turning to Windslow, he added, "And she's glad you're helping the coach. This wouldn't be a good time to disappoint your mother." Bill looked at his watch. "We better go. We can clean up the dishes tonight."

8: Jeers and Tears

At school, many of Windslow's friends made comments about the Sallyforth cheer heard over the public address system the day before. Most of his friends thought it was funny and great. Only a couple felt sorry for Marcy Sisedeli. Windslow asked them why they thought it was *that* Marcy. They pointed out Marcy Sisedeli was the only Marcy in the school. Windslow smiled when he thought of the cheer. He didn't really care much for Marcy. She might be one of the prettiest and most popular girls in the school, but Windslow thought she was snobbish, conceited and didn't care if she hurt someone's feelings by her comments. He figured it was about time someone turned the tables on her.

Windslow shut his locker and spun his wheelchair around. He couldn't roll forward. Marcy Sisedeli and her clutch of admirers blocked him.

"I know you're her friend," Marcy said, "but I can't imagine why. She and her sisters don't even belong in this school. They dress and act like they live in some homeless shelter or something."

Windslow pushed his chair forward, forcing Marcy and her group to take a step back. His face burned and his heart pumped hard. "They're not homeless. And if they were, that would have nothing to do with what they're like as people. It would have everything to do with us. Anyone with a real heart would do things to help them out. How'd that cheer go? Oh, yah. You're no smarter than a jumping rope, Marcy. I don't think the Sallyforth sisters should have said that. It was insulting to the rope!"

Marcy glared at Windslow. "I told my parents what happened and my dad talked to the school principal and cheer leading coach last night. My dad has paid for all the uniforms for the cheerleaders, and most of the sports teams." The volume of Marcy's voice rose. She put her hands on her hips and continued. "My dad is a very powerful man. So guess what. The Sallyforth girls will be able to try out for cheerleading, but I can guarantee you they won't make the squad this year or any year. My dad might even file a lawsuit against the school!"

"Oh," Windslow said and put one hand against his cheek, feigning surprise and shock. "That would be horrible. Why would your dad file a lawsuit? It's not illegal for you to be stupid and clueless is it?"

Most of Marcy's friends gasped. Two smiled and turned their heads.

"I'll get you both," Marcy said and stormed away, her circle of friends following.

For the rest of Windslow's day, between classes, his friends commented both about the cheer and about his run in with Marcy that morning. Even students he knew only by name gave him smiles and high-fives, as they walked past.

When he got to science class, Molly was already at their shared desk. Windslow wheeled to his spot just as the bell rang, signaling the start of class.

Molly leaned over to him and whispered, "We going to try out for cheerleader after school. We going to have fun and help-a team win lots a games."

Windslow smiled at her but didn't say anything.

Ms. DiMarco told them to take out their homework as she wrote on the board.

On a scrap of paper, Windslow scribbled, *Why haven't you been in Gabendoor? We need your help.* He slid the note to Molly and turned his attention back to Ms. DiMarco.

Molly looked at it, and wrote something. She folded the paper in half and slid it back to Windslow.

He opened the paper, smiled and shook his head. Molly had simply drawn a happy face.

When the dismissal bell rang, Molly jumped up. "I need-a get ready for cheer squad tryout. I see you at soccer," she said and skipped out the door.

Windslow slumped back in his chair, closed his eyes and sighed. He wasn't looking forward to soccer. Cheerleader tryouts were on the sideline of the soccer field. He opened his eyes, said goodbye to Ms. DiMarco, and headed for the locker room.

ꙮ

The soccer coach had piled a mesh bag full of soccer balls on Windslow's lap. Windslow wheeled his chair down the hall and out the door to the soccer field. The team was busy doing calisthenics to begin their warm-up routine. Windslow took the balls out one at a time and tossed them on the field. Hillary ran over and began kicking balls toward the other girls.

"Hey," Windslow called to his stepsister. "Molly is really acting funny and..."

With short controlled kicks, Hillary dribbled the last ball out on the field.

"...and, and... And I guess I'm the only one that cares," Windslow added, his voice trailing off.

From down the sideline and out on the field he heard laughter. Most of the girls on the field laughed. Hillary stood with her hands on her hips. Windslow turned to look where some of Hillary's teammates pointed.

Down the sideline, the cheerleading squad and their coach stood together in a group. Walking toward them were the Sallyforth triplets. Molly, Tillie and Nelly wore the same costumes. Each wore a pink ballerina tutu, yellow leggings with bold green horizontal stripes, and a white t-shirt with a happy face printed on the front. They held homemade pompoms fashioned from strips of Mylar balloon. The silvery pompom strands glistened and fluttered.

Windslow couldn't hear what the cheerleading coach was saying. She shook her head and waved her hands. Windslow could hear the squad's laughter. The look on Marcy's face said, pleased and satisfied. Marcy grinned as the Sallyforth sisters walked off the sideline and headed for the parking lot.

"They didn't even get a chance," Windslow said softly. He banged his fist on his wheelchair arm. He twisted his chair and was about to go after the Sallyforth sisters. The soccer coach yelled to him from the field.

"Windslow go get the other goal net. It's in the equipment closet."

Windslow held up his fingers, gave the coach an "okay" sign and headed for the locker room.

After practice, he and Hillary met outside the gym and hurried to the parking lot. Bill was already waiting for them. He told them Trish's memory had improved a little. Some older memories had come back to her. She did remember some events that had happened when she was dating him, but didn't remember being married or having children. Bill told them she was still confused. She had said something about having three uncles named Haggerwolf, Fernbark and

Larkstone and wondered why they had not visited her. Bill said he had played along and told Trish they lived in Australia and couldn't come. He told Windslow and Hillary he felt uneasy about telling Trish that, but it did seem to ease her mind.

Windslow glanced at his sister. She shrugged her shoulders.

During the ride to the hospital, Windslow's thoughts switched back and forth between worry about his stepmother and anger about Marcy.

At the hospital, Trish welcomed Hillary and him by name, the look in her eyes told Windslow she didn't really remember them. He gave her a long hug and sat at the foot of her bed.

"Where are your three friends, the triplet girls?" Trish asked.

"I guess they couldn't come," Windslow said. He told Trish and his dad what had happened at soccer practice and the cheerleader tryouts.

Trish laughed when Windslow described their homemade cheerleading uniforms.

"Oh, that is so like them," Trish said. "They don't take life too seriously, but yet they do. I wouldn't count them out yet."

"I don't know," Windslow said. "They had pretty long faces when they left the field. I think they're really disappointed. They haven't been acting normal lately."

Windslow looked at his stepmother for a moment and chanced a question. "Mom, how do you know so much about them?"

Trish gave him a long look. "I don't really know. Three words pop into my memory whenever I think about the girls.

The words are 'truth,' 'intuition' and 'secrets.' I don't know why and I wish I could remember more about them. Somehow I feel they're important." Trish glanced at Hillary and back to Windslow. "Of course, they aren't as important to me as you two are. You're my family. You're my children. Come on. I want another hug from both of you."

Hillary moved around to the other side of the bed, hopped on and stretched out along side her mother before giving her a long hug. Windslow wished he could do that too. He had to settle for a hug that lasted until his back muscles complained from the strain of him leaning forward so long.

Bill winked at Trish. "I'll get mine later."

Trish smiled. She grabbed Windslow's hand and held tight. "You're a good person to worry about your friends, Windslow. I'm sure they will be fine because they have you and Hillary as friends. Just tell them not to give up hope. Those girls help people see the truth through intuition, and there is always mystery surrounding them. Why don't you and Hillary turn the tables on them?"

"What do mean?" Hillary asked.

Trish looked at her and shrugged. "I don't know. The thought just popped into my head."

They chatted with Trish for another hour. She had many questions about what they were doing in school. By some of her questions, Windslow was certain his mom couldn't remember what grade they were in. He didn't care if she was bluffing at times. It helped him feel better just spending time with her.

On the ride home, he thought about his mother's comments about truth, intuition and secrets and turning the tables on the Sallyforth sisters.

The "mystery" comment bothered Windslow the most. The girls had always helped sort things out in Gabendoor. They had always been the ones to cheer everyone up. They were the ones that gave everyone hope. And right now, "hope" was what Windslow clung to.

Back at home in his bedroom, Windslow studied two hours before heading for bed. When he rested his head on his pillow, Windslow felt a lump, reached back and pulled out the *Book of Library Secrets.*

"Oh, this stupid thing," he said and turned on a light. Windslow flipped through the pages until he found new words.

Giving up's the easy way.
What words did Windslow's mother say?
Hope is hard to understand.
It's fleeting in another land.

Aberratia plays a part,
A temple where the stone will start.
ratStone brings them home again.
The future is where it began.

Hope will never work alone.
You won't find it in the stone.
Hope depends on what you do.
Finding hope is up to you.

"Great," Windslow said. He slammed the book shut and tossed it on the floor. Reaching to his desk, he grabbed his science book. "At least this one makes sense," he said and started reading.

Somewhere in the middle of "Properties of Matter," Windslow's mind wandered. He fell asleep and began his dream-slip thinking about laughing cheerleaders, Marcy's crooked smile and the disappointed look on the faces of the Sallyforth triplets.

9: Up Down or Nowhere

Windslow sniffed. Pungent smells from the nest and the faint stink of dog like creatures filled his nostrils. He opened his eyes. He thought the sky was gray at first. As sleep cleared from his eyes, he realized something covered the nest. It looked like thousands of fine threads stretched back and forth in every direction from one side of the nest to the other.

Someone moved beside him and Windslow looked, expecting to see his sister materialize from her dream-slip. Three forms filled in.

"Finally," Windslow said. Crowded next to him lay Molly, Nelly and Tillie.

"Hi, Windso," Molly said.

Tillie sat up, grabbed the strange netting like material covering the nest, and pulled. Nothing moved. "This not good," she said.

Nelly stretched, wrinkled up her nose and pinched her nostrils with her fingers. "It really smell good in here."

"Hey."

"Don't push."

"I not doing it."

The Sallyforth voices mixed together. Something pushed against Windslow. He shoved against the girls. Hillary's form filled in, adding to the already overcrowded nest.

Hillary sat up and held her nose like Nelly. "Oh, I'm so glad you're here," Hillary said. She released her nose and hugged the sisters.

"Are those dog things still here?" She asked Windslow.

"I don't know," Windslow said. He pulled at the sticks forming the nest's edge. He wasn't able to move any. He turned around and managed to wiggle to his hands and knees. "I can't see the ground. What's this thing over us?" He pulled on it as Tillie had. He pulled harder. The nest and tree swayed slightly but the covering held fast.

Windslow took his Swiss Army knife from his pocket, opened the longest blade and sliced at the netting. "I can't cut it," he said.

Windslow folded the knife blade closed and opened the slender saw blade. He sawed and poked and sawed. "This stuff is tough." He switched back to the knife blade and tried again. For all his effort, he was only able to make a small opening about three inches in diameter. He shoved his knife back in his pocket and twisted to get his eye close to the opening.

"What can you see," Hillary asked.

"Nothing but some kind of huge bird that looks like a vulture sitting on one of the higher branches."

"Let me see," Molly said and pushed closer to Windslow. As she wiggled her way forward. More protests filled the air.

"Ouch."

"Watch it."

"Get your foot off me,"

"That very bad thing," Molly said. "It blood buzzard. It spin out stuff like spider an trap stuff in nest. Nothing cut it but buzzard beak."

"Well," Hillary said and held up her small piece of wand. "Let's see what we can do with a little magic."

Tillie put her hand over Hillary's fingers and covered the wand. "That all a magic we have. This not time a use it."

Hillary pulled her hand away and closed it into a fist. "What do you mean? Why not?"

"Because we not--"

Molly put her hand over her sisters mouth. "Because," Molly said. "Because we not want to use it unless we need to. That wand very small an we need biggie magic to stop blood buzzard."

"It's just a stupid bird," Windslow said. While the others were talking, Windslow had been trying to make a hole through the nest. He put both hands around a stick he had partially exposed. He pulled, yanked and wiggled. As thick as his thumb, the two-foot long stick pulled free from the nest.

Everyone looked up when the nest shook and a shrill bird cry sounded.

Windslow looked out the hole in the netting and quickly sat back. He pushed his stick through the hole and moved the end around. Something yanked at the stick and released it. The nest shook again. Windslow pulled his stick back.

"Whoa," he said and showed the stick to Hillary and the sisters. "That bird clipped off the end of my stick. Look at how clean it's cut."

"Birdie have very sharp beak," Molly said. "It trap things in nest an snip out little holes. Then it snip at us. It try a make us bleed. We starve and bleed a death. Then it open up top enough a eat us."

Tillie put her hand back on Hillary's closed fist. "You not have enough magic. Birdie just clip an wait, clip an wait.

You use up all-a magic. Then it get lucky an clip you here an clip you there." While she spoke, Tillie poked Hillary's shoulder and neck. "Cuts not close up. Maybe we need magic to stop a bleeding."

"Maybe we don't need to worry about that at all," Windslow said and pulled more sticks loose. "I'm making progress. If I can make a big enough hole, we can go out through the bottom."

The nest shook again. The buzzard clipped a six-inch slice in the netting. Windslow jabbed his stick through the opening, angling each thrust in a different direction. A click sounded and Windslow pulled his stick out. He held up the four-inch long piece of wood. "It cut it again," he said.

The nest shook. Windslow cautiously looked through the enlarged hole. "The buzzard's back up on its branch."

"My brother's right," Hillary said. She wiggled in between Molly and Windslow, grabbed a stick, and pulled. "We need to go out through the bottom. Come on. Everybody help."

Windslow twisted around and kicked at the edges of the hole. Sticks cracked and shifted as the hole grew wider.

"Stop a second," Hillary said. She leaned down and looked through the hole. "Crud-o. The dog things are still there," she said. "Three are just laying there. The fourth one is watching us. He's drooling. Gross."

"Molly," Windslow asked. "Take a look. What are those things?"

Molly glanced down the hole. She sat back, folded her arms and shrugged. "I not see them a-fore. Charm-Mist Mountain have lot-a secret."

"Why aren't you three helping?" Hillary asked. She helped Windslow work at the growing hole.

"What good it do?" Tillie said and folded her arms like Molly. "Buzzer get us from up top. Doggies get us from down below. I think I just take a nap an wait. Then I dream-slip back a Earth and have some cocoa. Cocoa all-a time make me feel better."

"I not have some too," Nelly said. Like her sisters, she folded her arms and leaned back.

Molly sighed and closed her eyes. "Cocoa not make me feel better. There no hope. We stuck here. There nothing we can do. We stuck at home too. We not have hope-a be cheerleader either."

"What?" Windslow said and sat up. "Is that what this is all about? You're bummed out because you didn't make the cheerleading squad?"

"We not even get a chance," Tillie said. "Marcy not let us."

"I can't believe it," Windslow said and turned back to yanking out sticks. "You three are the ones who always tell us not to give up. You got me to realize that being in a wheelchair wasn't an excuse for me to use for not trying things. You three always help us figure out things."

Tillie looked at him. "We have lot a stuff to help us then. Now we only have one."

Molly opened her eyes. "Shush," she said to Tillie. "That suppose-a stay a secret."

Hillary looked up. "What stuff? What's going on with you three?"

"I think it's big enough," Windslow said. "Scrunch around so I can lay down."

Everyone wiggled and squirmed until Windslow could stretch his legs out and bend down through the opening in the bottom of the nest. "The dog things are gone" he said. "Oh, oh. I think I know why." Windslow sat back up. "It's those guys wearing the purple hoods. A bunch of them are here and there's some other guy with them."

"Welcome Molly," a voice called from the ground. "I know you're in there. I can sense you from here. I see you have your sisters with you. And you, lad. You must be one of the Children of the Wind. Is your sister here too? If she is, then this is quite a lucky day for me."

Windslow was about to look through the hole again. Molly grabbed his sweatshirt and pulled him back. "That very mean person," she whispered. "That Dead-door. He very biggest wizard. Now there really no hope left."

"Let me look," Hillary said. She still held the piece of wand in her hand. She shifted it up to her fingertips and wiggled next to her brother. Windslow edged back from the hole and let her lean down.

"Hello," Dreadlore called. "I assume you're Hillary."

"Ouch!" Hillary said and pushed herself back into the nest. She shook her hand. "He took my wand somehow. My fingers felt like I was holding a flame and I had to open them."

"That silly thing a do," Molly said. "We told you not a use it. Now look what happen. Now we stuck even worse."

"Molly," Windslow said. "I think you have some explaining to do and not much time to do it in."

Molly sighed. "Move back," she told him. "I need a talk a Deadborie." Molly leaned down the hole.

"Hi, big boss," she called.

Dreadlore yelled back. "I'll have my men get you down. I assume our bargain is still valid?"

"It still there," Molly said. "I need time a talk to my sissers."

"Make it quick," Dreadlore called.

Molly sat up.

"Well?" Windslow asked.

The three sisters looked at each other. Molly turned to Windslow and Hillary. "Long time ago we make bargain with Dread-gore. When he here, we only allowed a use magic one time a day. We got one time-a use it this day. We saving it to help mommy Trish again. That how we use it yesterday and a-fore."

"I knew you could work magic," Windslow said. "I've seen that blue light when you make stuff happen."

"Windslow," Hillary said. "We've got to save their magic. They need to use it on mom. What are we going to do?"

"We make new bargain," Molly said. She leaned back down the hole.

"Hey, Deadbore. I got new bargain."

Dreadlore called back. "If you're serious, then let me talk with Tillie. She has to tell the truth. You might not."

Molly pulled herself back up and whispered in Tillie's ear. Tillie leaned down the hole.

"You want us a go to Aberratia with you," She yelled to Dreadlore.

"That's right," He called back. "But there's more. I want you to take me to the Secret Library. I want you to help me find the ratStone and I want you to channel your magic with mine. I want the Children of the Wind to follow my orders too."

"Here what we do," Tillie yelled to him. "You go back a Aberratia. We meet you there tomorrow after next. Then *we* do all a stuff you ask."

"What do you think you can do in two days? Just give up now."

Tillie answered. "We give up a you now, then you not get all a things you ask for. That not good bargain for you. Think about how bad it be if Molly and Nelly and I be all-a time trouble for you. This way you got old bargain and new bargain with a Sallyforth sisters. That very good thing for you."

Windslow listened. He wished he could see Dreadlore's face. No one said anything. Molly smiled at Nelly.

Tillie called to Dreadlore. "Some wizzie guy tell me I not have much time a think things over. I running out of time with him. I need a answer for my sisers and me."

"Done!" Dreadlore yelled.

"They going," Tillie said. She sat up.

Molly and Nelly gave her a hug. "That very good job," Molly said.

"Good job?" Windslow said. "You gave him everything he wanted."

"No we not," Tillie said. "I do like Nelly. I twist things all up."

Molly grinned. "Library already gone. It not in Gabendoor anymore. We help him find ratStone, but not promise to let him have it. We channel magic with him, but when there no magic, there nothing to channel. We fix things up for you two. We tell him we agree. We tell him he got bargain with Sallyforth sisers, not with Children of a Wind. He not get very much. We get one more day and one more chance to help mommy Trish."

"There's only one problem," Hillary said, her head lowered to the hole. "Dreadlore and his men are gone, but the dog things are back. They're watching us from across the meadow."

"That's not all," Windslow said and pointed. "The buzzard was back." A hole the size of a dinner platter gaped in the netting. A tan hooked beak darted down and clipped away another piece.

"Let's get out of here," Hillary said. She turned around and lowered her legs through the hole. "I just wish I had that piece of wand."

"How bout this," Nelly said. She grabbed the end of a piece of wood protruding from the hole. "It Somber wood. Birdie do us a good thing. There lots of it here." Molly pulled out another slender stick. She pushed one into Hillary's backpack and handed the other to Windslow. "Now you both got new wands."

"Who said there's no hope," Hillary said. She dropped through the hole and onto one of the stout tree branches.

Windslow helped the triplets through, then followed. Hillary was already on the ground. Molly, Nelly and Tillie dropped down beside her. Windslow joined them and held out his wand. He muttered something and pointed the stick at the dog like beasts. Nothing happened.

"They not charged up yet," Molly told him. "They not absorb magic until wizard hold them. It take awhile yet."

"Great," Windslow said and put the stick in his back pocket.

Across the meadow, all four beasts stood. Instead of heading straight for the tree, they split into two groups, one circling to the left, the other right.

"It's like they're trying to herd us again," Hillary said.

Windslow took a coil of rope from his backpack. "I've never seen an animal that didn't want to get away when you tied it up. Let's see what these do. Start moving for the woods. If one gets close to us, I'm going to lasso it. Hillary, keep your wand ready. If you have to cast a spell, think small. If there's such a thing as a low power spell, we'll need one."

The group moved at a fast walk. The beasts on their right moved in closer. The beasts to their left moved slightly away.

"They moving us to cliff," Molly said.

Even though the beasts moved in closer, Hillary stayed on a straight line toward the forest. The beasts yelped and showed their teeth. One darted within ten feet of them.

Windslow twirled his rope over his head and threw. The beast turned away then circled back. Windslow pulled in his rope, coiled it, ready for another throw. The beast lowered its head, bared its teeth and darted close. Windslow's toss landed the noose neatly around the beast's neck.

Windslow pulled. The beast stopped, planted all four legs and strained against the rope. "I got him," Windslow yelled.

The other beasts broke the pattern and rushed to the beast Windslow had lassoed. It whined and bit at the rope. Windslow wrapped the end of rope around his waist to keep it from slipping out of his hands.

Suddenly the tension stopped. Windslow lost his balance and fell backward. The lassoed beast rushed at him. Windslow threw up his arm to shield his face. The beast's mouth closed around his arm. Windslow closed his eyes and clenched his teeth to withstand the pain. When he felt none, he opened his eyes.

The beast held his arm firmly in its mouth and pulled, dragging Windslow toward the cliff. Windslow looked at the beast's teeth. They bent like rubber around his forearm. The beast stopped after dragging Windslow about twenty feet. It let go of Windslow's arm, licked it three times and grabbed it again.

Windslow didn't struggle. He looked for his sister and the Sallyforth sisters. They stood huddled in a group. The other three beasts dashed around them in a tight circle. Hillary shook her wand, pointed it at the beasts and shook it again.

The beast pulling Windslow let go, ran behind him and grabbed Windslow by the belt. Walking backward, it moved Windslow with a series of short jerks. After moving him only ten feet, the beast let go, sat on its hind legs and panted. It whimpered, stood and grabbed Windslow's belt again.

"Ok, okay. I get the idea this time," Windslow said. When the beast stopped to rest again. Windslow twisted around, reached out and scratched it under the chin. The beast licked its long tongue over its teeth and snout. Windslow slowly stood and put one hand between the beast's shoulders. It walked slow, leading Windslow toward the cliff.

"They don't want to hurt us!" Windslow yelled. "They were herding us. Their teeth are like rubber. They can't bite you!"

Hillary stopped pointing her stick. All four girls sat on the grass. With slow steps, the beasts moved closer. When one was within reach, Hillary held out her hand. The Sallyforth sisters did the same. The beasts moved closer. One licked Molly's hand. The other two moved behind the girls.

Windslow stopped walking and waited for the others to catch up. The beast with Windslow led the way. When they neared the cliff, Windslow saw where the creatures wanted them to go; a narrow opening to what looked like a cave. At the entrance, the lead beast moved back with its companions.

"Well," Windslow said. "I suppose there's only one thing to do now." He ducked his head and stepped into the dark.

10: Jurassic Bunny

The opening wasn't as much a cave as an arched walkway cut through thirty feet of rock. It curved to the right and opened into a valley encircled by steep cliff walls.

"Whoa," Windslow said. "A hidden valley just like in a fantasy book."

"This place is huge," Hillary said. "You could fit a city in here."

They stood at the edge of a meadow, much like the one on the other side of the wall. The grass here looked a deeper green and the lush blades grew longer, nearly coming to Hillary's knees. Pink and yellow flowers grew in clusters and gave off a fruity scent. To their right, trees dotted the meadow with wide spaces between them. Farther away, the trees grew closer together and blocked the view.

"Molly, what is this place?" Windslow asked.

Molly shrugged. "We not know. We go lots a places in Gabendoor but not in Charm Mist. We never a-spposed to go there."

"Why?" Hillary asked. "It's beautiful here."

"If you know you're not supposed to go here," Windslow said. "Then you must know about it"

The Sallyforth sisters looked at each other. Tillie answered. "There lot-a places we know bout. There rules we half-a follow sometimes."

Hillary tilted her head to the side and wrinkled up her eyebrows. "You three get more mysterious every time we come to Gabendoor with you. Whose rules?"

"Um..." Molly said. "Rules of magic. Rules of Gabendoor. We-- Oof!"

Molly fell to one side, knocked off balance by the three dog-like creatures that had herded everyone to the cave entrance. They ran ahead, stopped and sniffed, their noses pushing aside blades of grass.

One long and two short whistles sounded from the direction of a clump of tall bushes one hundred yards ahead. Four snouts jerked up from sniffing the grass. Ears stood alert. The beasts dashed for the stand of lavender and blue bushes.

"Come on!" Windslow yelled. "Let's follow them."

Windslow started in the lead. His sister and the Sallyforth triplets quickly passed him. He caught up to them when they stopped at the bushes. Here the grass was shorter and looked mowed or clipped by something. The others stood looking at the thick foliage.

"Where'd they go?" Windslow asked.

"We lost sight of them," Hillary said. "I can't see any tracks and I don't see any openings in the bushes. Maybe they went around?"

"Look," Windslow said. He plucked a small tuft of black hair off one of the woody bush stems. He pushed the stem aside. "Here's the path." Without saying anything, he bent over and moved through the narrow opening in the thick stems and leaves.

The path snaked left and right then opened back in the meadow. "Whoa, land of the lost." Windslow said. "Look giant rabbits."

On this side of the bushes, the land rolled with gentle grass covered swells and flower lined low spots. From the nearest cliff wall, crystal water showered down the rocks, splashing into a large pond with a stream running from its far shore. Around the pond, oversized rabbits with curly hair hopped and grazed. Spaced out beyond the rabbits, the three beasts sat watching. When one of the rabbits hopped too far away from the pond, one of the beasts stood, ran, and herded it back to the group. Its task done, the beast retuned to its spot, sat back down, and continued its watch.

"They can't be rabbits," Hillary said. "They're three feet tall and they look like they have wool instead of fur. Their noses are wrong too."

Windslow shrugged. "Jurassic Easter bunnies maybe?" He took a step forward.

Hillary grabbed his arm. "Hold on. Those whistles didn't come from the wind. There's somebody here."

"That not very good," Molly said and pointed to the western sky.

They all turned. A large black cloud rolled high into the atmosphere. Like boiling soot, it rose and spread. In the distance, they all heard rumbling.

"Oh, oh," Hillary said. "I think I know what that is. Molly, does Gabendoor have any volcanoes?"

"Not afore now," Molly answered.

"The ground isn't shaking here," Windslow said. "I think we're okay, aren't we? I mean it's not going to rain boulders or anything is it?" Windslow yawned. "Crud-oh. Dream-slip time is coming, but it's too early. We haven't been here that long. Time is all screwed up."

Molly gave her own yawn. "We better find a place a sleep."

"I go get a couple bunnies to cuddle with," Tillie said. When she moved forward, one of the dog-beasts leapt to its feet and yelped at her. Tillie stepped back. "That not good idea. I cuddle with you, Nelly."

Nelly yawned. "I sleep right here. This very good place." Still yawning, she turned back to the bushes.

"The bushes are as good a place as any," Hillary said. She and the others followed Nelly.

ꟷ

The Wind-Climber watched the girl, and the people with her, duck into the cliff wall. The Wind-Climber knew the place beyond the cliff in the sheltered valley. She had been there before. It would be a difficult flight with the stone in her pouch adding extra weight. The cliff was high, but she was a Wind-Climber and there was always wind.

The furry brown creature gulped in air to form the airfoils between her front and hind legs. She drew in more air, puffing out her stomach. She would need to boost her flight. With a kick from her strong hind legs, she leaped into the air, gliding toward the cliff. At the wall, she drew in her wings, twisted her body and kicked to launch herself even higher. When her speed slowed, the Wind-Climber tightened her stomach and chest muscles, compressing the air in her chest chamber. Expelled from a small vent near her tail, the burst of air propelled her faster and higher. Tightening her glide, she circled back toward the cliff while she gulped more air. With another kick and boost from her air jet, she soared.

She felt the rush of wind that struck the cliff and bent upward like a thermal. Soaring in the updraft, the Wind-Climber watched the cliff's top ridge drop below her. The rest of the flight would be easy, a gentle glide into the valley. A tree near the waterfall would be a nice place to land and look for the girl.

A strange scent drifted with the wind. In the distance, a black cloud rose from a large mountain with a red glowing top. The Wind-Climber sneezed, pushing out the smell. She angled her glide and saw the girl and her companions ducking into a large oval of bushes. The Wind-Climber used a last jet of air to extend her glide. The last thrust would be just enough. On a high branch, she expelled the air from her wings, relaxed, and wrapped her furry tail around herself. Now she would sleep like the girl and the others.

ഇ൱

Hillary closed her eyes, ready to dream-slip. She wiggled, reached under her back and pulled out a stick that had been poking her. She closed her eyes again and waited. She could hear the others rustling. *Well, come on*, she thought to herself. *Let's dream-slip*.

She waited a few more minutes. "Windslow?" she said softly.

"What?"

"Oh, I was just checking to see if you were still here," she said.

"I here too."

"I here three."

"I gone."

Hillary opened her eyes. "What's wrong," she asked. "Why aren't we dream-slipping? I don't feel tired anymore." She rolled over to her side and looked at the others.

Windslow sat with his knees pulled up against his chest. All three Sallyforth triplets lay with their elbows on the ground and their chins cradled in their hands.

"Time shifted," a melodic voice said from outside the bushes. "You won't dream-slip for some time yet. Come sit by the fire."

Hillary emerged first. Something wasn't right. Night had come even though it had only been a few minutes. She shivered against the chill. In front of her, a boy and girl both about Hillary's age, stood holding hands. "Who are you?" Hillary asked.

"She's my sister, Faith," the boy said. He smiled at the girl. His brown eyes sparkled.

"He's my brother, Maxwell," the girl said. "Come with us. Down by the pond we have a fire to warm you."

Still holding hands, she and her brother turned and walked away. From the back, they looked nearly alike, brown hair cut the same, just above their shoulders. Woven headbands of multicolored wool held their hair in place.

Windslow looked at his sister. "What's going on? It can't be night. And I don't see any stars. Where did those two come from?"

"Sky got funny red glow over that way," Tillie said and pointed in the direction where they had seen the dark clouds earlier.

"I not want-a go by fireplace," Molly said. I stay here.

"Me staying with siser," Tillie said and sat down next to Molly.

"I go by fire," Nelly said as she plopped down by her sisters.

"Geeze," Windslow said. "What's with you three? You're acting goofy. I mean not goofy like usual. I mean you three always do crazy stuff and make me laugh and run straight into any adventure. I don't get it."

"Maybe Marcie go with you," Molly said. "Maybe she an cheerleaders want a sit by fire. I not happy right now. I not want-a go home."

Hillary squatted down in front of the sisters. "What do you mean, you don't want to go home. This is your home. Do you mean you don't want to go back to Earth? Don't let Marcy get you down. Let's go find out who those kids are."

"Girl got silly name," Tillie said. "We have lot-a faith in lots-a stuff. Now it all go away."

"Oops," Windslow said and un-slung his backpack. He pulled out the *Book of Library Secrets.* "This thing just sprung to normal size inside my pack. Let's see if it has anything new to say."

Windslow put the book on the grass and opened it. They all crowded around, watching Windslow flip through the pages.

"The book is full of wisdom," Maxwell said.

They all looked up. Instead of sitting on the grass near the bushes, they now sat in front of a small fire. The yellow and orange flames reflected off the pond. Across the fire, Maxwell and Faith sat on a log. The four dog like beasts lay curled at their feet. The fire reflecting in the beasts' eyes made them look red. One beast yawned and licked its snout before resting its head back on outstretched paws.

"How'd we get...?" Hillary said. "We were just over..."

Maxwell smiled. "It's simple. Either the fire and the pond moved to you or you moved to the pond. Either way, you will be more comfortable."

"You're quite safe here," Faith said. "What does your book say?"

"It's private," Windslow said and slammed the cover shut. "If you two are wizards, whose side are you on?"

Faith giggled. "We don't have any magic. At least I don't." She pulled on her brother's hand. "Do you, Maxwell?"

He shook his head.

Faith looked back at Windslow. "This place has magic. Things happen here as the magic wants them to happen. As my brother said, either it brought you here or moved the fire and us to you."

"What are those dog things?" Hillary asked. "Are they yours or do they belong to this place too? Why did they herd us in here?"

Maxwell patted one of the beasts. "They belong to Gabendoor. They are Shelterhunds."

"They not stink so much anymore," Molly said. She sat with her arms folded tight across her chest.

"They were very dirty," Faith said. "I bathed them in the waterfall. The magic sent them after you. You were all in great danger."

"How would you know that?" Hillary asked. She got off the ground and sat on a log near the fire. Windslow joined her. Even with the fire, she still shivered.

"The magic would not have sent the Shelterhunds. Sometimes the magic reveals things to us by reflecting images in the pond. We saw you in the tree. We saw the men coming up the mountain for you."

"What has your book told you?" Maxwell asked. "Here" he said holding out his hand. From his fingers dangled a multi-colored headband, like the one he and his sister wore. "This will help keep you warm."

Hillary gave him a long look. "Yah, right. At least one strip of my head won't be cold." Despite her remark, she took the band and pulled it down to her forehead. She looked at her brother and back to Maxwell. "It's like I just put on a sweater."

Faith smiled. She offered one to Windslow. "They keep you warm and keep you cool. We weave them from the wool of the heather-ears."

"You mean those oversized rabbits?" Windslow asked.

Faith and Maxwell looked at each other.

"Never mind," Windslow said. He looked at his sister, glanced at the Sallyforth triplets and opened the *Book of Library Secrets,* holding it balanced on his knees. It doesn't really say much this time. He read the new words aloud for the others.

Hope begins
With a cheer that wins.

"Like usual," he said, "It doesn't say much." He looked up at Maxwell and Faith. "Do you two have any ideas?"

The both shook their heads.

Faith stood. "It is from the Secret Library. You and your sister are the ones the book's wisdom is for." She walked to the Sallyforth girls and held out her hand, holding three more headbands. When the sisters stayed still with their arms folded, Faith placed a headband on each scowling girl.

Windslow turned when his sister gave a short scream.

"It's okay," she said. "I just got startled." She looked at Faith. "I think another one of your creatures just decided to join us."

"First overgrown rabbits," Windslow said. "Now it's an overgrown squirrel."

"It's not ours," Maxwell said. "It's a Wind-Climber. It must have been looking for you, Daughter of the Wind."

"Yes," Faith said. She returned to her seat next to her brother and took his hand. "Wind-Climbers find things and return them to people. You must have lost something. It has come to trade."

"I haven't lost anything," Hillary said. "Is it okay to touch it?"

"They are normally gentle creatures," Faith said. "What will you offer it?"

"Hi, little guy," Hillary said and cautiously reached out her hand.

"It is female," Maxwell said.

Hillary gave him a funny look. "I knew that. It's just a phrase." She stroked the creature's soft fur. The Wind-Climber purred as she ran her hand over it. With her other hand, she dug in her backpack. "Here sweetie," she said and held out a granola bar.

"Um... maybe you should unwrap it first," Windslow said.

Hillary lifted her hand from the Wind-Climber, ready to tear the silver and gold foil wrapper. Before she could, the Wind-Climber snatched it from her hand. It squealed as it turned the bright package over and over in its front paws.

"I guess she likes it," Hillary said.

The Wind-Climber stuffed its new treasure into its pouch and took three hops away from the log.

"What's it doing?" Hillary asked.

"Watch," Faith said. "It has accepted your trade. You'll see how it got its name."

The Wind-Climber stretched out its front paws. Hillary heard a series of small puffing sounds as the skin between the creature's front and back legs filled with air. It hopped forward, each hop higher than the last. The third hop brought it to the log Hillary sat on. She heard a loud "thud," when the Wind-Climbers hind feet propelled it high off the log. She heard a sound like air rushing from a tire. The Wind-Climber shot upward, soaring on its fur wings, until darkness surrounded it.

"Whoa, cool," Windslow said.

Hillary looked at Faith. "I thought it was going to trade me for something?"

"It did," Faith said. "It found something lost and put it where you will now find it. The trade has been made."

"This is all too confusing," Hillary said and yawned.

"This all silly," Molly said.

Maxwell leaned forward. "You know it's not silly. You know what's happening. What have you done with your hope?"

"Marcy take it," Molly said. "Mommy Trish need it. Gabendoor need it. We not need it. There nothing for us a do. There no hope for us for anything."

Maxwell snapped his attention to Windslow. "No," he said. "Don't discuss it. Just do it."

Windslow opened his mouth, hesitated and closed it again. "That's spooky," he said, "but all right."

"What?" Hillary said and looked at her brother. She yawned.

Windslow yawned, but didn't answer.

"Space has folded back again," Maxwell said. "Time is back in order; at least for now. It's time for all of you to dream-slip."

"We need to find a place..." Hillary's words trailed off. She didn't remember closing her eyes, but recognized swiftly entering a dream-slip.

II: Science and Hope

Windslow woke, got out of bed and hurried to get ready for school. He hoped to be up before Hillary so he could have a chance to help out more. When he neared the kitchen, he saw the lights on and could smell coffee. Inside the kitchen, Hillary already had lunches made. She stood at the stove and used a spatula to flip over a piece of French toast sizzling on a griddle. "How long have you been up?" he asked. He wheeled to the kitchen cabinets but stopped when he saw Hillary had already set the table.

"You can warm up some syrup," Hillary said and placed the last piece of battered bread in the skillet. "The bottle is already in the microwave."

It's already in the microwave, Windslow said silently, moving his lips to the words. He sighed as he pressed buttons on the timer. It was nice that his sister had everything ready but it annoyed him that everything was so perfect. He knew it was foolish to feel that way. He felt that somehow helping around the house would be like helping his step-mom.

"Good morning, kids," Bill said and helped himself to a cup of coffee. "Hillary, I appreciate all the extra work, but I don't want you getting sick. I'm worried about you getting enough sleep. You too, Windslow," Bill said. "I couldn't sleep myself last night, and peeked in on both of you. You were both tossing and turning. Windslow, you were muttering something in your sleep about rubber teeth. Hillary, you were talking in your sleep too. You kept saying something about magic books and trading granola bars."

"Have some French toast," Hillary said and shoved the steaming plate to her stepfather.

The microwave beeped.

"Syrup's done," Windslow said and opened the microwave door. He glanced at his sister.

"Wow, look at the time," Hillary said. She sat at the table and spread butter on her toast, poured syrup over it, and took a big bite.

Windslow did the same. "Yah, we better get a move on. Eat up dad."

Bill didn't say much more. He was half-finished with his breakfast when Windslow and Hillary both put their plates in the sink.

Hillary headed out the kitchen door. "I need to get my backpack," she said.

"Me too," Windslow added. "Meet you in the car, dad." He hurried out of the kitchen.

***

At school, the day went well until the last period. Windslow had just closed his locker when he heard Marcy's voice. He turned around and saw her and her gaggle of friends approaching. She had a smirk on her face and looked straight at him. Windslow turned his chair in the opposite direction, hoping to avoid her.

"Lost?" Marcy asked, her voice sweet, musical and sarcastic. "Your science class is that way," she said, tilting her head the other direction down the hall.

"Um... no," Windslow stammered. "I thought I needed something. I decided I can get it later." He turned his chair around.

Marcy blocked him. "You won't believe what your stupid Sallyforth friends have done. They upgraded their wardrobes. Messy Molly tried to show off her new outfit to me. I told her that dressing semi-normal wouldn't make a difference. She and her sisters still have no hope of even trying out for the cheerleading squad. She is so un-cool."

Windslow clenched his fists. His face burned.

Marcy stepped to the side.

Windslow looked down, trying not to move his head any more than necessary. He judged the distance, put his hands on his wheels and readied himself. "Marcy," Windslow said, "You'd be nothing without your friends. You couldn't intimidate a flea. In fact, a flea wouldn't even want to come near you. Do me a favor and step back. You're too close to my chair."

Marcy scowled at him. Her face flushed. She did exactly what Windslow had hoped she would do. Marcy stepped closer to his chair.

Windslow shoved on his wheels.

Marcy screamed. "You're on my toes! You're on my toes!" She shoved at his chair.

Windslow pushed on his wheels, rolled forward an inch and rolled back. He felt his wheel bounce over her toe again.

Marcy wailed. She dropped to the floor, her books and papers scattering to her side. Crying, she grabbed her foot. "I'm bleeding," she cried.

"Sorry," Windslow said. "Sorry! Are you hurt?"

"You idiot!" Marcy yelled. "You did that on purpose."

"No!" Windslow said and moved his chair away from her. "That's why I told you that you were too close to my chair. You shouldn't stand with your feet so close."

Mr. Garrick, the history teacher, came running from his room. He pushed through the group of girls and knelt down beside Marcy. "What happened?" He asked.

"He ran over my toe," Marcy said. Tears streamed down her cheeks.

"It was an accident," Windslow said. "I just got some stuff from my locker and Marcy came over to talk. I had to get to science class and told her to move back. When I started moving, she stepped closer instead. I ran over her. I'm really sorry. Is she okay?"

Mr. Garrick slipped Marcy's sandal off her foot. "Calm down, Marcy," he said. "I doubt your toe's broken. A little skin is scrubbed off." He looked up. "Everyone off to class. You too, Windslow. Come on, Marcy. I'll help you to the nurse's office."

"Can you move please," Windslow said to some of the students still gawking at Marcy. "I don't want to get any more toes."

The students moved back, making a path for Windslow. He hurried to science class. Behind him, he heard Mr. Garrick tell everyone to go on with their business.

Windslow tried to keep a concerned look on his face until he reached his classroom. He couldn't help but grin as he wheeled through the door and up to his spot in the front row. Everyone but Molly was in class. Her stool sat empty next to him. Just as the bell rang, Molly came running in and sat beside him.

Windslow took a quick look. Instead of the familiar clothes she normally wore, she had white sneakers, tight black jeans, a white shirt and black vest, all designer labels. Instead of spiky black hair that looked like she was a chimney-sweep brush, her hair swept back, glistening with gel. Windslow stared at her bright red lips before gawking at her dark eye shadow. "Molly?" he said. His mouth stayed open.

"You like my new clothes?" she asked. "I in high style now. My sissers too. We got all a popular stuff to wear. Now all-a girls like us like they do Marcy."

Windslow blew out a long breath and leaned close to her. "You look different," he said. "I don't think I like it. I liked you the way you were. You need to give up on being a cheerleader. You're being dumb. Clothes aren't going to change you."

Molly's smile fled. She stared at Windslow, tilted her head to the side and sucked in her lower lip. Turning away, she looked down and quietly folded her hands in her lap.

I'm so stupid, Windslow said to himself. He sighed again and flipped open his science book.

Ms. DiMarco handed out a worksheet with instructions for experiments that each team was to conduct in class. She wrote on the board and talked about polymers and compounds.

When it was time for Molly and Windslow to do their experiment, Windslow had to gather all the materials. Molly sat, still staring at her hands.

For the experiment they had to use borax, cornstarch, glue and water to form a polymer ball and then see if it would bounce.

"Molly, you know you could help a little," Windslow said. He measured borax and water into one beaker and cornstarch and glue into the other. "You need to watch this. We're supposed to record our observations."

"Leave me alone," Molly said.

Windslow leaned close to her so the other students wouldn't hear. In a loud whisper he said, "Molly, it's not fair to just sit there. You need to help."

"There," Molly said and flicked her finger toward the two flasks. A soft blue light swirled around the experiment and winked out. One flask sat empty. The other held what looked like a gooey mass of soft white putty. "Polymer done. I done. You do a-rest."

Windslow grabbed her arm and leaned close again. "Did you just use magic? If you did, then it was the magic you were supposed to be saving so you could help my mom."

Windslow sat up straight. Ms. DiMarco stood in front of his table. She picked up the flask, and examined it.

"Very nice work," she said and put the flask back down. "Start cleaning up, everyone. The period is almost over." She turned and walked back to her desk.

Windslow looked at Molly. She sat as before, her hands neatly folded on her lap. He was about to say something when he noticed a tear run along the side of her nose, leaving a track in her makeup when it continued across her cheek.

Windslow bit his lip. He had never seen Molly or her sisters cry before. They were always silly and confident, brave and upbeat, no matter how bad things were. His heart sunk. He wanted to say something, but words wouldn't form in his head. The school bell rang. Molly slid off her stool and ran from the classroom.

Windslow leaned back in his wheelchair. *What a miserable day*, he thought to himself. He waited for the last students to leave the room before heading for the door. He was going to stop at his locker, but decided not to. He didn't want to chance running into Marcy again. He pivoted his chair and headed for the gym and soccer practice.

Out on the field, he thought to tell Hillary about what had happened, but decided against it. He figured his sister would either be mad at him, or mad at Molly, or mad at both of them. Several times the coach had to yell at Windslow to get his attention. For the moments when there was nothing for him to do, Windslow sat staring into nothingness, his thoughts a hazy mix of feelings and emotion.

Windslow was glad when practice finally ended and his dad came to pick up his sister and him. Thankfully, Hillary didn't have much to say on the trip to the hospital. Windslow's stomach churned as he thought again about how Molly had wasted her magic on the chemistry assignment. He was worried even more when his dad didn't ramble on and on about how everything would be fine. Windslow decided that too much silence wasn't a good thing.

ꙮ

Windslow fidgeted in his wheel chair as he waited with his sister and father. When they got to the hospital, they couldn't go into his stepmother's room right away. Her doctor had wanted to have a family conference with them. The news wasn't good. The doctor talked about brain injuries, what doctors knew about them, and what they didn't. Windslow didn't care about all that. What he cared about was the news his stepmother had some kind of pressure on her brain. All the medical words didn't mean anything to Windslow. The look on his father's face told him what he needed. Things weren't going well. The doctor spoke about the possibility of some kind of brain surgery to release the pressure. They were going to run more tests in the morning. Windslow thought again about Molly using magic in science class. He didn't know much about medicine but was certain that magic was what his mother needed right now.

The nurse's voice pulled Windslow out of his thoughts. "You can come in now," she said from the open doorway to his mother's room. "She's sleeping. We sedated her so I doubt she'll wake up. Sleeping is good for her. She needs her rest. You shouldn't stay long."

Inside the room, Windslow looked at Trish. She slept on her back, her bed slightly inclined. She looked pale. He moved his wheelchair around the bed and near the window. Hillary eased herself up on the side of the bed and gingerly slipped her hand under her mother's to hold it.

"Hi," a soft voice said from the door.

Windslow looked up. Mrs. Christensen walked in with Molly, Tillie and Nelly. Bill took Mrs. Christensen's arm and walked out of the room with her. The Sallyforth triplets stayed silent and lined up, shoulder to shoulder against the wall. Hillary glanced at the girls and nodded, but didn't say anything.

Windslow bit his lip. He wondered why the triplets were even here. There wasn't anything they could do without magic. After staring at them for a few seconds, he leaned forward, rested his elbows on his knees, and used his hands to cradle his chin. He gave a sigh and looked at the floor.

They all looked up when they heard Trish's voice. "It's time for me to give this back to you," she said. Trish lay with her eyes open and head turned to face the Sallyforth Triplets. She raised her arm just inches off the bed and opened her hand. In her palm rested a soft glowing blue ball of light. "You gave this to me long ago. I haven't needed it. Now I give it back," she said. "Truth, secrets, intuition. Have you forgotten?"

"We just scared," Molly said, her eyes filling with tears. She held out her open hand. The blue light floated from Trish's hand to hers. Molly folded her fingers around it. When the light winked out, Molly used the back of her fist to wipe her eyes. “This lot-a hope and little bit of magic.” Molly sniffed and looked at her sisters.

Trish’s eyes closed and her arm fell back to the bed.

“What’s going on?” Hillary asked.

“Your mommy tell us we need-a be us,” Molly said. “But, that going to be very hard.” Molly walked to the side of the bed and stroked her fingers across Trish’s forehead. Molly’s fingers left a trail of blue light that quickly faded.

“She gave you magic,” Windslow said. “What did you do?”

Molly looked at him. “She not need operation now. She need lot of hope. Gabendoor need lot of hope too.” Molly glanced at Hillary and turned back to Windslow. “Mommy Trish and Gabendoor linked together. Only way-a bring hope is up to Children of-a Wind. What you need a do is very dangerous.”

“Dangerous?” Hillary asked. “How?”

“Hi, kids,” Bill said when he walked into the room. “We need to let your mom rest.” He didn’t say anything more and stood by the doorway as they all moved into the hallway, where Mrs. Christensen waited.

“I’m your ride tonight,” Mrs. Christensen said, looking at Hillary and Windslow. “Your dad wants to sit here with your mother a little longer. We’re all going to get some dinner on the way home. Windslow and Hillary, do you need anything from the store? We can stop along the way if you do.”

“Thanks, Mrs. Christensen,” Hillary said. “I think we’re okay. Windslow, can you think of anything?”

Windslow shook his head. As everyone moved toward the elevator, Windslow wheeled up beside Molly. He grabbed her sleeve.

"Sorry," he said softly when she turned to look at him.

Molly nodded, turned and silently kept walking.

Oh, crud-o, Windslow thought to himself. *What a mess.*

On the ride to the restaurant, Windslow's head filled with thoughts that mixed and jumbled together. He thought about the mystery of the Secret Library, what Maxwell and Faith had said about magic in Gabendoor. He tried to sort out what Trish had meant by the Daughter of Secrets, Maiden of Truth and Child of Intuition. While they ate dinner, Mrs. Christensen did most of the talking. Molly, Tillie and Nelly poked at their spaghetti, moving the noodles around on their plates more than eating. Hillary half finished her soup and salad. Windslow was the only one who really ate. When Windslow and Hillary got home, Windslow wanted to talk with his sister and see if she could help him sort anything out. She said she was exhausted and wanted to get to bed.

Windslow made some lunches for the next day. Back in his room, he flipped through the *Book of Library Secrets*, but found no new words and still had no idea what the words that did show meant. He closed his eyes and hoped his thoughts would stop scrambling in his head and let him sleep.

12: Aberratia

Windslow knew he had just dream-slipped. He stretched and opened his eyes, expecting to see the Shelterhunds and the hidden valley. One hundred feet in front of him stood the backs of small homes. It took him a few seconds to realize it was Eldervale. The normally whitewashed homes and golden brown thatched roofs all looked a dismal deep gray.

"What's all this stuff?" Hillary said from behind him.

Windslow twisted around and looked at his sister. She stood and stomped her feet on the ground as she used her hands to brush off the back of her jeans. Each foot stomp sent up a small cloud of gray dust.

"This awful," a voice said in front of him. Windslow turned back and saw the three Sallyforth sisters getting up from the ground. They had gray dust marking where they had made contact with the ground.

Windslow took his magic crutches from his backpack and used them to stand. He too was covered with the dust.

"I think it's ash," Hillary said. "It's all over everything."

"Mountain blow its temper," Molly said.

Tillie pointed to the west. "It from over that way. It big volcano."

"Is it going to erupt again?" Hillary asked. She looked in the direction Tillie pointed. Above the treetops, she could see a plume of gray black smoke rising in the distance. The clouds hovered in a tight group that looked like dark storm clouds.

Nelly sneezed. She rubbed her nose with her shirtsleeve. "It really close and so all-a lava going to burn everything here."

"Um... good," Windslow said. At first he was startled, but then remembered it was Nelly who had given the answer. "So we don't need to worry about a pyrotechnic flow or boulders smashing down or anything like that?"

"Not here," Molly said. "It very bad in some places. It bad enough here. All-a crops are ruined."

Hillary started walking. "I think we should find Granny Gilderbun and Grandpa Dimbleshoot. There are probably lots of people who could use our help right now. Dreadlore can wait."

"He not wait," Molly said. "Best way-a help ever-body is to fix things at Aberratia. We need a get rid of Dread-snore"

"An," Tillie said, "we need help a do that."

"An we not need a ratStone either," Nelly added.

Windslow hurried along behind the others as they approached the backs of the first homes. "This is all such a mess. What is the ratStone? I still don't get the deal with this Dreadlore guy."

No one answered.

They walked single file between two buildings and emerged near the town square. Its once beautiful white gazebo now looked old and gray. Water didn't flow in the fountain behind it. The water had a murky, oily look to it, almost like thin mud.

Many people sat around the fountain and gazebo. Just past the town square, more people gathered in front of several large tents that had once been white. Most people just sat, saying nothing and staring at the ground. Some women wept.

"There's Gilderbun," Hillary said and ran to her elderly friend who sat alone on the low rock wall surrounding the fountain. When Hillary reached her, they hugged. "Gilderbun, are you all right?"

"I am, dear," Gilderbun said. "Yesterday it hailed again. If that weren't enough to do most of the crops in, it started to rain last night. The trouble is it rained soot. Everything's ruined. Look at this fountain. The water's no good. We only have one well and the water from it has slowed to a trickle. Winter will be coming soon. But I don't know that we need to worry about that. I don't know how we'll survive until then. Even the little bit of livestock we have won't do us much good. The chickens are already sick. There's nothing to feed the goats. I just don't know what to do. No one has any ideas, except Dreadlore. He thinks he knows everything. The fact is, he's a fool."

"Where is he?" Windslow asked. "And where's Dimbleshoot?"

Granny Gilderbun looked up at him. "Dimbleshoot gathered up some of the men to see what they could do in the fields. He thought if we could get the soot off the tops of the plants, some of them might be all right. Dreadlore's men wouldn't let him. They said it was a waste of time and sent the men into the woods to forage for food and to check the streams to see if any of them are clean enough to use for water."

"Did Dreadlore go with them?" Hillary asked.

"No," Gilderbun said. "He went back to Aberratia, his temple. A lot of the villagers went with him. Dreadlore told them it's the only place that's safe. A few fools from the village went traipsing off to search for a rock Dreadlore called the ratStone. He offered a reward to anyone that found it."

"We got appointment," Molly said. "Tomorrow it time for us-a go see him."

"Oh my goodness," Gilderbun said. "You can't go there. It's too dangerous. If you three girls are determined to go, at least go alone. You can't take Hillary and Windslow with you."

"We aren't going tomorrow," Hillary said.

Gilderbun sighed and put her hand on Hillary's shoulder. "Thank goodness."

"We're going today," Hillary said and smiled at her brother.

"What are you up to?" Windslow asked.

"Tillie's bargain excluded us," Hillary said. "Dreadlore is expecting us tomorrow. He's not expecting us today. I think we should do a little spying and see what we can learn."

ഇരു

Heart-Thorn forest wasn't hard to find. All Windslow and Hillary had to do was follow the path trampled in the soot covered grass by the residents of Eldervale who had already made the journey. Along the way, other paths joined in, leading from other villages in Gabendoor. A blanket of clouds formed and released a soft slow rain. The drizzle turned the soot into mud. Although not deep, it was slippery. The rain spattered mud up on their legs and coated their tennis shoes.

Several miles inside Heart-Thorn forest, the soot ended abruptly providing an easier walk. Windslow and Hillary tried to leave the path and move through the forest. The undergrowth was too thick, the brambles too sharp and the ground too marshy.

"This is no good," Hillary said. "We can't get through this stuff and I don't even know if we're going the right way. We need to go back to the path."

"Not the way we look now," Windslow said. "We look a little out of place with our backpacks."

"Good point," Hillary said. She unzipped her magic pouch, stretched it out and stuffed both backpacks inside. After zipping it shut, she shrunk it back down and handed it to her brother. "It may be small, but I'm not carrying it. It's too heavy. You take it."

Windslow untied the twine he wore as a belt and lifted the long sack-skirt he wore. He stuffed the zipper pouch inside the front pocket of his jeans.

When they moved back to the trail, they encountered a group of men, women and children who had left Wartville and were on their way to the temple. Windslow and Hillary joined in without much notice at the end of the group.

The drizzle stopped, but the sky remained overcast. The group followed the path until the tangle of forest gave way to a circular clearing broad enough to hold several football fields. Rows of white tents stained by streaks of soot, huddled close to the trees and snaked around the perimeter. A thin haze of smoke mixed with faint odors. Laundry hung from tent ropes. Children silently tended pots suspended over small cooking fires. In the center of the clearing rose a stone pyramid, not like the ones in Egypt that Hillary had learned about in school. It was more like an Inca or Mayan temple. She could never remember which was which. She knew it had to be Aberratia.

Square stones, five feet per side, sat stacked like overgrown alphabet building blocks. Hillary counted twenty-five steps to the top where the pyramid leveled off to form a large plaza. In the plaza's center towered four stone rectangles, each at least ten feet tall.

"You. The new group!" someone shouted. "Over here."

Hillary looked. Several men wearing purple hoods stood next to a pile of rolled up tents.

One of them spoke again. "Take a tent and pitch it on the other side of the temple. Or, you can try to find one that's already up and has room in it."

Several of the hooded men chuckled.

Another said, "At least six people to a tent. No exceptions!"

"After that," The first man continued, "all children will gather firewood or tend to cook fires. Adults, report back here and we will assign you to a search group. You'll be hunting for the ratStone. If you find it, you get a reward. Teens, report to the west side of the temple for garbage and latrine detail. At dusk, all new arrivals will be tested for magic. Meet at the east side of the temple."

The group stayed silent. Most of the men and a few of the women picked up tents from the pile and began walking. There were no teens other than Hillary and Windslow. One of the hooded men looked at them. "What are you waiting for!" he yelled.

"Which way is west?" Windslow asked, trying to make his voice sound meek.

"That way," the man said and pointed.

Hillary and Windslow began walking. When they were out of earshot from the men, Hillary leaned close to her brother. "If this is supposed to be the only place where there is hope, then Gabendoor is in serious trouble."

"You've got that right," Windslow said. "Do you have a plan you want to share?"

"Not really," Hillary said. "I wish I did. Let's just improvise and see what happens. My biggest worry is getting out of here when we're done."

When they reached the west end of the temple, no one was there. "I guess there aren't that many teens in Gabendoor," Windslow said.

"They're probably smart enough to stay away from this place." Hillary grabbed her brother's arm. "Come on. Let's see what's going on around the corner. We came in on the north side. Magic testing is on the east side and garbage duty is on this side. Let's peek around the corner and see what there is on the south side."

At first, they stayed close to the temple wall. After a few steps, the worried they might look suspicious. "I think we need a couple of these," Hillary said. She walked to a pile of large wicker baskets and smelled one. "Eew, garbage," she said.

They both picked up a basket and headed for the south-west corner of the temple. Walking as if they were headed somewhere with a purpose, they rounded the corner.

A long line of men and women began at a trestle table near the middle of the temple's south side. The line stretched back to the tents. Behind the table, in a high backed chair, sat Dreadlore. On either side of him stood men with purple hoods. Fist sized stones of every color and shape filled baskets in front of the table.

At the front of the line, a man stretched out his hand. In it sat a gray stone speckled with quartz. Dreadlore held out a two-foot long metal rod with a ring on the end. The device looked like the outline of a metal lollypop. A four-pointed brass star swiveled inside the metal ring. Two of the star points functioned as pivot points. Blood red jewels tipped the top and bottom points.

Dreadlore leaned back and said nothing. One of the hooded men grabbed the stone and tossed it into one of the baskets. "Next," he said.

"They've all got stones," Hillary said quietly to her brother.

"Must be the ratStone search detail," he answered.

"You two," another man in purple called to Windslow and Hillary. "Bring those baskets over here and go dump some of these."

Windslow and Hillary both nodded. They kept their heads down, hoping Dreadlore would not recognize them. They put their empty baskets next to the others. They each grabbed one handle on a full basket.

"It's here!" Dreadlore yelled and stood up, nearly knocking his chair over. He held his metal wand close to the stone held out by a woman at the front of the line. The brass star spun.

"I win the reward," the woman shouted. "I win the reward. I found the ratStone!"

The people in line pushed forward.

"She found it," other voices called out.

Yells of "Let me see it," filled the air as more pushing and shoving turned the line into a push of bodies.

"Stop!" Dreadlore screamed. "Stop! It's not it. Not this one. But it's here. It's close." He moved around the table.

The crowd pushed forward. Arms stretched out, each hand holding a stone.

Dreadlore walked past the outstretched arms, and passed his metal wand over each hand. As he moved away from the table, the brass star slowed, then stopped.

"Come on, let's get out of here," Hillary said. She and her brother strained to lift the heavy basket. With awkward steps, they carried it around the corner. Out of sight, they dropped the basket and each grabbed an empty one from the pile.

"We need to get out of here," Hillary said and yawned. "We're going to dream-slip soon. I think the garbage detail needs to head for the exit."

"I've got an idea," Windslow said. He pulled his new wand from his back pocket and waved it over his basket. "Covered in pink, filled with odorous stink."

A piece of pale pink burlap appeared from the shimmer of Windslow's wand. It draped itself over his basket.

"Oh, that stinks," Hillary said and pinched her nose shut with her thumb and finger. "What did you make in the basket?"

"Nothing," Windslow said. "Just pure stench. Remember, teens are on garbage and latrine duty. We just switched jobs. The latrine crew needs to carry this basket out of the compound."

Hillary took her own wand and touched it to the tip of her nose. "Oh, that's better," she said and shoved her wand back in her pocket. "You're brilliant, little brother."

Windslow grinned, lifted the basket and started walking.

With Hillary close behind, he walked around the north side of Aberratia and headed for the path that led out through Heart-Thorn forest. When they reached the path, Dreadlore's men didn't stop them. Windslow hollered out, "Make way for latrine crew." Most of the men turned away. One waved his arm, motioning them to hurry. All the men pinched their nostrils shut.

A hundred yards down the path, Windslow tossed the basket into the woods. They hurried another quarter mile, their yawns coming more frequently. "This is as good as any spot," Windslow said and turned off the trail. He had to hold back vines and help Hillary climb over fallen trees. When they were out of sight from the trail, they stopped.

"This is going to be awful," Hillary said. She took her zipper pouch from her brother, expanded it and pulled out both of their backpacks.

"It doesn't have to be that bad," Windslow said. He waved his wand over a tangle of brambles. The thorny branches shimmered as if out of focus then returned to normal. "The tents gave me an idea." He waved his wand again. "Come on."

Windslow got on his hands and knees. He crawled through the small opening he had made with his magic. Hillary followed.

"Not bad," Hillary said. Her brother had used his magic to form a space inside the bramble patch that looked like an igloo lined with flannel. She started to laugh when she recognized the pattern. Small yellow ducks with black eyes dotted the light blue fabric. "You copied the pattern from your old pajamas. I remember seeing you wear them in lots of pictures from when you were little. You looked really cute."

"This is not funny and it's not cute," Windslow said. "It's practical." He stretched out and used his backpack as a pillow. He gave his wand another wave and the entrance closed. "I just held the words 'warm' and 'snuggly' in my head when I made the shelter. I did it for you."

Hillary yawned and stretched. "Well you did good." She settled back and closed her eyes. "Beat you home," she said and peeked at her brother. He was already gone.

13: Granola Treasure

Hillary woke from her dream-slip and looked at her alarm clock. It was 5 A.M. Before heading for the shower, she pulled her backpack from under her bed. She didn't want to take it to school with muddy soot stains.

Hillary stopped and smiled. She plunked down in her desk chair and leaned back. "No school," she said. "It's Saturday. Oh well, I still need to get this cleaned up."

She began taking everything out of the blue bag. She put her zipper pouch in her desk drawer. She didn't like leaving that out where someone might see it. Next came a small makeup bag, some candles and matches.

"What's this?" Hillary said. She took out a wad of granola bar wrappers the size of a large orange. She peeled the first wrapper away from whatever the rectangles of foil hid. As she normally did, she smoothed out the first wrapper. When it was flat, she folded it over, ran her finger along the crease and folded again. She repeated the folding until she had made a tidy square of folded wrapper. She tossed the wrapper in her wastebasket.

She peeled off another wrapper and folded it like the first. "I didn't eat this many granola bars. I bet this is some stupid trick of Windslow's." Her curiosity building, Hillary folded back the last pieces of foil to see what it hid. "Whoa," Hillary said. "This can't be real."

Gingerly picking up the amber jewel, she turned it over and over in her hand, examining the polished facets.

"How'd this get in my bag?" she said softly and put the jewel on her desk. "Wow, if it is real, either I'll be the richest girl in the state or I'll have one huge diamond ring." Hillary looked again at the flattened sheets of granola wrapper. On one, she spotted long cinnamon-brown hairs. She thought for a minute and remembered what Faith had said. "The trade has been made," Hillary said, repeating the words. "This is what the Wind-Climber traded me."

She slowly shook her head in wonderment. "Well, I guess it's not going to be a ring, and so much for being rich."

"Why are you up?" Bill called from the hallway. "It's sleep-in day."

"Just habit," Hillary called back. She grabbed her zipper pouch, put the stone inside and put the pouch back in her drawer. Hillary stood, pulled on her robe and turned back to her desk. She took her zipper pouch from her drawer and shoved it under her pillow. She turned toward the door, turned back, grabbed the pouch and shoved it under her mattress. "That's no good either," she said staring at her bed. She pulled out the pouch shrunk it down, and stuffed it in the pocket of her robe.

Hillary heard her brother say something in the hallway and then heard the bathroom door slam. "I guess nobody is sleeping in," she said to herself and began straightening up her room.

ꟻᴐ☙

The morning went by fast. They all pitched in to clean the house and work on laundry. Lunch was a delivery pizza. In mid afternoon they all agreed there was more to do, but were anxious to visit Trish.

They arrived at the hospital and hurried up to Trish's room.

"Hillary, Windslow." Trish said and held out her arms. "I missed you."

They both gave her hugs, then moved so their dad could have his turn.

"How are you feeling today, dear?" Bill asked. "You look good."

"Oh, right," Trish said. "I don't have any makeup. I'm in this stylish hospital gown and have tubes and wires connected everywhere. I look simply fabulous." She turned to Hillary. "So when's the first volleyball game?"

"Um, it's soccer," Hillary said. "We have a scrimmage on Tuesday."

"Of course, it's soccer," Trish said. "I knew that. Lot's of things are still very fuzzy for me. So, kiddo," she said looking at Windslow. "Anything new in Gabendoor?"

"Um... ah..." Windslow stammered. He glanced at his sister and back to Trish. "Ah, yah. Ah, lots of stuff. Everything's going fine."

Hillary looked at her step-dad to see his reaction. Thankfully, he just shrugged his shoulders.

"So, how's the food?" Hillary asked, hoping to change the subject.

"Soupy, flavorless, but satisfying," Trish said. "Oh dear, my headache is coming back." Trish frowned. Wrinkles formed across her forehead as she winced against the pain. "You're all getting a little blurry too," she said.

Bill pressed a button at the end of a cord that ran from the wall to Trish's bed. "We'll get the nurse to take a look at you. Here, have some water." Bill picked up a white foam cup from the bedside table and held it out to Trish.

Trish leaned forward to take the straw in her mouth. She stopped before it touched her lips. "Ouch," she said. "It hurts to move my head and suddenly I'm really sleepy." Slowly she settled back on her pillow.

The nurse came into room. Both Bill and Trish told her what happened. "I'll get you another pain pill," the nurse said. "You'll have some dizzy spells off and on. I don't think the headache is anything to worry about, but you should get some rest. Listen to your body. If it's telling you to sleep, then sleep."

"All I've been doing is sleeping," Trish said.

"Sleep is good for you." The nurse said and scribbled something on Trish's medical chart.

Bill leaned over to give Trish a kiss. He stopped, grabbed her hand and kissed her palm.

"What kind of a kiss was that?" Trish asked and closed her eyes.

"I didn't want to hurt your head," Bill said. "I think we'll skip the goodbye hugs, too."

"All right," Trish said, her voice soft. "I'll see you all tomorrow. I think I'm starting to dream-slip now anyway."

Bill followed Hillary and Windslow out of the room. He sighed when they got on the elevator. "I'd like to say she's doing really great," he said to them. "But you're not kids anymore. You'd know I wasn't being honest. I don't know what to tell you."

"You don't need to tell us anything, dad," Windslow said. "She is getting better. We just need to have hope."

"And we need to do this," Hillary said. She gave her dad a long hug.

Back in the car, everyone was quiet. Bill drove them to a little bar and grill at the edge of town for spicy chicken wings and French fries. Bill asked a few questions about Hillary's soccer scrimmage, and if either of them were thinking of dates for the homecoming dance. Hillary said she hadn't been asked by anyone and Windslow said he didn't plan on going. Bill told them a social life was important. Hillary was glad he didn't have more questions. She liked soccer, but started to think that it was cutting into her social life. She did want a date for the dance but didn't even have a boyfriend. She decided she had more important things to worry about.

Hillary was tired when they got home. She was already in bed when she remembered she hadn't told Windslow about the gem. "Oh, well" she said and closed her eyes. "I'll tell him in Gabendoor."

ꙮ

Hillary enjoyed dream-slipping. She marveled at the stars and planets as she rushed by them. She recognized Cassiopeia, which she knew marked the halfway point to Gabendoor. Molly had said that when they passed Cassiopeia, they also crossed into a different dimension in time. Hillary guessed that was why she never remembered that part of her dream-slip.

This time, Cassiopeia loomed closer than ever before. The stars that formed it blinked out and back on, as if someone was playing with a light switch. *That was odd,* Hillary thought. Up ahead, she recognized Earth. Confused, she felt her eyelids get heavy. She couldn't fight her sleepiness and closed her eyes. When she opened them she was in her bed, at home, on Earth.

Hillary sat up and looked at her alarm clock. "It's 9A.M. What's going on?" She jumped from bed, pulled on her robe and headed for her brother's room. His room was empty but his bed looked slept in.

"Did you dream-slip?" he asked from behind her.

Hillary turned around. "No. I got to Cassiopeia then ended up back here."

"Me too," Windslow said. "All we need is another weird thing to deal with."

"Hey," guys," Bill said from the end of the hallway. "Good to see everyone slept in this time. How about I take us all out for some brunch. Then we're going to stop and check out a car lot. After that we'll go to the hospital and maybe finish off the day with a movie. How's that sound?"

"Car dealerships aren't open on Sundays," Windslow said.

"I know. We're just going to do some window shopping." Bill looked at his watch. "How about we leave around 11? Will that give you two enough time to get ready?"

"Fine with me," Windslow said and headed for his room.

"I get to pick the restaurant," Hillary said and headed for the bathroom.

ജ്വ

Brunch was nice. The mood was a little lighter than it had been. They laughed about how they'd need to learn how to wash dishes again when Trish came home because they were eating out so much. At the car dealership was the only time Windslow and Hillary had another chance to talk about not dream-slipping and their concern. Neither of them had any idea what was wrong or if they would dream-slip that night. They did smile at the way their dad pushed his forehead against different van windows and shield the sun with his hands. He moved from van to van, looking inside and saying things like, "Wow, this one has a navigation system," or "Look, the back seat in this one folds down into a bed," or simply,

"Cool." Windslow and Hillary did look in the vans, but had to pretend they were more interested than they really were.

When they got to the hospital and rode the elevator up to Trish's floor, Bill was still talking about horsepower, engine torque and fuel economy. Before they went into Trish's room, they stopped at the nurses' station to see if there were any messages from the doctor or if there was any change in Trish's condition.

The nurse assigned to Trish that day said the headaches were gone but Trish was sleeping even more, and for longer stretches. Sometimes, they had trouble waking her and stopped giving her sleeping pills. Almost as an afterthought, the nurse said that Trish was talking a lot in her sleep.

When they walked into Trish's room, she was asleep. Bill sat in the chairs on one side of Trish's bed. Windslow moved his wheelchair to the other side. They simply sat quietly, watching Trish sleep.

Several times Trish turned her head back and forth and muttered in her sleep. Bill had whispered to Windslow and Hillary asking if they could understand anything Trish was saying. Both Hillary and Windslow said they couldn't, even though Hillary did recognize some of the words. She was certain "hugger woof" was Haggerwolf and "ferf park" was Fernbark. Hillary was worried that "bed bore" was Dreadlore.

After sitting for an hour, a nurse came in to check on Trish. The nurse said they would wake Trish up at dinnertime and then let her sleep more if she wanted to. Bill nodded as he listened. After the nurse left, he motioned Hillary and Windslow to follow him out into the hallway. "I don't know that there is much we can do but watch her sleep. I think we should go home. I'll have the nurses tell your mom we were here."

Back in the car, a more somber mood like that of the last few days, returned. Hillary's thoughts returned to worrying about not dream-slipping and the link between her mother and Gabendoor. At home, she and Windslow both hurried to get things ready for school and headed for bed, wondering what this night would bring.

ഇ൦ജ

Hillary woke refreshed but late. She had slept well, but again she had not dream-slipped. Other than being rushed, the morning had been the same routine as the last few days with Trish in the hospital. Hillary only talked briefly to her brother. He had not dream-slipped either. Hillary forgot to tell him about the strange jewel. She brought it with her to school, tucked inside her zipper pouch with the pouch buried at the bottom of her backpack. Even in class, she kept her backpack on the floor against her leg so she would feel it right away if someone moved her bag. I'm being paranoid, Hillary thought to herself when she got to science class.

Before the bell rang, Hillary had a chance to speak with Ms. DiMarco about gemstones. Ms. DiMarco said that would be an interesting research project Hillary could do for extra credit.

"I'm not really interested in that right now," Hillary said. "I just need a quick opinion." Keeping her zipper pouch inside her backpack, Hillary unzipped it and took out the strange jewel. She held it up. "I know it isn't a diamond. I'm guessing it's just glass. What do you think?"

"Goodness," Ms. DiMarco said. She chuckled. "If it was a diamond, it would become the most famous one in the world. Where did you get it?"

"With mom in the hospital, we've been cleaning out some stuff. I found it in a box in the attic. What do you think it's made of?"

"Well, here's an easy diamond test. A diamond is so refractive, it doesn't transmit light like a magnifying glass or prism. I can see my fingers through your gem, so we know it's not a diamond. Let's try something else." Ms. DiMarco turned to a workbench filled with electronic equipment. She flipped on several switches. "Oh dear," she said.

"What's wrong?" Hillary asked.

"The equipment is going crazy. Look at all the dials. I better shut these off. Here," she said and handed the jewel back to Hillary. "I had better have someone look at the circuit. I hope there wasn't a power surge. Some of this equipment is very expensive. We'll have to test your jewel tomorrow."

"Um... no thanks," Hillary said and put the jewel away. "I guess I will take you up on your extra credit offer. You got me kind of curious now."

"Well good," Ms. DiMarco said. "That's what a teacher is supposed to do. Good luck."

Ms. DiMarco turned to the class. "Get out your workbooks," she said and began class.

When class finally ended Hillary slung her backpack over her shoulder and headed for her literature class. In the hallway, she saw Marcy. Hillary wanted to stick out her tongue. Instead, she held her head high, looked straight ahead and walked brusquely past her. After literature, came social studies and then her favorite time of the day; soccer practice.

ᘛᘚ

"Hey, bro, hang on to this for me," Hillary said. On the side of the soccer field, she handed Windslow her backpack.

"Stick it in you locker," Windslow said.

"No. I've got something important in there. It's something from Gabendoor. I don't want to take any chances with it."

"What is it?" Windslow asked and took the backpack.

"I'll tell you later."

The coach blew his whistle. Hillary turned and ran out on the field to join her teammates. Windslow looked down the sidelines to where the cheerleaders held their practice. He was relieved, yet sad, not to see the Sallyforth girls.

"We up here," someone called from behind him. He turned to see the triplets sitting in the bleachers. All three sat with elbows on knees and chins resting on their hands. Molly waved. "We come a support Hillary. She still our friend. Got any eggs? Maybe we throw them at Marcy."

Windslow laughed. "If I did, I'd throw them myself."

"Why they coming here?" Tillie asked.

Windslow looked back to the soccer field. Led by Marcy, the cheerleading squad walked down sideline. They stopped in front of him.

"We have a cheer for you," Marcy said and lined up with the other cheerleaders.

Standing in a row, they shook their pompoms, jumped, spun around in a full circle, and began their cheer.

There's an ugly little girl and her name is Molly.
She won't grow up and still plays with her dolly.
A girl named Tillie dresses pretty silly.
She smells kind of awful like a goat named Billy.
The one named Nelly has a big fat belly.
Wherever she goes, she has stains on her clothes.
They won't stay up late because they never have a date.
They'll never have a chance for the Homecoming Dance.

"Yea, yea, yea," they all cheered together and then laughed.

"Oh, very funny," Windslow said. "So do you think their mother will come in and complain to the principal like yours did? Well, I doubt it. The whole family has more class than that. And your crack about the Homecoming Dance is wrong. I asked them. I invited them to the dance. I'm dating all three of them."

"Well," Marcy said and gave Windslow on over-sweet look. "I hope they'll show up at the dance and not run away like they just did."

Windslow looked over his shoulder. The bleachers were empty. He looked back at Marcy. "They just stopped by to say hi to me. They had stuff to do. And you girls have something to do too. It's called 'practice.' You're all out of sync and you move like a bunch of stupid robots."

"Oh," Marcy said and clutched at her heart, mocking Windslow. "Your words are so cruel. They've hurt me so bad." She held one arm across her face. "Come, girls," she said, her voice syrupy sweet. "I do not wish to cry in public. My feelings are so wounded."

The girls laughed and giggled as they followed Marcy back to their practice area.

"I hate her," Windslow said under his breath. He turned around, hoping he could spot Molly or her sisters. All he saw was a blue van and a couple of other cars in the parking lot.

After practice while he and his sister walked to the parking lot, he told Hillary about Marcy and the cheerleaders. He left out the part about inviting the Sallyforth sisters to the Homecoming Dance.

"Where's Bill?" Hillary said.

The blue van's horn honked. Both Hillary and Windslow ignored it.

Windslow looked at his watch. "I hope nothing's wrong at the hospital. Dad's usually not late."

The horn honked again.

Windslow gave it a quick glance.

"Let's start walking up to the road," Hillary said. She plunked her backpack onto Windslow's lap. "Here, carry this for me," She said and started walking. "I'm worn out from practice. I think the coach worked us too hard. I don't want to be worn out for our first soccer game."

The blue van rolled up behind them. Its horn gave two short beeps.

"Go around," Windslow yelled and waved his arm.

Toot, toot.

Hillary spun around. "Bug off, moron!" she yelled. "Oh, oh," she said in a softer voice.

"Wow, cool!" Windslow shouted. He spun his chair around and shoved hard on its wheels.

Bill walked around from the driver's side of the van. He grinned at Hillary. "I didn't quite hear what you said."

"Um... I said is that blue or maroon?"

"Nice try," Bill said. "Well, come on. Let me give you the tour."

Both Windslow and Hillary said, 'wow' or 'cool,' at least twenty times as Bill showed them the new family van. They played with the power wheelchair ramp, squabbled over the remote control and headphones for the DVD system. Bill laughed when Hillary tried to figure out the handicapped controls that would enable Windslow to drive.

"I want my permit. I want my permit," Hillary said over and over as she bounced up and down in the driver seat and twisted the steering wheel back and forth.

"Enough," Bill said. "Would all passengers please take their assigned seats? The Windgate-Summerfield van is scheduled to depart. First stop, Mercy Hospital."

ꙮ

The mood was light hearted on their drive to the hospital. Neither Windslow nor Hillary asked about Trish. Most of what they said was still, *ooh*, *ah* or *cool,* as they continued playing with all the options in the van.

Windslow was the first to ask, after he had moved from the van to the curb without help from anyone. "How's mom? Did you tell her about the van?"

"I told her," Bill said. He pressed a button on the key fob. The van honked once and the lights flashed. "You know with a head injury, you can have your ups and downs."

"So translated," Hillary said, "that means she's not doing so great today."

Bill nodded. He moved behind Windslow and pushed him toward the entrance doors. "So to speak," he said. "She's unconscious again. Her memory started coming back a bit. She's not really in a coma, but then again, she's not really not in one."

"You're not making sense, Dad," Windslow said.

"The doctors aren't sure what's going on. It's as if she's stuck in a dream and won't or can't wake up. She's muttering things in her sleep that don't make sense. She does say your names though. I guess she woke up in the middle of the night and asked one of the nurses if you two were all right. She told the nurse she remembers part of the accident, but her memory is as if she were watching it from outside her body."

"What's she say in her sleep?" Windslow asked.

"She keeps repeating some gibberish about Gabendoor. I tried to search for it on the Internet but came up with nothing. It must be a couple words she's stringing together. You two are better with computers than I am. Maybe you can find something when we get home."

When they reached the floor Trish's room was on, they stopped at the nurse's station. Bill asked if there had been any change. Windslow asked if there had been any visitors. The nurse answered, 'no,' to both questions.

In Trish's room, they all stayed silent. Bill leaned against the wall. Windslow heard his dad sigh heavily. When he looked at his dad, Bill had his hand over his eyes. Hillary sat on the opposite bedside and held her mother's hand. Windslow wheeled up against her bed and took her other hand. They all looked when Trish muttered something in her sleep.

"Gaboar... Slip... slipping... Lost. Put them back, Windslow. Help him, Hillary. Lost... stars gone..."

"Any of that mean anything to either of you?" Bill asked.

Both Windslow and Hillary shook their heads. Windslow leaned closer when he felt his mother squeeze his hand. Her eyes flickered open for a moment, then closed. "Closer," she said in a faint wispy voice. Both Windslow and Hillary leaned as close as they could.

"Lost in dream-slip... stars gone... put them back." Trish stopped speaking. Her head turned back and forth. She licked her lips and spoke again in the same wispy voice. "Hillary has it. Windslow... full of hope... don't let go. Teach them all. I want to be home." Trish's breathing steadied. Windslow felt his mother's grip on his hand relax.

"I think we should go," Bill said.

Windslow looked up. "Aren't we going to wait and

see if Mrs. Christensen and the Sallyforth girls come and visit mom?"

"No," Bill said. "I called their house. Molly answered. She said everyone was sick with the flu or something and they wouldn't be able to come. I know they're your friends, but you can't expect them to be here every night. I think it's great they've come as much as they have." Bill moved to the door. "Come on. Let your mom rest. We'll go get some dinner. Hey," he said, trying to make his voice sound cheery. "How about we stop at a store and buy a movie? Then we can check out the DVD player in the van. And we'll use the navigation system to get us home."

Hillary gave Bill a hug. "We know the way home, dad." She stood on her tiptoes and kissed his cheek. "By the way, dad, you'll never make it as an actor."

Windslow felt good when he saw a genuine smile spread across his dad's face. Windslow's own smile didn't last long. It slid from his face when he thought about Molly not coming. He wondered if she had used up her magic again today on something stupid.

"Come on, kiddo," Bill called.

Windslow's thoughts snapped back to the present. He tried not to frown as he thought about his mother's words while he, his stepsister and father headed for the parking lot.

ꕥ

Dinner and the new van were both good diversions. They kept Windslow's thoughts away from his mother, the Sallyforth triplets, Marcy, Gabendoor, and the magic *Book of Library Secrets.*

At home, he and Hillary spent some time in her room, comparing notes. Hillary showed him the amber jewel she had received in trade from the Wind-Climber. Windslow thought it was pretty, but not part of what they needed to do in Gabendoor. For both of them, not having any idea for a plan frustrated them. They did check the book, but nothing new had appeared. From memory, they tried to piece together the words their mother had spoken in her sleep. Neither of them came up with a theory both of them could agree on. Tired, Hillary put the gem in her desk drawer and told Windslow she wanted to finish her homework and get some sleep.

In his own room, Windslow opened his backpack to get out his homework. He tossed the *Book of Library Secrets* on his bed. He had to do some research using the Internet. When he was done, he clicked on science news. There was an article about how scientists think they discovered an anomaly in space. The scientists say it may be evidence of curved space. Apparently, several stars past the constellation Cassiopeia had shifted location. The scientists were still analyzing their data.

Windslow closed his web browser. "Hey, guys," he said as if talking to his computer monitor. "Next time I dream-slip to Gabendoor, I'll take a look for you. It's not out of my way."

Windslow chuckled to himself and did the last of his homework. He packed his science and history assignments back into his backpack. Turning to his bed, he reached for the *Book of Library Secrets.* It lay open close to his pillow. He was certain it had been closed when he tossed it there. Placing the book on his lap, he looked at the open page and the new words that had not been their earlier when he and Hillary had checked.

So many clues yet to unravel.
Send the stars back so a mother can travel.
It's not up to eight, it's just up to one.
Crowds will all cheer but his work is not done.

At first, he just stared at the words. Windslow's eyes opened wide. He looked at his blank PC monitor, back to the book and nodded his head. Softly he said, "Mom's stuck in a dream-slip. That's what she was trying to tell us. She's trapped. She's not here and she's not on Gabendoor. She's stuck in between!"

Windslow looked again at the other pages and clues. "It's the ratStone," he said. "It's the key. Somehow the stone warped space, or time or both or something. I've got to figure out who the eight are, and the two and... Crud-o," he said and slammed the book shut. "As clear as usual."

Twisting around, Windslow looked at his closed door. He wanted to tell his sister what he had figured out. Glancing at his alarm clock, he decided it would have to wait until they were together in Gabendoor.

Worried he might be too excited to sleep, Windslow got ready for bed. When he pulled his covers up, he began taking long slow breaths to stay calm. Thoughts flitted in and out of his mind. Frustrated, he reached over to his desk and grabbed his music player and ear-buds. As the music played, his thoughts settled. The music in his head stopped when he saw Cassiopeia.

14: Dreadlore

When Hillary dream-slipped, the stars normally streaked by until she passed Cassiopeia. Tonight her flight through space slowed, as it had the last two nights when neither she nor her brother completed their dream-slips. She seemed to simply float, not moving in any direction. She tried to clear her thoughts but couldn't. She felt like she was half-asleep and half-awake; stuck in a dream. "Gabendoor," she whispered.

The star field began to move, spinning slowly around her as if she were in the center of a galaxy. The silver points of light swirled faster, making her dizzy. "Gabendoor," she said again.

How odd, Hillary thought. She looked down and saw herself floating in the star field, detached from herself, yet not. She watched an amber glow expand from her backpack. The glow surrounded her then spread out like a beacon to illuminate a tiny planet far past Cassiopeia. Somehow, she knew that planet was Gabendoor.

Her eyelids heavy, Hillary blinked. She no longer saw herself, the amber beacon, or the far away planet. Instead of fighting to keep her eyes open, she let them close and could feel herself moving through space again.

Hillary chanced another peek, and found it easy to open her eyes. Her dream-slip complete, she woke inside the little flannel thorn hut her brother had made the day before. Hillary stretched before glancing over to where her brother had been. The air shimmered as his shape filled in.

"That was so weird," Windslow said. "It was like I was dreaming inside a dream-slip. I dreamt I got lost. I saw you and you pointed this huge flashlight and I knew where to go. Very strange."

"I had the same kind of dream," Hillary said. "Enough things have been going wrong and now something is going wrong with dream-slipping. We got here, but we still don't have a plan and we don't know what to do. So what's the point of it all?"

Windslow sat up. "I think I figured some things out," Excited, he scooted next to her and told his sister about the page in the book and what he though Trish's words meant. "We've got to find that stone."

"You're right, but we already knew that. Everyone wants the stone. Tillie promised Dreadlore she and her sisters would help find it. It's obvious, from what we saw the other day, that Dreadlore has everybody out looking for it. So, okay, wave your wand and let us out of this hut. We'll go get the stone, flatten out space again and go get mom out of the hospital. Then when we get home, we'll check the mailbox. I bet we won the lottery too."

"Don't be like that!" Windslow snapped. "That's all I need. The Sallyforth girls have given up. Who knows where the wizards are. Most of the people on Gabendoor are giving up. We need to stick together and find that stone."

"Yah, right," Hillary said and looked away from her brother. "What hope do we have? Be realistic."

"Maybe all of you should have spent some looking at a wheelchair and wondering if you'd ever walk again. Maybe you should spend some time thinking about life as a cripple. Maybe all of you should all just crawl off in corners and feel sorry for yourselves. Why don't you dream-slip home and go play video games until mom comes home. That will really help things."

"Stop preaching at me," Hillary said.

Windslow waved his wand. The door appeared, letting in a puff of fresh air. "When I broke my back, I did a lot of thinking. I decided it's like there is this line. On one side of the line is hope. On the other side of the line is nothing. When you're on that side, you've given up. Which side are you on? If you gave up, I think you should stay here because there's nothing you can do."

Windslow crawled through the opening and stood. He waited for a moment but refused to look behind him. He didn't hear any sounds; no footsteps, no clothes rustling, nothing. He retraced his steps from the night before and headed for the road. *Now what,* he thought to himself.

Windslow emerged from the trees and tangle of brush. "Wow," he said and watched the disorganized column of people walking toward Aberratia. The ground shuddered. People stopped walking. Screams filled the air. Many of the people got down on the ground. Behind him, trees swayed. He heard the sound of cracking wood as dead branches shook loose and crashed to the ground. Instinctively, he bent over, put his arms over his head and rushed to the road.

The ground shuddered again. Windslow nearly lost his balance. "Hillary!" he said and spun around, only to bump into her. She grabbed him and held on tight.

"I decided I don't like earthquakes," she said. "And I don't like giving up."

The ground gave a slight tremor. Someone in the crowd yelled, "We'll be safe at the temple!"

People on the ground stood and hurried down the path and joined in with others who already rushed ahead.

"Hi, Windso and Hillre," a voice called.

"I hi too.

"Bye."

Both Windslow and Hillary turned to look the other direction. In the line walked the Sallyforth triplets. Hillary and Windslow ran to them.

"What are you doing?" Hillary asked and gave the girls a group hug.

Molly answered. "We got appointment with Bed-Snore."

"We promised," Tillie said.

"This be best-est day," Nelly added.

"Well, we're not letting you go alone," Windslow said.

Windslow and his sister joined the sisters in line. As they walked, he told them about the new words in the book and what he was sure he had figured out.

"That right," Molly said. "We know that before. We know mommy Trish stuck in dream-slip. We use-a magic to help all-a things wrong with her except that. She get well now, but she still stuck."

"I not feel like crying right now," Nelly said. She blew her nose on her sleeve.

"Don't do it that way," Tillie said and handed Nelly a tissue. "Marcy use tissue. We need-a learn how a have manners."

"Argh!" Windslow yelled. Several people on the trail looked at him. "I am so tired of hearing you three talk about Marcy. You three were the coolest girls I know until you started letting Marcy get to you. What's wrong with you! If you're going to keep acting like this then stop calling me your best-est boyfriend! The four of you go sulk someplace. I'll do this alone!" Windslow picked up his pace and moved up in line, away from the girls.

Behind him he heard Tillie say, "Then Marcy right. We not have-a stay up late, cause we never get a date."

Windslow groaned and walked even faster.

The line slowed and just ahead of him, he saw the clearing and the temple. As before, hooded men greeted everyone.

"Take a tent and pitch it on the other side of the temple. Or, you can try to find one that's already up and has room in it" one of the men said. He sounded like a recording, repeating the same speech to everyone. This time, there were more people, more tents, more of everything.

Windslow pushed past him. "Get out of my way. I'm here for an appointment with Dreadlore."

"Grab him!" someone yelled.

Windslow had only taken five steps when two men grabbed him by the arms.

"Sure you do," one of the men said. "We'll take you right there."

"Stop fooling around," the other man said to his partner. "Let's tie him to a tree until Dreadlore decides what to do with him."

"You had better tie us all up," someone said from behind the men. Windslow craned his neck to look over his shoulder. He recognized the voice. It was his sister.

"She's not with me," Windslow said.

"That right," another voice said.

Windslow looked past his sister. Behind her stood the Sallyforth sisters.

"She not with him," Molly said. "She with me."

Tillie pointed at Hillary. "I not with her too." She pointed at Molly. "I with her."

Nelly put her hands on her hips. "Well I not with my two sisers and I not with the Children of a Wind, cause that not who they are."

The two hooded men glanced at each other. "It's them," both men said at once.

"All of you over here," one man said. He walked toward the tents. Windslow, Hillary and the Sallyforth sisters followed. The second man walked behind them.

Just past the tents, the lead man stopped. To his partner he said, "You guard them. I'll go talk to Dreadlore."

"Guard them with what?" his partner asked and held out empty hands.

The first man shook his head. He ran to the tent pile, grabbed a tent pole and hurried back. He handed the long pole to his partner. "With this," he said, turned and ran toward the temple.

The second man held the pole out pointing it at the group. "Sit down!" he yelled.

"We hear you," Molly said. "You not have-a yell."

"Good," Windslow muttered as he sat down. "At least a little spark of the Molly I knew."

"We hear that too," Tillie said.

"Chill, brother," Hillary said.

Windslow rolled his eyes and folded his arms across his chest.

They didn't wait long. A group of ten hooded men marched toward them from the direction of the temple.

"That's your escort," the man guarding them said. "On your feet."

With little said, the group led them to the temple, and around to where Dreadlore sat at his table. Just as yesterday, a long line of people holding stones snaked from the table to the woods.

"Oh no," Hillary said and pointed to the plaza at the top of the temple. "It's the wizards."

Windslow looked. A group of women and men stood on the plaza's perimeter. They all faced outward and held hands, spaced apart as far as the clasped hands would allow. Each person wore a wooden headband filled with wooden spikes sticking out like fingers. Wooden spiked bracelets wrapped around every wrist. Nearly everyone stood with their eyes closed. Many looked weary, their heads bent down, chins resting on chests. Shackles on their legs chained them to the plaza.

"It's Haggerwolf, Larkstone and Fernbark," Windslow said. "Why are they chained? What are those spiky wood things for?"

"They like antenna," Molly said.

"Not like a bug have," Tillie added.

Molly looked at her sister. "I telling it," she said.

"Geeze," Windslow said. "Everybody's got a temper today. Molly, what kind of antenna?"

"They somber wood," she said. "They like super-size magic wand. They help wizzies build up magic faster. They make wizzies be like magic battery. They all hold hands to link all a power together. Then Dreadlore can use them to do very big spells."

Windslow wanted to yell to the wizards, but doubted they would hear him.

"You!" Dreadlore yelled to one of his men. "Here, take the probe. Check the stones." He held out the metal wand

Windslow had seen him use yesterday. Dreadlore used both hands to slick back his hair. The sleeves of his purple robe slid down his arms, revealing matching tattoos on his forearms. Windslow recognized what they represented. The stars and connecting lines represented the constellation Cassiopeia. With long strides, Dreadlore approached.

"Promise fulfilled," he said and nodded at the Sallyforth Triplets. Dreadlore stretched out his hand to Windslow. "Now we meet formally, Child of the Wind, Son of the Summer Storm."

Windslow shoved his own hands in his jean pockets.

Dreadlore extended his hand to Hillary. "My pleasure, Child of the Wind, Daughter of the Summer Breeze."

Hillary looked at Dreadlore's hand. "Have you washed that today?" she asked.

Dreadlore folded his hands together. "So much for civility," He said. "Follow me for a little demonstration."

Dreadlore walked to a broad set of steps that led up the slope of his Temple of Aberratia. Without saying anything, he climbed the stairs. Windslow, Hillary and the Sallyforth triplets followed. At the top, two women in the group of collared people released their held hands. They stepped back, making room for Dreadlore and Windslow's group to pass.

"Close the circle," Dreadlore said.

The two women moved back into place and joined hands, completing the circle.

"Now," Dreadlore said. "Let's make sure everything is clear. You will take me to the Secret Library. You will help me find the ratStone. You will channel your magic with mine and the Children of the Wind will follow my orders too."

Nelly answered, "That right."

Molly answered, “Almost right.”

Tillie answered, “Nope.”

Dreadlore paced forward stood directly in front of the sisters. He leaned down over Tillie. “Explain,” was all he said.

“We agree a take you to Library, but Library not anyplace anymore. It gone,” Tillie said. “We help a find ratStone, but not Hillre and Windso. When we promise, we say we, not all-a us. We channel magic with you, but we only get a use magic once each day. That what we promise you last time and you still hold us to that.”

“Ha!” Dreadlore shouted and spun around. Tillie had to duck to keep from being hit by Dreadlore’s robe as it flared out. He walked forward and turned back around. “I release you from your previous promise. You’re free to use magic more than once a day, but only to help me. Agreed?”

“Let see,” Tillie said. She flicked her hand in the air. A small sparkle of blue light formed at her fingertips and winked out. “Promise is gone. Poof, it not there anymore. We get a use all a magic you need to help you.”

“Good,” Dreadlore said. “Now tell me about the Library.

Tillie scratched her head. “It complicated. Library let you go, then it go away from that place. It not there anymore.”

“Where is it?”

“Like all a time. It up in Nellie’s room behind the clock.”

“You told me that once a long time ago. At least I know it’s not your sister we’re talking about. Who is Nellie and explain what you mean, it’s behind the clock?”

Tillie glanced at Molly.

Molly nodded.

"It Nasty Nellie," Tillie said.

Dreadlore's eyes opened wide. "The Nellie in the old nursery rhyme?"

Tillie grinned.

Dreadlore took in a long breath. He let it out and recited the rhyme.

Nasty Nellie lives in a well.
Ask for a wish.
It will cost you a spell.

Use your wits if you hope to survive.
To get out of the well,
while you still are alive.

"That right," Tillie said. "She have clock in her room. Behind clock is little magic book. Inside book it always tell where library is."

Dreadlore paced back and forth in front of the group. He stopped, turned and looked at Tillie again. "What about the stone? And those two," he asked shifting his gaze to Windslow and Hillary.

"We help look for a stone. That part okay," Nelly said.

Windslow broke into the conversation. "She doesn't speak for us," he said. "We're not helping you." Windslow's hand moved quickly. He snatched his wand from his back pocket and pointed it at Dreadlore. The wand turned to ash like a burnt match and crumbled.

"Nice try," Dreadlore said. "But useless." He turned to Hillary. "Show everyone your wand, dear."

"I'm not 'dear'," Hillary said. She reached for her wand. She screamed and jerked her hand away from her pocket. A small brown snake fell to the plaza stones. It slithered away a few feet and burst into flames that quickly disappeared.

"That's not much magic," Dreadlore said. "Frankly, I'm a little disappointed. I've heard so much about the Children of the Wind, I thought you'd be more than just a couple teenagers from Earth. Let me show you magic."

Dreadlore walked around them and stopped in front of the two women that had made the opening. They released hands. Dreadlore stepped in-between them and turned to face Windslow and Hillary. He took the hand of each woman bedside him, closing the circle again. One of his men ran forward holding a wooden crown with eight points. He placed it on Dreadlore's head.

"Can't you afford something a little fancier?" Windslow asked.

Dreadlore smiled. "It's somber wood. A skinny little stick isn't a very efficient or powerful wand. The magic of Gabendoor works through the wood, not the shape. With all of my followers linked to me, the amount of magic at my command is greater than any wizard has had at any time on Gabendoor."

"Followers, ha!" Windslow said. "*Slaves* is more like it. My wizard friends aren't followers of yours."

"You mean those three used up retired old men that know you? They agreed to help if I promised not to kill you and your sister. Actually, it doesn't matter if you are willing or not. All you need to do is hold hands to channel magic. Watch."

The temple shuddered. Windslow hoped an earthquake would shake it apart. He glanced at the trees. They weren't swaying. The only thing moving was the temple. Down on the field, people stopped what they were doing, faced the temple and dropped to their knees as if in worship. Windslow felt the temple rise.

After a few minutes, the movement stopped, the people stood and resumed whatever they had been doing. Some shouted out praises to the "Great Wizard Dreadlore."

"What did you do?" Hillary asked.

"Aberratia is higher now, complete, and in position again. A Long ago," he said, pointing at the Sallyforth sisters, "three girls and some other wizards sunk it in a swamp. Then they fooled me into a battle that trapped me in a book. With my temple restored, I can do some other tricks. Turn around and look at the obelisks."

In the center of the plaza stood four stone rectangles, each ten feet tall. Three rectangles arranged close together each held a colored gem, one black, one green and one orange. Across from them, one more rectangle held a gem colored black with red flecks in the stone.

Dreadlore walked back to the circle of linked wizards. He held out his hands and completed the circle.

Windslow heard a crackling sound and spun around to look at the circle of stones. Blue lightning crackled as the long strands of magic stretched toward the center of the space they formed. When all four strands met, they streamed upward and gave off a low-pitched thrumming sound.

"Enough," Dreadlore yelled and opened his hands, breaking the circle. A clap of thunder sounded. The magic stopped. He walked back to Windslow and Hillary. "I can move planets with that much power. The problem is, it's like using a sledgehammer to crack open a nut. You get the nut open, but you destroy it in the process. The ratStone is the key to controlling all that power."

"You not so sure," Molly said. "No one know how a ratStone supposed a work. Nobody even know what it look like."

"I don't care!" Dreadlore yelled at her. "It won't look like just an ordinary stone. Maybe it looks like a rat. Maybe it has a rat shape. Maybe is has a rat shape etched into it. The legend failed to say anything about that!"

Dreadlore moved in front of Hillary and Windslow. "I can't use my power to pluck a petal from a flower, but I can use it to destroy the mountain the flower grows on. I can use that power to obliterate you and the three wizards you seem to be fond of. I can sever your spinal cord," he said looking directly at Hillary. "I can make you just like your brother with one difference. I'll use magic to let you both feel pain; pain so extreme, you'll wish you were dead."

"All right," Windslow said. "We'll help. We'll look for the stone. We'll do what we can to help Molly and her sisters with Nasty Nellie. But, you have to release Haggerwolf, Larkstone and Fernbark."

"Ha!" Dreadlore said. "Not a chance. I need those wizards to channel for me."

"Agreed," Hillary said. "You have what you wanted, but only if you at least treat our wizard friends better. Make sure they get enough to eat and enough sleep."

"Agreed," Dreadlore said.

"Then let us out of here," Windslow said. "We have work to do."

Dreadlore bowed at the waist and swept his arm out in a grand gesture. "You are free to go," He said. "I'll give you three days. Then I stop giving Haggerwolf water if you haven't made progress. The next day, no water for Larkstone. The day after is Fernbark's turn. If five days pass, I begin a little torture."

"You promised," Hillary said.

"Ah, but as the Sallyforth sisters did when they twisted words, and as I'm sure Nasty Nellie will do, I've done my own little twist. I promised to let them sleep, to feed them and not kill them. That's all. The only hope for them is for you to find the ratStone and the Secret Library."

Hillary glared at him. "You... you..."

Windslow interrupted. "You made your point," he said, finishing Hillary's sentence but probably not the way she was going to. He grabbed his sister's arm. "Come on. Time to go."

Windslow led his sister down the temple steps. He stepped carefully, a little unsteady on his weak legs. She stomped her way down, making her anger obvious to everyone. The Sallyforth sisters said nothing.

Windslow didn't let go of his sister's arm until they reached the trail leading back through Heart-Thorn forest. "Your time to chill," he said to his sister. "You won the battle. We only agreed to help look for the stone and help the Sallyforth sisters. You got Dreadlore so mad and so focused on his own word tricks that he didn't pay attention. We never agreed to channel. We didn't promise to do anything we weren't going to do anyway."

"So what good is all that." Hillary said. "I'll tell you. It's worthless. What hope do we have? Did you see that power? Did you see what he did to your wand and mine?"

"Yah, I saw. I was there," Windslow said and began walking. He yawned. "We need to find some somber wood and start charging up some new wands." Windslow yawned again and turned around. Walking backward, he looked at Hillary. "I told you before, either give up or try. And when I say *try*, I mean try your best. And you three," he said, looking at the Sallyforth sisters, "I just don't understand you anymore. You know, this is going to sound like something one of you would say to me. You'd tell me we have a path we are walking on. There are other paths in the woods. We could make a path through the woods. As long as there is a path we can take another step on, we're doing something. As long as we are doing something, anything, there is hope. If there isn't any hope, then it's time to stop walking!"

"Those just words," Molly said. "You not know how ever-thing make us feel."

"I don't care!" Windslow shouted. "When we were with Faith and Maxwell, I had a thought and was going to say something. It's like Maxwell read my mind. He told me, 'Don't discuss it. Just do it.' I forgot all about that until now. Molly, Tillie and Nelly, if you want to be cheerleaders, stop whining about it. Just do it!"

"Oh, you're just full of advice," Hillary said.

"And you too, sister," Windslow snapped back at her. "You have magic. I have magic and the triplets have... Hey," Windslow said. "Was that promise you made long ago a deal to only use magic once between the three of you, or once each?"

The triplets looked at each other. They all shrugged.

"So you might have three uses each day when you aren't around Dreadlore?"

Again, the triplets glanced at each other. "We never try it," Molly said.

Windslow threw up his hands. "I can't believe it. Speaking of magic, how come you three never use a wand?"

"We not need one," Molly said. "We different. Mommy Trish different too. She not need one either."

Nelly folded her hands on top of her head. "I so cheerful and happy."

"Me too," Tillie added.

Still walking backward, Windslow's heels hit something in the path. Twisting and shuffling, he tried to keep his balance. His gyrations weren't fast enough. He fell. He grimaced, expecting to hit the ground hard. Instead, he landed soft and floated along, keeping pace with his sister.

"I'm special too!" Hillary shouted. She jumped up and down. She pointed her fingers at Windslow.

With no effort of his own, he rose, tipped back vertical, and lowered to the ground.

"I did that. I did it," Hillary said, still jumping. "I tripped you and everything. Oh, sorry, bro."

Windslow stumbled realizing he was still moving forward and needed to use his feet. "Hey, it makes sense," he said. "You inherited it from your mom. Too bad I'm just a step son."

"It not special like that," Nelly said. "It special because Gabendoor decide it. Like Faith and Maxwell say in meadow, Gabendoor do what it want sometimes."

"It like you say," Molly said to him. "You just got to do it sometimes if you want a find stuff out. You make a good cheerleader."

Windslow looked at her, nodded, and held out his open palm. He blinked his eyes. Blue light flashed in his hand where now sat a double cheeseburger. "Cool," Windslow said. He took a bite and quickly spit it out on the side of the road. "Tasted like plastic," he muttered.

The Sallyforth girls laughed. Hillary gave him a smile that turned into a long yawn. "Dream-slip time, everyone. We had better find a spot."

"I know a comfortable place nearby if you don't mind yellow ducks," Windslow said. Behind him he heard;

“Rah, rah, rah, we getting back on track. Let’s hear a yell.”

“Quack.”

“Quack.”

“Oink.”

15: Stand Up and Holler

Hillary stretched and looked at her alarm clock. "Early, late, late, early," she muttered. "It would be nice to be back to normal, but at least we dream-slipped again."

Because she had a bit of extra time, Hillary cleaned out her backpack. She liked having it tidy and arranged. She couldn't understand how Windslow could just jam everything in his. She decided not to leave the gem from the Wind-Climber at home but took it out of her zipper pouch and placed it on her desk. Leaning down to look at it at eye level, Hillary rolled the jewel from one facet to the next and examined the surface. When she rolled it again, she giggled. "Wow, I can see myself." Hillary sat back up. She had rolled the jewel over a flattened piece of granola foil she hadn't thrown away from yesterday. "Oh, when it sits on the foil, it reflects like a mirror," she said. She rolled it to the next facet. "That can't be," she muttered. In the octagon shaped, flat top, she clearly saw an image of Haggerwolf. Hillary rolled the jewel again. She saw Fernbark.

"This is incredible," Hillary said and checked all eight facets. "Me, Windslow, the three wizards, and the Sallyforth triplets," she said, her voice soft and whispery. Glancing at the clock, she put the gem back in her zipper pouch and the pouch in the bottom of her backpack. "I've got to show this to Windslow," she said. Hillary slipped on her robe and began getting ready for school.

On the van ride to school, Bill said he was excited about watching the soccer game after school. When he dropped them off, both Hillary and Windslow rushed off to class.

Hillary didn't give the gem another thought throughout the day. Her mind was on soccer and the scrimmage with the team from Rutherford school. It felt good when friends walked past and wished her luck but she was worried about the match.

The day seemed to rush by. Two hours before the end of school, Hillary started feeling "butterflies" in her stomach. She paced back and forth in the locker room waiting for the rest of her team to get ready. The coach gave them a short "pep talk," and they headed out to the field.

***

Windslow wheeled up and down the sidelines. Everything was ready. Twice he had gone back into the equipment room just in case he had forgotten anything. There wasn't really much for him to do once everything was ready. He helped the coach keep notes, made sure the water bottles were filled, and did anything else the coach needed help with. Both teams were out on the field warming up. Behind Windslow, the bleachers had filled early, more with parents than with students. Soccer was popular at school, but more students came to conference games than to a scrimmage. When Marcy and the cheerleaders came out, the crowd cheered and applauded. Each of the cheerleaders gave a little yell, leaped in the air, did a little kick, and shook their pompoms. Marcy did a couple cartwheels and people clapped. Windslow looked around. He didn't see the Sallyforth sisters, but he did see his dad, sitting halfway up the tiered seats.

The teams were well matched. Hillary's side scored one goal in the first period. Now with only fifteen minutes left in the game, the score was still one to zero. Marcy and her cheerleaders swished their pompoms as they took position again in front of the bleachers. Marcy led the cheer, one her squad had been using all afternoon.

1 cent,
2 cents,
3 cents,
A dollar.
All for our team,
Stand up and holler!

Most of the spectators in the first thee rows did stand and yell. A few people stood in the mid section. In the back rows, people did yell, but didn't stand.

"Whoo, hoo," Marcy yelled and did another cartwheel. "Let's hear it everyone." She and her squad lined up elbow to elbow and gave another of their stock cheers.

We've got the talent.
We've got the spirit.
We've got the fans.
So let us hear it.
Whoo, whoo!
Let us hear it!

Response from the crowd was about the same as before. Everyone seemed more interested in just shouting out encouragement to whichever player they had come to watch. When Windslow heard Bill's voice yell, "Go Hillary, go!" Windslow usually added in his own shout, "Come on Hillary! Score! Score! Score!"

"Let's hear it, let's hear it," Marcy yelled. "Stand up and shout."

This time the crowd did stand. There were cheers from the other side as the team from Rutherford scored a goal.

The cheerleaders gave another cheer.

Go team.
Go team.
No time to rest.
We're going to win.
Yes, we are the best!

This time no one in the crowd even seemed to acknowledge the cheer.

At the far end of the bleachers, spectators pointed. A few laughed. Others stood to look where the group pointed. From around the bleachers marched the Sallyforth sisters. Each wore the same outfit they had fashioned for the cheerleading tryouts last week.

Windslow grinned. Instead of a somber walk, the three girls skipped arm an arm, their pink ballerina tutus swishing together. They skipped in unison, legs covered in yellow leggings with bold green horizontal stripes keeping in step. They had added pink lips to the happy faces printed on the front of their t-shirts. Their homemade Mylar pompoms gave off flashes of silver reflected light.

Marcy and her squad stood and glared.

Molly held up a cardboard megaphone decorated in blue glitter stars. She held the small end of the cone to her lips and yelled. "Our team not know how good they are! We need a tell them!"

Bill stuck his fingers in his lips and let out a loud whistle. "You tell 'em, Molly!" he yelled.

"Hi, poppa Bill," Molly called back through the megaphone.

The crowd laughed.

Molly's sisters lined up beside her. They jumped and spun in mid air. When Molly's feet hit the grass she yelled into the megaphone.

All-a our cheers
Are waiting for ears.
We got one
An it sound kind-a dumb!

The crowd laughed again.

Molly continued, this time her sisters chiming in.

If we gonna win
We got-a begin.
We want a goal
So kick it through the poles.

"If you want a goal, then you got-a let-a team know!" Molly yelled. "We try it again."

The crowd stood. Molly began the cheer. The crowd joined in.

If we gonna win
We got-a begin.
We want a goal
So kick it through the poles.

At the end of the cheer, Molly and her sisters jumped up and down. The crowd cheered. Out on the field Hillary yelled, "Go Sallyforth! You rock!"

The cheer from the crowd rose in pitch and ended with hands clapping, whistles and shouts.

Molly yelled again. "We got a score it one a one. Our team have a chance till the game is done."

"Come on! Come on!" Windslow hollered, not knowing what else to yell. If he could stand, he would have got out of his wheelchair. The pace of the game had changed. There was barely five minutes left and the score was tied.

Marcy and her squad pushed up in front of the crowd. She and the other girls gave the same cheer they had used at practice the other night.

There is an ugly girl and her name is Molly.
She won't grow up and still plays with her dolly.
A girl named Tillie dresses pretty silly.
She smells kind of awful like a goat named Billy.
The one named Nelly has a big fat belly.
Wherever she goes, she has stains on her cloths.
They don't stay up late because they never get a date.
They'll never have a chance for the Homecoming Dance.

The crowd booed. Bill began chanting, "Sallyforth, Sallyforth!"

Molly and her sisters pushed in front of the cheerleaders. "This time we do what we say," Molly yelled.

Stand up and down.
Stamp both feet.
We gonna win.
This soccer meet!

"Ever body, do it again!" Molly called.

The crowd chanted along. They stood. They sat. They stomped their feet, over and over, ending each round with "whoops," and "whoo-hoo's."

Molly and her sisters led them in another cheer.

We not need a rest .
We always try our best.
Udder team don't know it.
But they going to blow it.

The crowd stood. A few people yelled. The action on the field stopped. A Rutherford player was given a warning.

Molly and her sisters gave a cheer.

Spin all-a round and
Ruffle your hair.
We gonna win cause we always play fair.

The action resumed. Hillary's team had the ball in the corner of the field by Rutherford's goal. Possession of the ball changed several times as each side struggled to gain control. A Rutherford player kicked it free and passed the ball to a teammate who sent it flying toward midfield.

Molly used her megaphone.

Proud of your player?
Then stomp your feet.
Yell out her name.
She can't be beat!

Feet stomped. The crowd yelled out names. Windslow added his calls to his dad's alternate yells and whistles, "Go Hillary! Go Hillary!"

Hilary's team sent the ball back to the corner. Windslow gripped the arms of his wheelchair. His sister stood twenty feet from the net. Her teammate kicked it from the corner; a high arching kick. Hillary ran, trying to position herself for a head-butt. Windslow new she couldn't make it. The ball would be too high. Hillary twisted, leaped and kicked, nearly doing a back flip.

The crowd roared when her foot connected with the ball. They screamed even louder with the ball sailed between the tip of the goalie's fingertips and the top bar of the net. The bleachers shook from all the foot stomping and jumping.

On the field, players danced and hugged each other until both coaches moved on the field and began lining up the players. The girls from both teams walked in opposing lines, slapping outstretched hands in congratulations for a fine game.

The bleachers emptied, with families hurrying over to congratulate the team. Many people stopped and spoke with the Sallyforth sisters. Windslow watched people pat the Sallyforth girls on the shoulders, shake their hands or chat briefly with them. Windslow had trouble pushing through the spectators. When he found his sister, neither of them said anything. They simply hugged.

"You were fantastic, Hillary," Bill said. "I can't believe you made that kick. You were... and then you... and I thought... and... and... You were awesome! And the Sallyforth girls. They were such a hoot!"

"I know," Hillary said. "It was so cool hearing everyone yelling our names and stomping and jumping and stuff. It's like it got my adrenaline going. They were so great. Come on, I want to go say hi to them and then I need to head to the locker room."

"You'll have to say hi later," Windslow said. "I just saw them go."

"Okay," Bill said. "You two go do what you need to do. I'll be out in the parking lot waiting for you. We'll stop in at the hospital so we can share news about the game with your mom and then get some dinner."

Windslow headed out on the field to start collecting nets, and balls. Hillary rejoined her team and headed for the locker room.

ꙮ

On the way to the hospital, they all talked about the game, Hillary's winning kick and the fun cheers from the Sallyforth sisters. At the hospital, the mood changed. The nurse told them Trish was asleep and had been most of the day. They did wake her to eat, but she still seemed confused and talking nonsense. The nurse told Bill, they were checking with some new specialist who had ordered additional tests.

Dinner and the ride home were somber. Hillary nearly dozed off in the van. At home, she went straight for bed. Windslow made his best attempt at starting a load of laundry. He wasn't sure what to do with what. He dumped all his dark clothes in together with a heaping cup of detergent, twisted the dial to "Super Wash," and hoped for the best. He didn't realize how tired he was until he was finally in bed. He knew falling asleep tonight wouldn't be any trouble. He also knew, any trouble to be had would be waiting for him in Gabendoor.

16: Nasty Nellie

Windslow woke first and watched his sister's form shimmer and fill in. He moved over, to make room for the Sallyforth triplets, assuming they would dream-slip back to the thorn hut too.

Hillary sat up and rubbed her eyes with the back of her fists. "Well," she said. "Just like last time, I have no idea what to do."

Windslow sat up on his haunches. "I do. We need to find Nasty Nellie's well and find that book that tells where the Secret Library is. Then we need to look for the ratStone." Windslow looked to his left and right.

"What are you looking for?" Hillary asked.

"The Sallyforth sisters. I want to get started, but nobody ever said where we could find Nasty Nellie. We could start looking for the stone, but I think we'd just be wondering around wasting our time."

"You'd think they'd be here by now," Hillary said. She adjusted her backpack. "Why don't you get the door open? The girls will find us. They always seem to show up when we need them."

"Well we need them now," Windslow said. He wiggled his fingers and a section of the thorn hut wall vanished, leaving an oval shaped opening.

When they were both outside, Windslow wiggled his fingers again and closed the opening. "That's been a great little hiding spot," he said and headed for the road.

"Whoa," Windslow said when he emerged from the trees. A scraggly line of people filled the road in both directions. Some people pulled small handcarts piled with belongings. Others, had wheelbarrows. Still others carried huge makeshift packs on their shoulders. They were all headed for Aberratia.

No one said anything. Cart and barrow wheels squeaked. Tired footsteps made soft plopping sounds. Here and there, a child whimpered until hushed by an adult. The sound of coughs mixed in with the general din.

Windslow and Hillary walked against the flow, keeping to the edge of the road. After twenty minutes of walking, a woman nearing them pushed back a hood that had covered part of her soot smudged face.

"Gilderbun," Hillary yelled and hurried to her friend.

"Oh, children," Gilderbun said, giving each of them a hug. "You're a good sight to see. We had no word of you and we were worried."

"Why are you going to Aberratia?" Windslow asked. "Where's Dimbleshoot?"

"He stayed back to help the stragglers," Granny Gilderbun said. "Everyone is headed for Aberratia. It's about the only place left. The mountain started spewing out more soot and ash. This time there were chunks of hot stones. A thatched roof isn't much protection against that. I'm afraid Eldervale is gone. It burnt to the ground. The fountain was still clogged with mud and all we could do was stand and watch it burn. The only place where there is any hope is Aberratia. The talk is, Dreadlore is using his magic to shield Heart-Thorn forest and Aberratia. He has a circle of wizards, like they used in olden times."

"Circle of slaves, is more like it," Hillary said. "He's got Haggerwolf, Larkstone, Fernbark and about fifty other people all chained together to channel magic."

"Well," Granny Gilderbun said. "Whatever he is doing still holds out some hope. There's not much of that left. It's like the legend said."

Fright town
Night town
Things that aren't right town.

Night death
Right death
Choice becomes plight death.

"Think about that," Granny said. "People are saying that fright town and night town and all the things that aren't right are about what's happening now. We've had hail, then heat, snow, wind, earthquakes and the eruption."

Windslow nodded and chewed on his lower lip as he listened to Granny continue.

"I have to agree, things aren't right in Gabendoor. And the part about choice becomes plight. That fits going with going to Aberratia pretty well. There's nothing any of us can do."

"Well, we can," Windslow said. "That's why we're here."

"You two children are wonderful, but what can you do? There's only two of you."

"No," Hillary said, "There are eight of us; me, Windslow, the three wizards and the Sallyforth sisters."

"Granny," Windslow asked, "Do you know where Nasty Nellie's well is?"

Gilderbun stared at him before answering. "Stay away from her. Why would you even ask about such a horrible person?"

"She's part of the puzzle; part of what we need to do," Hillary said.

Gilderbun sighed and nodded her head. "That shouldn't surprise me. But if I tell you where to find her, promise me you won't ask her for a wish."

"I think that's why we need to see her," Hillary said.

"No, dear, that can't be right." Gilderbun said. "Once a man wished for a bag of gold. Nasty Nellie made his wish come true. The bag formed in his stomach. It killed him. People have wished for love, and found it, but the loved one died within a day. Examples go on and on. No one has ever survived. A lot of people have tried. A lot of people thought they could outsmart Nasty Nellie. A lot of people are dead because they tried."

"It makes some sense," Windslow said. "We never get asked to do anything easy. So, will you tell us how to find her?"

Gilderbun nodded. "It will be easy. Follow the trail half way back to Eldervale. You'll come to a fork that heads off to the West. Take the fork for a mile and follow the trees."

"We're in the middle of a forest," Windslow said. "What do you mean, follow the trees? There are trees everywhere."

"You'll know," Gilderbun said and gave him a hug.

Hillary took her turn at a hug. "We'll take care of each other," she told Gilderbun.

ꙮ

Hillary and Windslow followed the trail. They wove through the line of travelers. A few people told Windslow and Hillary they were headed the wrong way. They both nodded and kept walking. When they reached the fork, they headed west down the tree lined path.

"Now what," Windslow said. "There aren't any more turns or anything and the trees all look the same."

Hillary shrugged.

Another hundred yards around a bend, Hillary stopped and pointed. "There's a little side path. Do you think we should take it?"

"I don't know," Windslow said. "It could just be a deer trail or something."

"Um, I don't think so. Look at that tree."

Windslow looked where his sister pointed. About ten feet off the ground in the center of the trunk, the bark pinched and twisted together to form a face. "It almost looks like some guy is pushing his face out from inside the tree," Windslow said. "Look at the eyes. They look like they're made of glass or something. It's creepy."

"There's another one up ahead." Hillary pointed farther up the path. "That one looks like a woman. I hope they aren't from real people."

"I don't want to find out," Windslow said and kept walking. "This has got to be the right way."

Hillary nodded and moved a little closer to her brother as they walked. They rounded another bend and stopped.

The path opened to a small circular grove. In the middle of the sparsely spaced trees sat a well made of tan colored blocks of stone. Each tree in the grove held an anguished face pressing out from the bark like the trees on the trail. At the well, two stout support beams supported a hand-crank and roller coiled with weathered brown rope.

Windslow leaned over the side of the waist-high stones. "I don't see any water, but there is a bucket." He stood back straight. "What do you think we're supposed to do now; make a wish?"

"I remember how the rhyme went." Hillary recited the poem.

Nasty Nellie lives in a well.
Ask for a wish.
It will cost you a spell.

Use your wits if you hope to survive.
To get out of the well
while you still are alive.

"So I guess we just shout out a wish. I don't think it's like you throw in a coin or anything."

"Who's come to my well?" a grizzled voice called up. "Who has come to visit sweet Nellie? I think it's the Children of the Wind, so I do. Call down your wish and I'll grant it to you."

Windslow leaned close to his sister and spoke softly. "I don't think it's this easy, and I don't trust her. All we need to do is get that book."

"Oh, you want my book," Nellie called up the well. "It's here behind my clock on a shelf. You'll need to come down and get it yourself."

"This is not good," Windslow said and slipped off his backpack. "Do you think you can lower me in that bucket?"

"What? You?" Hillary said. "You're not going down with your legs and all. I mean, I don't usually say anything about what you can and can't do, but let's face it. You need crutches. You can't really run very fast and well... if you have to jump or something..."

"You don't think you're going?" Windslow said.

Hillary nodded. "Yes I am. I don't want to start an argument by saying I'm smarter than you." Hillary leaned forward and gave her brother a kiss on the cheek. "Call us equal in that department. But I'm the one on the soccer team. I can run, jump and kick. I'm going. You crank."

"I don't think you'll be playing a soccer game down there. Maybe we should both go down."

"Dah... Who's going to crank?" Hillary said. "Maybe I should take back that kiss."

"All right," Windslow said. "But if you aren't back in half an hour, or if I hear anything funny, I'm coming down after you. I can shinny down the rope."

Hillary leaned over the well. "It's me, the Daughter of the Wind. I'm coming down."

Nellie called back. "Welcome Hillary-Windgate Summerfield. Is your wish for me to help your mother? Or is your wish something other?"

"This is creepy," Hillary whispered to her brother. She boosted herself up on the wall and dangled her legs down the well.

Windslow cranked the bucket up until Hillary could get one foot into it. She grabbed the rope and eased herself off the wall. "I'm ready," she said.

Windslow turned the crank and lowered his sister into the well.

"You can stop," Hillary yelled after only a few feet. "There are metal rungs here. I can climb down."

The bucket stopped. Hillary carefully grabbed one of the metal ladder rungs sticking from the wall. She pulled herself over and eased a foot onto a lower rung. With slow steps, she climbed down.

She could see well enough. A faint green glow filled the well. It came from the moss that clung to the stones. Thirty feet below, she could see the bottom. "There's a tunnel that heads off to my left," she called up to her brother.

"Which way is your left?" Windslow called back.

"Um... north! I'm at the bottom now." She swallowed hard and took a step forward.

17: The Big Bang

Hillary looked down the tunnel. Just as in the well, soft green light provided illumination. "Ew," she said and pulled her hand away from the wall. "Slimy."

Even though there was plenty of room, she ducked her head. She didn't want to chance brushing her hair against the ceiling. The tunnel curved left, right, straightened and ended at a gate that looked like the door to a jail cell. Past the iron bars she could see a large high domed cavern furnished with everything to make it a home.

Tall wooden cabinets with a mix of doors, drawers and shelves sat against the wall. A long counter space held crocks, murky colored glass jars, piles of books, papers, pot, pans and a clutter of things Hillary didn't recognize.

A large fireplace sat in the far wall. A small fire and large pile of glowing embers added orange and yellow light to the green color from the moss. Some sort of liquid bubbled and burped in a shiny copper pot hung from a long metal arm over the fire.

"Come in, come in," Nellie's voice called from somewhere.

Hillary pushed on the iron bars. The hinges squeaked as the door opened. She took a step forward.

Something felt odd. It was as if the air was thick and it gave Hillary the feeling she had when she was walking into a strong wind. After two more steps, the slight pressure went away. The image before Hillary changed.

The cabinets were still there, but not made of smooth polished wood. Long bones fastened together formed doors and drawer fronts. Stacked skulls of different sizes supported the countertop. The books, paper and clutter were still there and so was the fireplace, but it had changed too. Instead of natural river stones stacked and cemented in place, the face of the fire pit held carved blocks; each carved in relief with an anguished face, just like on the trees along the path.

The pot over the fire was the same shape but not shiny copper, but black and covered with baked on drips and spills. Where an inviting stuffed couch had sat in a corner, now sat an arrangement of driftwood stacked with dry brown grass. In the middle of the cavern stood an octagon table with legs made of antler and its top of rough-hewn planks. Four chairs, with food stained seats and backs, looked less than inviting. Small jars, clay pots, tiny piles of small bones and tangles of dried roots covered half the table.

Not sure what to do, Hillary walked to the table. She looked at one of the seats and decided to stay standing.

"Sit and stay for a while," Nellie's voice called from a passageway off to one side. "I'm just arranging my dress. I like to look nice when I greet a new guest."

Hillary picked a chair that would let her look toward the passage. She took a handkerchief from her backpack, spread it on the seat and sat down. The tabletop was clear of clutter where she sat, but looked greasy so she folded her hands in her lap. After a few moments, she heard soft footsteps. Nellie walked into the room.

She wasn't what Hillary had expected. She imagined Nellie as a wrinkled old lady who would walk stooped over and might even have a cane. The woman who walked from the passage looked middle aged with smooth skin and jet-black hair pulled back in a ponytail. She wore a white long-sleeved shirt and black leather vest, black leather skirt and mid-calf boots. Hillary did notice, Nellie walked with a slight limp.

Nellie took a seat across from Hillary, leaned forward and rested her arms on the table. "Well, girl," Nellie said, "what is your wish?"

"I don't know that I have one," Hillary answered. "You see, I thought about it. I thought a lot. Anything I wish for you can change around. I could wish that my mother recovered. If she only recovered for an hour, that would fulfill the wish. I could wish to be happy for the rest of my life, but you could make my life short."

"I'm not here to play games." Nellie said. "Everything you ask for could all work the same. Ask me a wish and pay me a spell. Then I'll let you out of my well."

"Let's try it this way," Hillary said. "I came here because you have a book up in your room. It tells where the Secret Library is. That's what I came for. That's not a wish. I'm simply telling you why I'm here. No wishes. Simply let me look at that book. Oh, and I'll give you a spell, depending what spell you want. So let's just get this over with. What do you have in mind for a spell so we can trade?"

Nellie leaned back and gave a long crackling laugh that fit better with the image of an old hag. She reached inside her vest and pulled out a long butcher knife with a silver blade and sleek black handle. Hillary sat back when Nellie stabbed it into the tabletop. The blade vibrated from side to side when Nellie released the handle and slapped her hands flat on the table.

"You'll be my dinner. What I can't eat I'll feed to my cat," Nellie yelled. "I'll put your face on an elm tree along the path after that."

"I don't think so," Hillary said and wiggled her fingers to work a spell. Blue light sparked from her fingers and stretched toward Nellie. Halfway to the woman the magic formed into a soft ball and hovered in the air.

"Oh, good," Nellie said. She jumped from her chair and hurried to her countertop. Snatching an empty jar, she hurried back. Carefully she slipped the jar over the ball of magic, and snapped on the lid. Sitting back in her chair, she held the jar up and examined the light. "Ah, a fine bit of magic," she said. "I'll accept it as a gift. If you'd like to try some more spells, be my guest. Your magic won't work very well, but try your best."

Hillary stretched across the table and yanked the knife free. She gave out a scream. The knife changed into a foot long cricket. Hillary held it by the back legs as it wiggled in her grasp. She let go. It dropped to the table, back in the form of a butcher knife.

Nellie snatched it up and stabbed it back into the tabletop.

"All right, I'm out of here," Hillary said. She shoved back her chair and ran for the metal grating at the doorway. She yanked hard, but it wouldn't move.

"Sorry, dearie," Nasty Nellie called.

Hillary yanked again on the metal bars that covered the doorway in the cavern. Frustrated, Hillary tried magic but nothing happened. She turned around and pressed her back against the bars.

"Let me see," Nasty Nellie said. She pulled the knife from the table and used the tip of the shiny blade like a spatula. She dipped it into a small orange clay pot in front of her and carefully lifted the knife back out. On the tip sat a teaspoon of silver powder. Nellie grabbed an empty shallow bowl, held it up and blew against the clay to clean it out. She set the bowl back on the table and tapped the edge of the blade on the bowl's rim to deposit the powder.

"A little puff-toad tongue," she said and used the blade again to transfer black powder from another jar into the bowl. "Oh, and eye of crow, and bark from the thorn-heart. I can't forget, this." Nellie held up a smoky colored glass bottle. She pulled the cork and sniffed. "Yes, this is it," she mumbled and poured two drops into the bowl. Again, using the knife blade, she stirred her mixture.

A thin curl of purple smoke rose from the concoction. Nellie fanned the knife blade through the smoke, pushing it toward Hillary. "Bring her to me," Nellie said as if talking to the smoke and stabbed the blade back into the tabletop.

Hillary watched the curl of smoke come closer. When it was a foot away, Hillary turned her head to the side and held her breath. She looked down and watched the smoke wrap around her wrist. Hillary blew out the breath she had been holding and carefully drew in another.

The smoke made her arm tingle. It pulled at her as if it were a leash. In Hillary's mind, she wanted to resist but couldn't. The smoke guided her by the arm as Hillary walked back to the table. When she sat, the smoke disappeared.

"The bargain is a spell for a wish," Nellie said. "I'll give you some time to think while I mix up a new dish." Nellie took the dish and tipped it upside down, tapping it gently at the corner of the table. She blew in it as before and placed it in front of her.

Hillary wasn't sure what to do. She watched the old woman use the knife to dip more powders from the array of jars, pots and flasks in front of her.

"All right," Hillary said. "I've come up with a wish. What do you want for a spell? Or how about a potion? Would you like a potion from Earth?"

Nellie looked up. "From Earth, you say?" She nodded her head. "That could make my day. Done! Give me your wish."

"My wish," Hillary said, "is that you don't make any potions or spells or whatever you do that will hurt me." Hillary folded her arms across her chest and smiled.

Nellie waived her hand in the air. "Wish granted," she said. "Give me the potion."

"Well," Hillary said. "I don't know that you have all the ingredients." Hillary chewed on her lip for a moment. She wasn't sure she could remember the formula she wanted. She thought it odd, that right now, she was really wishing she had paid more attention in science class. "Okay, you need sulfur. It's called brimstone sometimes. It's yellow and you might find it around a volcano. It smells like rotten eggs."

"Ah," Nellie said. She got up from her chair and moved to her cluttered countertop. After shoving jars and pots aside, she came back with a small glass bottle. Burning egg stone, she said.

"Use your knife and measure out two and a half parts."

Nellie did as instructed. She looked up at Hillary and waited for the next ingredient.

"Take some charcoal from your fire and grind it up very fine," Hillary said.

Nellie used a small mortar and pestle to grind the charcoal and measured it into the sulfur.

"This will be the hard one," Hillary said. "You need saltpeter. It's pale yellow and looks like brushes or hairs sticking up from the ground in bat caves. If there aren't any bat droppings then it isn't the right stuff."

"Bat beard," Nellie said, her eyes lighting up. She rummaged in a cabinet and brought out a small wooden box. She ground the contents in her mortar, and measured one knife-tip into the other two ingredients.

Now, you need a piece of paper or parchment.

Nellie ripped a sheet from a book on her table. She held it up. "Will this work?"

"Yes," Hillary said. "Dump the powder on the paper and then fold the paper in half. Now fold all the edges in and roll it up tight so it looks like a paper stick."

Nellie did as instructed and held up the finger sized roll of paper.

"That's it," Hillary said. "If you used the right stuff, and didn't mess up mixing it, then it's ready."

"Ready for what?" Nellie asked. "What does it do?"

"That wasn't part of the agreement," Hillary said. "You'll have to figure that out. But I'll tell you it does have something to do with fire. You'll need fire to make it work." Hillary shoved her chair back and was relieved when nothing prevented her from standing. "I'll be going now," she said and turned toward the barred doorway.

"We're not done," Nellie said. "Sit back down and we'll have some fun."

Hillary ignored her and grabbed the bars again. She pulled and kicked. The bars wouldn't move. She felt something at her wrist. The curl of smoke was back. Hillary's thoughts fogged in her mind. She relaxed, turned and let the smoke guide her back to her chair. When she sat, the fogginess lifted. "What about my wish!" Hillary demanded.

Nellie looked up from the rolled paper she still held. "I didn't promise to let you go. There might be more about his potion I want to know. And, you did get what you wished for. I didn't hurt you when I brought you back from the door."

A sound like someone dropping an armload of firewood grabbed Hillary's attention. She looked at the pile of driftwood.

The wood and straw moved. The lengths of weatherworn wood clacked and clattered, tumbling in the air. Pieces smacked together. The straw swirled as if caught in a small whirlwind. When the pieces stopped, they formed a cell. The door swung open.

Nasty Nellie stood and pulled the knife from the table. She pointed it at Hillary. "I don't think I should let you wander about. You're not leaving here. There's no way out. I don't want to cut you or slice you just yet. So get in that cage while I get everything set."

Hillary stood. Instead of heading for the cage, she walked in the other direction.

Nellie, the table and the chairs moved with Hillary, all of them twisting around in the room as if they were all mounted on some sort of turntable or merry-go-round.

Nellie laughed. "I don't like people getting too close to me," she said.

Hillary kept walking. Nellie and the table kept turning. Hillary stopped when Nellie's back faced the fireplace.

"You win," Hillary said. "Burn the end of the paper tube with a candle."

"Hah, ha, ha. Hah, ha, ha," Nellie called out in delight as she stood from the table and did a small dance in a tight circle. She grabbed a candle and lit the wick in the fireplace. She looked at Hillary before touching the flame to the tightly rolled paper.

Hillary got ready to duck and to run, hoping she had remembered the formula correctly. There were many 'if's.' Would it work if Nellie used the right ingredients? If, it worked would it give Hillary an opportunity to flee? And, two more 'if's' she thought of. If it worked, would there be a chance to get the book? If it worked, would Hillary be able to get the metal grate open? Ready to move fast, Hillary watched the flame darken the end of the paper.

BAM!

Hillary ducked under the table. She looked up and saw a cloud of black smoke. From behind the smoke, Nellie screamed. Hillary leaped for the grating. With one foot planted against the wall, she grabbed the bars. Nothing moved. From behind her she heard Nellie.

"You dreadful girl! You were clever in your wish. If I could hurt you now, I would. You would feel daggers sticking in your brow. That's how my fingers feel now. Come back and sit in your chair. I'll teach you a couple of my potions if you dare."

Hillary didn't have a choice. She felt the smoke grip her wrist again. This time it didn't gently lead her to the table. This time she didn't feel in a fog. This time the smoke yanked her hard and invisible hands shoved her down to sit.

Across from her, Nellie stood. She held one arm around a bucket of water, holding it tight to her chest. She soaked the fingers in the water. Black smudges covered her face.

Nellie moved to where she had sat, but stayed standing. She put the bucket on the table and kept soaking her fingers. With her left hand, she yanked the knife from the table and began mixing a potion in the bowl. "This one uses fire too," Nellie said. She grabbed the candle and dripped wax into her mixture. With the knife tip, she scraped up a small dab of the softened wax mixture and flicked it at Hillary.

Hillary used her arm to shield her eyes. She didn't feel the wax hit her. "I think you missed," Hillary said, aware she might be taunting Nellie.

"I don't miss," Nellie said. "It doesn't matter much where the wax lands. It's done its work. Look at your hands."

Hillary held out her hands, first looking at her palms and then at the backs. She gasped when she looked closely at her fingertips. Blood formed around her fingernails. The flow continued. Hillary held her hands out over the table. Blood dripped from her fingers and pooled on the tabletop.

"This will help," Nellie said and mixed more powders. This time she flipped the small bowl upside-down. Hillary saw the bowl move. The lip pushed up. Out came three small brown lizards with spiky skin and thick pink tongues that looked more like something a frog would have. They scurried across the table, heading for her.

"They like blood," Nellie said. "They want to nurse at your fingertips. They'll help suck the blood out of you fast. It won't hurt, but you won't last."

Hillary gave a scream and tried to push away from the table and stand. Something held her in place. She screamed again when she felt something on her finger. One of the lizards had her finger in its mouth. Hillary yanked it off, threw it on the floor and kicked it toward the fire. She looked for the other lizards. One was on her arm, the other on her leg. She grabbed and sent them flying toward the fireplace.

The dish clattered. Three more lizards crawled out from under the bowl.

Hillary held her hands out. She raised her elbows and lowered her fingers so the blood would drip instead of running down her arms. The growing size of the puddle worried her.

Nellie picked up the knife and dipped the blade into a tall vase. "You have a wish granted," Nellie said. "I just fixed my blade so you won't feel a thing. My cutting won't hurt you. It won't even sting."

Both Hillary and Nellie jumped and screamed when the metal grating crashed to the floor.

"Oops... Sorry," a voice said. "We break your door. We not mean a do that. It was stuck."

"You three!" Nasty Nellie yelled.

Molly, Nelly and Tillie walked into the room.

"Hi, Nassy," Molly said.

Tillie waved. "Hi, Hillre. Windso waiting for you."

"Hi, nobody," Nelly added.

She and her sisters spread out around the room.

"She's bleeding me to death," Hillary said, frantically looking from girl to girl.

"You okay," Tillie said. "I don't think a color right. Darker red be better."

"You almost near death," Nelly Sallyforth added.

"Hey, Hillre," Molly called from across the room. "Close a eyes, stick finger in a mouth and taste it."

Hillary looked at her hands, back to Molly and back to her hands again. When she closed her eyes, a small tear rolled down her cheek. Hand shaking, Hillary raised her fingers to her mouth. She touched one finger with the tip of her tongue. She paused. She put the whole finger in her mouth. Hillary opened her eyes and looked at her fingers. She stuck two of them in her mouth.

Hillary scowled and twisted her head to look at Nasty Nellie. Hillary looked down at the pool of blood on the table. With her pointer finger, she drew a line through the puddle of blood. Hillary could feel her finger on the wood. Her finger didn't leave a trail in the blood as she had expected.

Closing her eyes again, Hillary took several deep breaths, drawing each one in through her nose and blowing out through her mouth. When she opened her eyes, there was no puddle of blood on the table. Her hands were dirty with two clean fingertips where she had sucked on them. She looked at the dish. A piece of plant root stuck out from under the lip.

Hillary looked back up at Nasty Nellie. She had changed. Nellie was no longer a middle-aged woman dressed in leather. Now her form fit her raspy voice. She stood stooped over with gray hair and wrinkled skin. A wrinkled dress with some sort of faded pattern replaced the leather vest and skirt. A dirty apron drooped across her paunchy stomach.

"This time you're in my domain," Nasty Nellie said looking at the Sallyforth Triplets. "This time the outcome won't be the same. Your magic doesn't work down here." Nellie grabbed her knife and held it out.

"That okay," Molly said. "We use your magic then." She pointed at the knife and said, "Croak, croak."

The knife turned into a bullfrog. Nellie held it by the hind legs. It jerked in the air trying to escape her grip. Nellie dropped it. It landed with a *Thunk.* Returned to a knife, the shiny blade stuck in the table again.

Nasty Nellie hobbled to the fireplace and grabbed the iron poker. Its tip glowed red from the heat of the fire. "We'll see who ends up being the winner. I'm going to cook you all for dinner."

"Oh, goodie," Tillie said. "I like a cook. Our mommy teach us how. I get a help."

"Not me too," Nelly said and skipped over to the countertop. "We not need this, an this and this," she said as she began rummaging through a pile of pots, pans and cooking utensils.

"I need lot of pepper on me," Molly said. She grabbed a medium sized jar filled with black powder.

"I do a pepper," Tillie said and tried to grab the jar from her sister.

"Leave everything alone!" Nasty Nellie yelled. "Don't touch that. Put that down!"

Molly and Tillie wiggled and twisted, each trying to get control of the jar. The cork top flipped up. Nelly swung at it with a frying pan and sent the cork sailing at Nasty Nellie.

Nasty Nellie ducked.

Nelly Sallyforth yelled out, "Fair ball. Runner on first!" Still holding the frying pan, she ran to the driftwood cage. "Safe!" she hollered and banged the pan against the wood. She jumped back when the framework teetered and collapsed back to a jumble of wood and straw.

Tillie won the struggle for the pot. "I do a seasoning," she said and scooped out a fist full of pepper. "You need some," she said and threw the pepper on Molly's hair.

"You need a salt," Molly said and grabbed another pot with a metal top poked full of holes. She shook salt on Tillie's head.

"Do here too," Tillie said and held up her arms.

Molly shook salt under Tillie's arms, on her back and down her legs.

"Get away from there!" Nasty Nellie hollered and ran toward them.

"We need a season Nelly too," Molly said. "We use a measuring spoon." She grabbed a handle that stuck out from a pile of books and papers, topped with another large jar. Papers and books tumbled. The jar landed sideways in the floor. Tillie grabbed the cork stopper and threw it toward her sister. Nelly banged the lid with her fry pan and yelled, "It a homer." She ran past the table. Her sisters chased after her, Molly shaking salt at her and Tillie tossing out handfuls of pepper. Hillary backed up against the wall near the fallen metal grading.

"Oh no!" Nasty Nellie cried. "My jar of eyeballs."

Spewed out from the fallen jar, small round objects littered the floor like a can of spilled olives. Nasty Nellie dropped to her knees and grabbed the jar. She picked up an eyeball. She blew it off before plopping it back in the jar and grabbing another.

"Hey, what this for?" Molly asked.

Hillary looked. The small girl had climbed one of the cabinets, she shook a small cloth bag. The contents gave off a clinking sound.

"Don't shake that!" Nasty Nellie yelled. She scooped up the remaining eyeballs and cradled them in her apron. "Get down from there."

Molly jumped. The cabinet door she had been holding onto broke, the bones that formed it clattered to the floor. The shelves behind it broke loose. Jars, crocks, utensils, bags slid from their places. Some crashed to the floor. Other's plopped and oozed. Sheets of paper, scribbled with formulas, floated across the room. Salt and pepper covered nearly everything.

Hillary stayed close to the wall. When Nasty Nellie had her attention on the girls, Hillary darted into the passageway where Nellie had come from. The tunnel-like passage sloped upward. The end opened into a small bedroom. Hillary spotted what she had been looking for. She ran to the grandfather clock behind the bed. Hillary pulled the clock away from the wall.

"Crud-o," Hillary said. "There's nothing there." She ran her hand over the hewn rock wall. "Wait," she said and looked at the back of the clock. She grinned when she spotted thin gaps in the wood, outlining a rectangle. She tried to pry the lid open. It wiggled but wouldn't move. She pushed and felt it slide upward. "Ah, ha," Hillary said and moved the lid, uncovering a hidden compartment. Inside she found a thin red leather book about the size of a journal.

She shoved the book into her backpack and pushed the clock back into place. Quickly she headed back to the main room.

The room looked like a cyclone had gone through it. The pot from the fireplace lay upside down near the table. Molly, Nelly and Tillie sat on top of the black cauldron. Each of them held a large wooden spoon.

"Where's Nasty Nellie?" Hillary asked.

Muffled sounds came from the pot. It lifted a half inch from the floor and moved sideways a foot. All three girls banged on the pot with their spoons.

Hillary laughed and pointed at the pot.

The three girls grinned.

"You need a go," Molly said. "Nasty Nellie still dangerous. She have lot a traps outside a well. We keep her here until you gone. Then we go out a back way."

"All right," Hillary said. She was going to tell the girls to be careful, but didn't. She knew that they could take care of themselves. "Have fun," she said instead.

The girls banged on the pot.

Hillary laughed again, headed down the tunnel and climbed from the well.

18: Start from the Middle

Windslow helped his sister climb out of the well. "How'd it go?" He asked. "I was so relieved when the Sallyforth Sisters showed up. They pretty much just walked out of the woods, said hi and climbed down into the well."

"I'll have to fill you in later," Hillary said. "I'll just say they were back to being their normal selves. It was dangerous, but hilarious too. The important thing is I got the book. At least I think I did. I haven't opened it yet."

"Let's see it," Windslow said.

Hillary pulled it from her backpack. Together they knelt on the ground and opened the book.

"Wow," Windslow said, "it has locations for other things too. Watch for anything about the ratStone."

Hillary flipped through the pages. "Okay, here's what we need, the Secret Library of Gabendoor. Look, one entry is crossed out."

The page began with, "Start from the middle and read to both ends." The next entry, crossed out in dark ink read;

.tree spider-vulture the from mile one North .range Charm-Mist the in up High Walk between two crossed oaks to cross the magic barrier.

A new line in fresh ink read;

.fulfilled purpose its, Gabendoor from Gone Back to the stars, it is no more.

"Great," Windslow said. "Another book that can't just say something out straight."

"Um, Windslow you know how sometimes clouds look like things?"

"Yah," he said.

"Well, I think you should look behind you. There's a cloud that looks like a turtle and it's getting close."

"Hillary, this isn't the time to be..." Windslow paused when he turned around and looked. Low hanging dark clouds had moved in. From the leading edge, a cloud mass had thrust out from the rest. It rolled and boiled, taking the shape of a turtle with front clawed feet sticking out at angles from the side. Its neck and snout stretched out even farther.

"That's awesome," Windslow said. "It's a snapping turtle."

"Clouds don't bite off tree tops," Hillary shouted, "and it's coming straight for us."

As the cloud-turtle drew closer, wind blasted ahead of it. The snout kept snapping as it raced forward and grew in size.

"Get behind the well," Windslow yelled against the wind.

Hillary grabbed the book and shoved it in her back pocket. Windslow grabbed her hand. Together they moved around to the other side of the well. The snout snapped at one of the uprights that held the roller and rope. Splinters and chunks of wood clattered against the stones. The broken timber pushed out some of the stones, leaving a hole in the well's wall. The image vanished and simple clouds swirled around Hillary and her brother.

"That was weird," Windslow said. He stood and put his hands on a stone forming the lip of the well. The stone moved then toppled. He and his sister moved back. A third of the wall crumbled, rocks and chunks of mortar tumbling onto the grass. The second support timber teetered before falling across the rubble.

Hillary shoved the book back into her pack. "Molly told me that Nasty Nellie might have some surprises for us outside the well. I guess that was it."

"*Surprises* is plural," Windslow said. "Look at that," he said and pointed at another shape forming in the clouds. "It looks like an arm with a closed fist."

The arm extended. The ground shook when the fist flattened a six-foot circle of grass. The arm raised, ready for another strike.

"I'm not going to just sit here," Windslow said. "Get ready to run. After I take care of this one, let's head back to the path and get out of here." Windslow pointed a finger and yelled, "Rain mix," Heavy rain fell directly over the fist. The water drops spattered off the clenched fingers.

"I think now would be a good time to run," Hillary said. She darted out from behind the well and headed for the trees. Windslow stayed close behind.

The ground shook again when the fist slammed down where they had been standing.

Hillary stopped and turned. "How about this," she said. Hillary pointed her fingers and called out, "Fire to burn away the mist!"

Her magic fire engulfed the fist. It quickly fizzled out. The fist rose, struck the ground again and turned to fog, blown quickly away by the wind.

"Let's keep going," Windslow said and grabbed his sister's arm. "We're almost at the trail. Magic doesn't seem to be the answer."

"I think it's just the spells we're picking," Hillary said. "The clouds are magic so we need to be more creative."

"Or we need to move faster," Windslow said. "Let's see how clouds do in a tree lined trail."

"Here comes your answer," Hillary said. She stopped and turned. A flat bottomed shark with a gaping mouth skimmed down the trail.

"Crud-o," Hillary yelled. "I dropped the book!"

Twenty feet behind them, the book lay in the center of the path. Hillary ran and dove to the grass. Her outstretched fingers touched the book. At the same time, her brother landed beside her and the lower shark jaw scooped them off the ground.

Hillary screamed.

Windslow tightened his grip around his sister. He could feel them being lifted in the air. Grayness surrounded them. The wind tore at his clothes and tumbled both of them like dry leaves.

"There aren't any teeth!" Windslow had to yell loud over the roaring wind. "Did you get the book!"

"Don't let go," Hillary yelled back. "I've got it. What's happening?"

"I'm not sure. We're off the ground. I know that much. I'll try a spell."

"Be careful," Hillary yelled. "Falling a couple thousand feet, isn't a solution!"

"I'll do a parachute. What do you think?"

"Go for it," Hillary hollered.

Windslow adjusted his grip then tried his spell.

Clouds release and let us go.
A parachute to lower us slow.

The grayness thinned. Something jerked Windslow and Hillary into an upright position. Windslow looked up and saw a white canopy with long strings running down to a harness that held both his sister and him. "It worked," he said.

"We're a thousand feet up," Hillary said. "Twist a little bit. I'm going to shove the book in your backpack. I want my hands free."

"All right –whoa!" Windslow yelled. The wind blew them nearly sideways. Part of the parachute collapsed. Hillary screamed as they dropped. Their fall stopped with a jolt when the canopy filled with air again. The wind swirled and spun them around.

"I don't know about this," Hillary said. "The storm is pulling us back up. We're going higher and look!"

Beneath them, a long column of cloud formed the shape of a snake's head. A small bolt of lightning forked out of its open mouth. Its coiled shape spiraled toward them.

The parachute harness disappeared. Windslow and Hillary dropped into the snake's open mouth.

Their fall slowed. As before, the thick gray cloud kept them from seeing anything but each other. They spun and tumbled.

"We're going back up," Windslow yelled.

"How do you like playing with Nellie," Nasty Nellie's voice sounded from all around them. "I always find a way to win. The ground is waiting for you. I hope you drop in."

Hillary clutched her brother. "That's not funny," she said, barely loud enough for him to hear. "I love you, Windslow," she said in a louder voice.

"Whoa," Windslow yelled when he felt them both drop. "I need to say something too," Windslow said, his lips nearly touching Hillary's ear. "Journey wind!"

The gray clouds whirled around them, tighter and tighter, faster and faster. Hillary and Windslow seemed to float now. The wind controlled the clouds, whipping them in a tight spiral that held Windslow and Hillary as if inside a cocoon.

The wind stopped, Hillary and Windslow lurched forward. They both sprawled across the grass and skidded to a stop. Windslow turned his head to look for his sister. Hillary groaned and pushed herself up to her knees. "Good spell choice, brother." Hillary said. She stared at Windslow and then burst into laughter.

"What's so funny?" Windslow asked as he sat up.

"You forgot one of those quirks about traveling in a journey-wind."

"What are you talking about?" Windslow asked.

"Take a look at your clothes."

Windslow looked down at himself. The jeans he wore were unbuttoned, unzipped and pulled up barely above his knees. Each of his feet stuck halfway into small white tennis shoes. He looked at his shirt. Only one button held the material stretched across his chest.

"Oh, crud-o" Windslow said. "These are your clothes."

Hillary stopped giggling long enough to tell her brother to turn around.

Windslow spun around, kicked off the tennis shoes and yanked off the jeans, which he tossed over his head. In return, his own jeans hit him in the back of the head. He tossed the shirt after the jeans. He slipped on his own shirt, did the buttons and slipped into his tennis shoes. "Can I turn around yet?" he asked.

"Ready," Hillary said and tossed him his backpack. "Where are we?"

Windslow stood. "I don't know. Let's figure it out. I didn't consciously have any place in mind when I cast the spell. But I must have had something in my head or I don't think the spell would have worked."

"I know where you were thinking," Hillary said. She squatted down and patted her knees. The shelterhund ran to Hillary and nearly knocked her over. "Hi, sweetie," she said and petted the large dog-like beast who tried his best to lick her face. Hillary stood. All we have to do is follow our guide. "Take us to Maxwell and Faith," Hillary said to the shelterhund.

"Yah, right. Like it understands English," Windslow said.

Hillary simply smiled as the beast trotted around the brush. When she walked past her brother she looked back over her shoulder. "Well, are you coming?"

Windslow shouldered his backpack and followed. On the other side of the brambles, he saw Faith and Maxwell sitting on the logs by their campfire where he and Hillary had met them before. All around the pond behind the fire were stacks of squash, heaps of potatoes and large wooden bins holding carrots.

"Whoa, what's with all the food?" Windslow asked as he sat down on a log.

"We've been harvesting," Faith said. "The volcano ruined the villagers' crops. My brother and I started harvesting from the meadows and valleys here in the mountains. There is more food than just this. We need your help to get it to the villagers."

"We can round up lots of help," Hillary said. "We'll get the villagers and have them bring their carts. Or maybe they should start moving up here into the mountains. They're all just hanging around Aberratia right now."

"Oh, no. That won't work," Maxwell said as he shook his head. "The mountains are magic and Gabendoor wouldn't let all the people come here. Besides, they need to rebuild what they have to restore their hope."

Windslow slipped his pack off, slid down to sit on the ground, and used the log as a backrest. "You said you needed our help. You expect us to haul all this down to Eldervale do you?"

"Not exactly," Faith said. "There's an easier way. If you open Larkstone's magic zipper closet in Eldervale, you can reach through to here. We'll hand you the food in baskets. It will be like moving everything a couple feet."

"Well, there's a problem with that," Hillary said. "And we have more than a couple of other problems too. First, Dreadlore has Larkstone. Second, we were supposed to find out where the Secret Library is. We got a book from Nasty Nellie that's supposed to tell where it is, but we can't read the book. Then, there is the problem of finding the ratStone. Things are a bit of a mess right now. Aren't they," she said, looking at her brother.

"Hillary's right," Windslow said, "but we still have lots of hope. So that just means we have a lot to do and not much time to do it in."

"I knew you understood," Maxwell said. He gave Windslow a big smile. "I'm so glad you helped the Sallyforth sisters regain their spirit. I knew you could."

"How did you know about that?" Windslow asked.

Hillary looked at them both. "What are you two talking about?"

Faith moved beside Hillary and patted her on the knee. "It's not important. What is important is your problems. As your brother says, you do have a lot to do. But I don't understand some things. You said you got the book you needed from Nasty Nellie, but you can't read it. The words should be very plain."

Hillary reached over and pulled the book from her brother's backpack. "We can read it," Hillary said. "I mean read the words and things. We just can't understand it." Hillary flipped the book open. She drew her finger across the page as she read the first line of crossed out words.

.tree spider-vulture the from mile one North .range Charm-Mist the in up High Walk between two crossed oaks to cross the magic barrier.

She read the new words, again following with her finger.

.fulfilled purpose its, Gabendoor from Gone Back to the stars, it is no more.

"See," Hillary said. "Some of it is gibberish, just like in the other books that have shown up from the Library."

"You're not following the instructions," Maxwell said.

Hillary looked up at him. "What instructions?"

"There at the start of the page," Maxwell said.

Windslow scooted up next to his sister. "You mean here where it says to start from the middle and read to both ends? Isn't that just part of the puzzle?"

"No," Maxwell said. "Those are the instructions."

"Dah," Windslow said and smacked his palm against his forehead. "So, okay then," he said and started counting words. "All right, I've got it. So the one that's crossed out would read like this." Windslow read the words aloud.

High up on the Charm-Mist range north one mile from the spider-vulture tree. Walk between two crossed oaks to cross the magic barrier.

"And the new line would be this."

Gone from Gabendoor its purpose fulfilled, back to the stars, it is no more.

"Close enough," Maxwell said. "That's one thing accomplished. You can give the book to Dreadlore. There is no more Secret Library on Gabendoor."

"What," Hillary said. "No more Secret Library?"

Faith nodded. "Yes, it is true. The Library has gone back to the stars as the book says."

"But," Hillary said and held up her hands. "All the knowledge it held. And... and... the other magic books and things."

"Don't worry," Faith said. "The building has gone. There are still books. There is still knowledge. There are other books."

Windslow grabbed at his pack. "Speaking of other books," he said. "I just thought of something." He pulled out the *Book of Library Secrets* and thumbed through the pages. He stopped, twisted the book around and pointed. "There. Look at that." On the page he pointed to the words read:

Start from the middle and read to both ends.
ratStone begins where will it end?
Strength from a sister and love from a brother
Should they survive could bring hope for a mother

"The sentences aren't goofed up like in Nasty Nellie's book but this passage starts the same way. I thought maybe the part about reading to both ends was a clue or something."

"It might be." Hillary said. "Don't give up yet, brother."

"It's more than a clue," Maxwell said.

Faith smiled at him. "They're about to understand."

Maxwell nodded.

"I've got it. I've got it," Hillary said. "ratStone is capitalized funny. Start from the 'S' and read to both ends. That makes it *STAR STONE*. We're looking for a Star Stone. That would fit with what we know about the temple in Aberratia." Hillary giggled and gave Faith a quick hug.

Windslow held his hand up to Maxwell for a high-five.

Maxwell looked at Windslow, smiled and held his own hand up.

Windslow gave a short laugh. "I thought everyone knew high-fives," Windslow said and explained the gesture.

Maxwell grinned and smacked his hand against Windslow's.

"This feels so good," Hillary said. "We're making progress."

"We still don't know what the Star Stone looks like," Windslow said and yawned. "And we don't know how to use it."

Hillary finished her own yawn. "And, we need to rescue the wizards so we can use Larkstone's zipper closet. I don't think that's going to be so easy."

Hillary and Windslow yawned together.

"You're about to dream-slip," Maxwell said. "Get comfortable. When you dream-slip back, Gabendoor will take you to your flannel hutch."

Windslow slid down on the ground, folded his arms and closed his eyes.

19: Makeup and Makeover

Both Hillary and Windslow overslept Wednesday morning. Bill had to wake them by knocking on their bedroom doors. They all made it into the van just slightly behind schedule. Bill promised no speeding. They did make it to school on time. Windslow wished he had time to look at the *Book of Library Secrets*. He wondered if there were more riddles he could figure out. He did decide to make a fake Star Stone. He just wasn't sure how. At the start of each class, he began with a little day dreaming, trying to come up with an idea. Twice that day, dreaming got him in trouble and he decided it could wait until soccer practice. He settled into his spot in science class and waited for the bell. Molly came bouncing in at the last moment and hopped up on the stool next to him.

"How you like this new outfit?" Molly asked.

Windslow looked at her. "You look... you look very ah... normal."

"Boys just never know how a say things right," Molly said. "You suppose a say I look hot. I get all a stuff at a second finger store. I don't know why they call it that."

"Second hand store," Windslow said. "They call them fancy names now like worn a bit and stuff. You look pretty cool. I mean you look hot."

"I get a jeans for just two dollars and my blouse and sweater for just five dollars each. See, the blouse still have a tag on it. It never been worn before. An then Mommy Christensen take us to craft store. I sew on all a sparkly stuff on my jeans myself. I learning how a sew and mommy Christensen going to teach us how a cook too. We not doing all that stuff with magic anymore."

"Shush," Windslow said. "You're going to get us in trouble. Mrs. DiMarco is getting ready to start."

"I do my homework without magic too," Molly said and took papers out of a folder. "It not that hard a do."

Windslow just rolled his eyes and shook his head.

The subject of the day was more about conglomerates and compounds. That did give him a chance to think a bit about a fake star stone. But he still didn't have any ideas. At the end of class, he headed for his locker. Molly stayed on his heels, talking about other things she was going to learn to do without using magic.

Windslow groaned when he got to his locker and saw Marcy heading his way. She and her group of friends stopped in front of him. Marcy stood with her arms folded tightly around herself. "I suppose you're happy now," she said. "I complained to my dad about what happened at the soccer scrimmage. He told me to, quote, live with it. Then he told me I should apologize to you and Molly. Well, you're both here, so here's your apology. I'm sorry. That's it. Now were done."

"We not doing any more cheering," Molly said. "You a good cheerleader. You a best cheerleader. We not have all a moves. We not have a good voices and we not very good dancers," she said. "My sisers and I just want a be pop-alar like you. Then Windslow help us decide we need a just be us. I sorry to you."

Marcy stood, her eyes wide open with almost a look of shock on her face. "I ah... I.. I don't know what to say. I mean, your cheers were pretty cool. Ours have been kind of lame. We just used the ones that have always been used."

"Work together then," Windslow said. "Let Molly and her sisters help you guys dream up some new stuff."

"Marcy no how a do that herself," Molly said. "Ever-body say how pretty Marcy is. No one say how smart she is. She very smart girl. She not need my help."

"You really think I'm smart?" Marcy asked, her face aglow.

"I think you're smart too," Windslow said. "And you look cold. Here take this," he said. From his locker, he took the headband that Maxwell and Faith had given him. He held it out to Marcy. "It might not fit your fashion, but it's pretty cool... warm actually. Try it on. It's like wearing a sweater. You don't need to put it on your head. You can wear it on your arm."

Marcy slipped the woven band over her wrist. "Wow," she said. "It *is* like putting on a sweater. Where did you get this?"

Windslow nodded his head at Molly. "A friend of Molly's makes them. You can't get them in stores."

Marcy slipped it off her wrist and put it back on as a headband. "Wow," she said again. "Thanks, Windslow and you too Molly." Marcy looked at the floor and then back up to both Windslow and Molly. "You know, people give me things to get on my good side or to try to impress me. This is the first time I got something from anyone just because they were trying to be nice." She looked at Windslow again. "I mean... That's why..."

"You looked cold," Windslow said and looked at his watch. "And I have to go. I need to get to the locker room. I'm late."

"See you at a hospital," Molly said and walked away.

As Windslow rolled down the hallway, he heard Marcy's friends behind him.

"That is so cool."

"Let me try it. Wow, it is warm."

"I want to get one."

"It's my turn."

"I bet we can find them on the Internet."

Windslow almost laughed. *Girls are so weird,* he thought.

ஐ

Soccer practice and the ride to the hospital were uneventful. Bill said he had stopped in to visit Trish in the mid morning. She was still asleep so he went to work, stopped in after lunch for about half an hour and no change. Windslow and Hillary didn't ask any questions and Bill didn't offer much more in the way of conversation.

At the hospital, Mrs. Christensen greeted them in a small waiting room down the hall from Trish's room. Mrs. Christensen told the Sallyforth girls to visit only a few minutes and said she would wait for them here.

Together, Bill, the Sallyforth girls, Windslow and Hillary entered Trish's room. She lay on her back sleeping. The girls spaced themselves around Trish's bed, each girl gently sliding up to sit without waking her. Bill leaned against the wall. Windslow wheeled his chair up near the headboard. No one said anything.

Windslow saw Tillie make a small motion with her fingers. He looked back at his stepmother. She opened her eyes, yawned and pushed herself up a bit. "Oh, I'm so glad you're all here. I've been so lonesome. Hugs everybody. Bill, you first." Hillary had to move to let Bill lean over Trish. They hugged for a long time and kissed twice. Hillary and Windslow took their turns next, and then the Sallyforth sisters.

"I can't get out of this dream," Trish said. She looked directly at Windslow. "I know you'll find a way." She turned to Hillary. "The big game! You were the star I hear. So tell me about it."

"Who told you about the soccer game?" Bill asked. "I was kind of hoping to tell you all about it. Hillary was fantastic. Go ahead. Tell her, Hillary."

"Why you told me," Trish said and looked up at her husband. "I know I'm sleeping most of the time, but my awareness seems to come and go. Sometimes I know I'm sleeping, but I can hear you talking to me. It's like you're talking to me in a dream. Then other times I'm totally inside my dream and seem to be aware of things happening in other places."

When Trish said, "other places," she squeezed Hillary's hand. Hillary looked at her brother but didn't say anything about it.

"Oh, girls," Trish said, looking at the Sallyforth triplets. "I'm so glad you're back to normal."

Hillary looked up at her dad. He had a funny look on his face but didn't say anything.

"Um..." Windslow said. "So, Mom, you remember us now and everything?"

"I do," Trish said. "I still don't remember the accident though." Trish yawned. "Oh, oh. I feel the dream pulling at me again. I'm trying to stay awake, but... but..." She looked at the Sallyforth sisters. "I'm afraid the only thing that would keep me from falling back asleep is a little magic."

Hillary closely watched the three girls. She saw Nelly's hand move.

"Oh, goodness," Trish said. She blinked her eyes and yawned. "There must be magic in the air. I think I'm fighting the drowsiness off."

They all turned when a knock sounded at the open doorway.

A middle aged, dark haired woman peeked into the room. "I'm sorry to bother you," she said. "My name is Mrs. Follen. This is my son, Hunter." A young man with curly, sandy hair leaned out from behind her.

"Hi," He said and ducked back out of sight.

"Mrs. Summerfield, I've been trying to stop by to thank you for saving my daughters. They were the girls on bicycles that you kept the truck from hitting. I don't want to interrupt. Like I said, I just wanted to thank you, but you've always been sleeping when I've come by. That's all. I don't want to disturb you any longer."

"No, no, come in. I'm Bill Summerfield, Trish's husband."

Mrs. Follen nodded. She and her son walked into the room. The Sallyforth girls moved to the end of the bed to make room. Hillary moved and stood next to her dad. She could feel her pulse rise when Hunter stood next to her.

"Hi, I'm Hunter," He said. He held out his hand as if to shake and quickly pulled his hand back.

"I know," Hillary said. She watched his face flush and looked away when she felt her own cheeks starting to warm.

Mrs. Follen took Trish's hand. "Thank you so very much," she said. "From what my girls and the police said, that truck would have hit my daughters." She let go of Trish's hand, took a hankie from her purse and wiped her eyes. "I'm sorry," she said. "I still get a little emotional whenever I think about it."

"That's all right," Trish said. She held out her arms. "We just finished group hugs. I think I still have one left."

Mrs. Follen gave a short laugh, leaned down and hugged Trish.

Molly bounced off the bed and moved to Windslow. "I think we all need a hug." She said. "Ever-body, hug whoever you close to."

Tillie hugged Nelly. Molly hugged Windslow. Hillary stared at Hunter. He stared back. Hillary started to lift up her arms then quickly turned and hugged her step-dad. Bill reached around her and shook Hunter's hand.

"We had better go," Mrs. Follen said. "I hope we can see you again sometime when you're out of the hospital. My daughters want to meet you. Maybe my family can treat yours to dinner sometime."

"We'll plan on it," Bill said.

"Hunter go to Rutherford," Tillie said.

"Um yah," he said. He looked at Hillary. "You were awesome in the soccer scrimmage. My sister is on the Rutherford team. I mean I wish they had won, but I couldn't stop watching you. I mean not because you're pretty and stuff, but because you're a good player and because... I... I'm sounding like a dope." He said, blushing from ear to ear. "Maybe I'll see you around or something. I mean sometime. I mean when our team plays you again. I mean... I gota go." He quickly walked out into the hallway.

The Sallyforth sisters giggled. Bill looked at Hillary, tilted his head, gave a tight little smile and winked at Hillary. She quickly looked away.

"I had better catch up with my son," Mrs. Follen said. "I'm so glad to have met you. Thanks again. Bye everyone."

Mrs. Follen gave Hillary a smile as she walked past her and out the door.

"That was nice of her," Trish said and yawned. "Sorry, I'm getting the sleepies again. And I'm so hungry."

Hillary saw her mother look at Molly and shake her head. "Save it," her mother said. Molly lowered her hand.

"Save what?" Bill asked.

Trish yawned longer and deeper this time. "Oh, nothing. I'm just rambling."

"I'll call the nurse and see if we can get you some dinner," Bill said. He turned for the doorway.

"Too late, dad" Windslow said. "She's already asleep."

Hillary adjusted the blankets and gave her mother a small kiss on the forehead. "We should go too."

"All right," Bill said softly. "Dinner at the steak house tonight. I'm feeling hungry too." Out in the hallway he invited Mrs. Christensen and the Sallyforth girls to join them.

Mrs. Christensen said maybe another time. She said she was teaching the girls how to cook and they had groceries in the car.

ജ്ഞ

On the ride to the restaurant, Bill said he was glad Trish had been able to stay awake for at least a little time. He said the doctors had talked about a condition called narcolepsy, but were ruling it out. Apparently, people with narcolepsy fall asleep at the drop of a hat. He also commented that Hunter was a good looking boy. Hillary smacked her brother when he said something about Hunter's fascination with a certain soccer player.

They had been home for about half an hour. Hillary had just changed into pajamas and had put a couple clips in her hair. She was headed for the kitchen for a drink of milk when the doorbell rang. "I'll get it," she said and headed for the door.

Hillary opened the door. On the front step stood Hunter, holding two boxes in his hands.

Hillary's mouth dropped. She blinked. "Just a second," she said and slammed the door shut. She pulled the clips from her hair and shoved them in the pocket of her robe. She looked at herself in the entryway mirror and fluffed her hair, brushing her bangs back. She gave a soft groan, sucked in a breath, blew it out and opened the door. Hunter stood as if he hadn't moved the whole time.

"Um... these are for you," he said and shoved the two boxes into Hillary's hands. "I mean for your family. They're pies. My mom thought you might want some dessert. We didn't know what you liked so we got two." He pushed his hands into his jean pockets. "Well, I guess I'll go now."

He had just started to turn when Hillary blurted out, "No! I mean not until I can say thanks." She leaned sideways to look past him. "Is your mom out in the car? Did she want to come in?"

"No, she let me come by myself."

"You have your license?" Hillary asked.

"Yah, I just got it. I'm a year ahead of you, I think. Actually this is the first time my mom has let me drive by myself. Um... you're smashing the pies," he said.

"Oh," Hillary said. She had held the boxes so tight one had a crinkle along its side. She shrugged. "Um... this is nice of you. Nice of your mom... and nice of you too... of both of you... of your family. Did you want to come in?"

"I have to get home or mom will start worrying about me."

"Hi, Hunter," Bill said from behind Hillary. "Well Hillary, are you going to invite him in or just stand there?"

"I did. He can't. Look. Pies."

"Thanks, Mr. Summerfield," Hunter said. "I need to go. See you," he said and turned to the driveway.

"Here," Hillary said. She twisted, gave the boxes to her step-dad and turned back to the doorway. She waved when Hunter backed out of the drive.

"Cherry and apple," Bill said. "Smart kid. He picked my favorites. So are you going to stand there all night, or come have some pie with me?"

"I want cherry," Windslow called from the living room.

Bill turned around and headed for the kitchen. "I wonder if we have any ice-cream."

"We do if Hillary didn't eat it all," Windslow said.

Hillary wasn't really paying much attention to her brother and father fuss over the pies. She faced the driveway but stood with her eyes shut, imagining Hunter standing at the door. Her thought made her smile. *He is so cute.*

20: Images

Windslow woke first. He sat up in the flannel thorn hut he had made in Gabendoor near Aberratia. Hillary's form shimmered and filled in. Before her eyes fluttered open she mumbled something about cherry pie and cute.

"Hi," Windslow said, but decided not to tease her.

"What do you mean, 'hi'," Hillary said. "You've never said 'hi' before when we dream-slip."

Windslow rolled his eyes. "Okay, then how about, hey sis, do we wait for the Sallyforth sisters or get started ourselves?"

"I don't know." Hillary sat up. She took a small makeup mirror from her pocket and used it to check her hair. "What do you think?"

"I think your mind isn't totally on Dreadlore and what our plan should be. We'll need to give him the book. Then we're off the hook for that task. I was thinking about the Star Stone. After we got home from dinner last night, I dug around in my closet and found this." Windslow reached into his pack and pulled out a fist-sized chunk of glossy black flint. "I got this a couple years ago when I was in Scouts. I was going to try to make some arrowheads. I haven't seen much flint in Gabendoor. It's shiny and cool looking. I thought maybe I could use magic and change the shape a little."

"But it won't do anything. Dreadlore checks all the rocks with that funny copper wand he has. I don't think you'll fool him."

"I think I have a chance," Windslow said. "I made this too." He held up a loop of copper wire with a flat copper disc in the center. "Let me try my spells first."

Windslow pointed his fingers at the rock. He didn't say any words aloud. His lips moved silently as he cast his spell. Small clicking sounds like stone hitting stone sounded as bits of flint flaked off from around the flint. Windslow smiled and held it up for Hillary to see. The changes gave it the rough shape of a five-pointed star.

"Real stars aren't pointed," Hillary said, "but it does look cool." She took it from her brother. "Ouch, the edges are sharp," she said and handed it back. "What about his stone checker?"

"I think I have that figured out too," Windslow said. His lips moved as he cast his second spell. "Hold my copper wheel up."

Hillary held up the copper wire and disc. Windslow moved his stone close to the copper. The quarter-sized copper spun in a whirl. Windslow moved the flint away and the spinning slowed.

"Maybe it will fool him," Hillary said. "Either way, we need to free the wizards and get Larkstone and his zipper closet back to Eldervale. I don't think we should wait any longer. Let's go and see what happens."

Outside on the path, the three Sallyforth sisters waited for them.

"Very nice," Hillary said.

Windslow looked at his sister. He wasn't sure what she was talking about.

The Sallyforth girls jumped to their feet. Each of them slowly turned around.

"I love the sequins," Hillary said. "Did you guys do them yourselves?"

"Nope," Nelly said.

Tillie nodded and held up her hand to show off a small bandage wrapped around one finger. "We learn a sew." She said.

"We do it all. We sewing now an last night we cook a-sketty and we make meat balls too. It really good."

"A-sketty?" Hillary said. "Oh, spaghetti."

"That what we say," Molly said.

Hillary walked close and peeked at the label on the inside collar of Nelly's shirt. "Nice brand," she said. "You all three look so cool."

"They look hot," Windslow said and rolled his eyes.

All three girls smiled. Hillary gave him a funny look.

"Okay," Windslow said. "The fashion show is over. Any ideas for Dreadlore?"

As they walked, Windslow showed them the stone he had made. He told them using it was the only idea he could come up with. He did have a question for them about the other night at the hospital.

"You used magic to help mom pull out of her dream-slip, didn't you."

"I did," Tillie said.

"Not me too," Nelly added.

"Mommy Trish tell me a save mine," Molly said. "So I still got one left."

"I heard her say that," Hillary said as they approached the entrance to Aberratia. "Mom seems to know about what's going on here."

"She know some," Molly said. "In her dream-slip sometimes she come very close to being here. Then she go back to Earth. Then she go back to in-between. That where she stay mostly."

"Tents are over there," the first guard barked at Windslow, Hillary and the sisters.

Molly marched up in front of him. She stood so close, he backed up a step. "You suppose a recognize us!" She shouted at him. "How many times we have a walk in and out, out and in, up and down a-fore you remember? We on special assignment for Dreadlore. You suppose a know that!"

"Oh, sorry," the hooded man said. "I'm just so used to seeing so many--"

Tillie interrupted him. "You suppose a pay attention. Maybe your purple hood need bigger eye holes. Go back a work. We going to see Dreadlore. We not tell him you goofing off. You very lucky. And you need a sew some sequins on your hood. It look much better that way." She held up her finger. "See? I stick myself with a needle last night. I doing these sequins on my jeans."

"Thank you guard," Windslow said and grabbed Tillie's arm. "She likes to talk a lot. Thanks for passing us through." Windslow gave a short salute.

The guard stared at him for a moment before mimicking the same salute. "Yes sir," the guard said and turned back to watch the road.

"Well," Hillary said, "We've got him fooled. I don't think Dreadlore is going to be as easy. Let's get on with it." She moved up beside her brother.

As they approached Aberratia, Hillary moved behind Windslow. There were too many people to walk beside him. Refugees had pitched tents nearly to the temple. People looked up at them as Windslow and his group passed. There weren't many cook fires going. The faces Windslow saw looked thin and dirty. Windslow wished he could tell them there would soon be plenty of food in what was left of Eldervale.

At the first row of steps leading up to the plaza, Windslow finally got a glimpse of the three wizards. They sat hunched over, their backs facing outward.

At the top, Windslow didn't see Dreadlore. "Wait here," he told Hillary and the triplets. "I'm going over to the wizards."

He had only taken two steps when he heard Dreadlore's voice.

"So you survived Nasty Nellie," Dreadlore said. His voice came from behind them.

Windslow turned around. The wizard, the legend called the Beguiler, pushed between Windslow and Hillary. Hillary moved to make room. Windslow stood still and bumped shoulders with Dreadlore. Dreadlore moved close to the tall rectangles of stone before turning around. He put his hands on his hips. "Well," he said. "Where is the Secret Library? Where is the book that gives its location?"

"Not that fast," Hillary said. "I want to see the wizards. I want to make sure you held your part of the bargain."

"What would it matter," Dreadlore said. "If you've got the book, it's easy enough for me to take it from you. If you don't have it, not much would change. What are you going to do if the wizards aren't here? Will you break into tears and run away?"

Men wearing purple hoods laughed.

Hillary took a step forward. Windslow quickly stepped in front of her. He reached into his backpack and pulled out the red leather bound book. He gave it a toss. It landed with a *flop* at Dreadlore's feet.

"Oh, your disrespect hurts me so much," Dreadlore said. "How can you be so cruel?"

His men laughed.

"Pick it up," Dreadlore said.

Windslow stood still.

"I pick it up," Molly said. "But I throw it a lot harder and in a different direction. I wonder how high I can throw it. I get a use one magic today. Maybe this good time a use it."

Dreadlore looked at her for a moment before directing his gaze to one of his men. "Pick it up," he repeated.

The hooded man scrambled to Dreadlore's feet, grabbed the book and handed it to the wizard.

"The library is gone," Hillary said. "Read it for yourself."

Dreadlore held the book open. "It's gibberish or written in code."

"A child could read it," Windslow said. "Try reading the instructions first. You start in the middle of the sentence and read to the left and then to the right. You read to both ends."

Dreadlore gave Windslow a piercing look before looking back at the page. Dreadlore fanned through the rest of the pages, closed the book and threw it back to the stone floor of the plaza.

"It's useless!" he screamed.

"It not useless," Tillie said. "It gone."

Dreadlore spun around and slammed his fist against one of the obelisks. He stood still for a moment, his head tilted down as if looking at the ground. He slowly raised his head, took his hand off the obelisk and turned back.

"What about the ratStone?" he asked, his words slow and controlled.

"There isn't any ratStone either," Windslow said.

Dreadlore's eyes widened. His face turned red. He doubled up his fists.

"Before you blow a cork," Windslow said, "It's not the ratStone you want. You see, it works the same way. You start from the middle and read to both ends. Start with the capital S."

Dreadlore gave Windslow a puzzled glance before looking out over the crowd. He nodded his head as if in thought. "Star Stone," Dreadlore whispered.

"It won't hurt to say it louder than that," Windslow said. "Yes it's a Star Stone, not a ratStone. And I have it."

"You have it?" Dreadlore said, his eyes wide. He smiled. "Give it to me. Give it to me now!" he said and held out both hands.

Windslow reached in his backpack. Dreadlore's men lowered the long copper tipped pikes they held. They pointed them at Windslow.

"Don't move," one of the men said.

Dreadlore waved his hand. "It's all right. What could he do, anyway?"

The men lowered their spears. Windslow took out his fake Star Stone and placed it in Dreadlore's hand. "Get my wand," Dreadlore said, not taking his eyes off the shiny black flint. He turned and walked toward the obelisks.

One of his men ran down the steps and around to the side of the temple where a line of people stood, each hopeful they had found the ratStone. He grabbed the copper wand, and returned. Nearly out of breath, he handed it Dreadlore and stood back.

Dreadlore held the wand over the black flint. The copper wheel spun.

Windslow grinned.

Dreadlore frowned, turning to the man who had fetched the wand. "Pass your hand between the stone and wand."

The hooded guard slowly passed his hand, as instructed. The copper wheel stopped spinning when his hand was directly between the wand and stone.

"Hold the wand," Dreadlore told his guard.

Dreadlore moved his own hand close to the stone. Staring at Windslow, Dreadlore threw the flint on the plaza floor. It shattered into large chunks. He held both hands high.

Windslow flew backward, as if a football player had thrown a block into him. He sat on the cold plaza stones, his arms stretched out behind him and his legs spread. Windslow struggled to take a breath. Feeling something trickle down his chin, he wiped his face with the back of his hand. Blood smeared his knuckles.

"Leave him alone!" Hillary screamed and took a step forward.

Dreadlore pointed at her.

Hillary let out a loud "oof," when Dreadlore's magic hit her in the stomach. She landed hard on her back and close to her brother. Rolling to her side, she drew her knees up to her stomach.

"I'll get you for that!" Windslow hollered. He didn't make it to his feet before another burst of magic slammed him back down.

The men with pikes hurried over and placed the copper tips of the long poles against Hillary and Windslow, keeping them pinned to the ground.

"Hey, Dead-door," Molly said. She moved to stand between Dreadlore and her fallen friends. "Better check a wand. Why it spinning if black rock a fake. Maybe you bust a Star Stone."

Dreadlore turned around. His guard held out the wand. The copper disk slowly turned on its axis.

"No!" Dreadlore said. He dropped to his hands and knees and crawled along, carefully checking each chunk of flint. He flung aside each piece that didn't change the speed of the copper disk.

One discarded piece slid across the stone floor, stopping when it hit Windslow's hand. He palmed the sharp chunk and slipped it into his back pocket.

"Get out of my way," Dreadlore yelled at Hillary.

She struggled to her feet and helped Windslow stand.

"It's not the flint," Dreadlore muttered and stood. When he moved closer to Hillary, the disk spun."

"I think I have what you're looking for," Hillary told him.

"What?" Windslow said.

Hillary glanced at her brother and back to Dreadlore. "I'll give it to you if you promise to let us go."

"Give it to me or I'll take it from you." Dreadlore looked over his shoulder. "Guards!" he shouted. Two of his men moved closer in. "Get ready to skewer them both on my order."

The men lowered their pikes. "I'll make this easy," Dreadlore said. "Give me the stone or I'll take it off your dead body."

"I think this good time a do what he says," Molly said to Hillary.

"It's in my pack," Hillary said. She un-slung her backpack, lowering it slowly to the ground. Reaching inside, she pulled out the amber eight-sided gem the Wind-Climber had given her. When she held it out, her finger pressed against one of the facets.

The chained wizards and magic users that lined the perimeter of the plaza gave a collective gasp. From down on the ground, voices started yelling and hands pointed at the obelisks. Both guards lowered their pikes.

Four streams of magic flowed from the gems atop the obelisks. They met in the center of the space between them to form a large cylinder of light, five feet in diameter and nearly six feet tall. In the center of the light stood the image of Hillary. There were no colors, only varying shades of light to dark green, yet the shading provided lifelike detail.

"It's one of the maidens," someone yelled from down on the ground.

Another voice yelled out, "One of them is back."

Hillary moved her finger. The magic flow sounded a crackle and winked out, the image gone. Hillary hoped she could remember the order of the images she had seen when she rolled the gem over the granola bar wrapper at home. Not sure if her experiment would work, she slid her finger to the next facet. With a thrumming sound, the magic cylinder of light reappeared. This time Windslow's image filled the space.

From below, voices called out.

"The Beguiler?"

"No, it's the Child of Intuition."

"Maybe the Keeper of Knowledge."

More voices joined the others along with cheers and yells.

"Give me that!" Dreadlore said and grabbed the stone

from Hillary's hands. As soon as it left her fingers, the image winked out.

The calls and yells from the crowd first hushed, then grew louder.

Dreadlore held the gem up high, pointing it at the center of the obelisks. He shoved his hands forward, as if thrusting the gem at some invisible object. Lowering his hands he closed his eyes and mumbled. He looked up to see the four streams of magic joined as he had joined them many times before without the Star Stone. He pointed the gem at the apex. Nothing changed.

Dreadlore spun around. "Form the link," he commanded. Each person wearing one of the somber wood spiked headbands, grabbed the hand of the person on either side of them.

"Hillre not use a link," Molly said.

"I don't care what she did or didn't do," Dreadlore said, his voice loud. He held up the gem again. Nothing changed. He stepped to the wizards and used one hand to link himself to the circle. Holding the gem high again, he closed his eyes and then opened them. Nothing had changed.

"Let Hillre try again," Tillie said. "Unless you going to smack her more."

Dreadlore moved back in front of the group. "If it's something you suggest, little Miss Sallyforth, then I don't know that it's really something I'd want to do. What else do you have in here?" He shook Hillary's pack upside down. Out dropped lipstick, hand sanitizer, a canister of pepper spray, tissues, a small sewing kit, a water bottle and several granola bars. Dreadlore kicked them aside. He grabbed Windslow's pack and dumped it. Out fell rope, a folding knife, a package of licorice, a water bottle and Windslow's magic zipper pouch. Dreadlore pulled the zipper and reached inside.

"Where did you get this"" Dreadlore asked, holding up the *Book of Library Secrets*. He looked at Tillie. "You said the Secret Library is gone."

"It gone," Tillie said. "That book show up all by itself, afore the Library go. It give itself to Windso and Hillre. It belong a them."

"Nothing belongs to them," Dreadlore said. He flipped through the pages and smiled. "This book is full of clues." He looked at Hillary and Windslow. "If you two figured it out then so will I. I don't know that I'll need you after all. But, just in case," he said and turned to his men. "Tie their hands and chain them over by their wizard friends."

Dreadlore shifted his attention back to the book. He stormed forward. The people linking hands quickly made a gap for him to walk through and he headed down the steps.

"Get over there," one of the guards said, prodding Windslow with the pike. Windslow reached for his pack.

"Leave it," the guard barked. "Get moving. All of you. Now!"

Escorted by the guards, the Sallyforth sisters led the way, walking along the line of linked magic users, heading for Larkstone, Fernbark and Haggerwolf.

21: Gabendoor

The people who formed the link of wizards and magic users around the temple perimeter all released hands and sat. No one said anything. Looking at their faces Windslow could tell they were weary, probably not well fed and certainly not well cared for. The guards had left Windslow and Hillary tied and chained their legs. The chains ran to the same iron loops that held the wizards captive.

As soon as the guards left, Windslow used the piece of flint from his shattered fake Star Stone, to cut the ropes.

Larkstone, Fernbark and Haggerwolf all looked thin.

"Your beard's all messy," Hillary said and plucked at Haggerwolf's whiskers. "And you, Larkstone, just look at your robe. And you... and you, Fernbark." Hillary's voice wavered. Tears filled her eyes. She gathered them together in her arms, hugging all three at once the best she could.

"Oh, stop crying," Haggerwolf said. "It's not all that bad."

Windslow didn't believe Haggerwolf and knew by the way his sister still hugged them that she didn't either.

When Hillary leaned back and wiped her eyes, Windslow gave each elder wizard a hug. The Sallyforth sisters did the same.

"We're going to get you out of here," Windslow said.

"That would be a little difficult and not be the best plan," Larkstone said.

"I had granola bars and water," Hillary said. "Dreadlore took them from me. Are you hungry? Do you need water?"

"Hillary, dear," Haggerwolf said. He cupped her face in his hand. "Dear child. Dear, dear Daughter of the Wind. We'll be fine. Listen to your brother. If we just sit here and feel sorry for ourselves, it will be a long and pointless wait. We saw what happened with the ratStone. Hillary, you were able to work it."

"You must tell us everything that's happened," Fernbark said. "How did you find the stone? How did you learn to work it?" He looked at the Sallyforth sisters. "What must Hillary and Windslow do next and how can we help?"

"We not sure this time," Molly said. "We caught up in it too. Book and stars say that most stuff up to Windso."

They all looked at him. Windslow shrugged his shoulders. "Well, we do know it's not the ratStone. The spelling is goofy. It's the Star Stone. You'll have to ask Hillary about how it works. She surprised me with her trick." He looked at his sister. "How *did* you do that?"

"I don't know about the image," Hillary said. "I've had that gem for a long time. I just thought it was a pretty stone. At home, I discovered that when you put a piece of aluminum foil, mirror, or something that reflects behind it, something happens. There are eight main facets. When I held foil behind them, a picture of a persons face would show up in the top of the gem. There are eight facets and eight faces."

"Who inside there," Tillie asked.

"Well," Hillary said, "me, Windslow, you Molly, Tillie, Nelly, and you three," she said looking at the wizards. "The eight facets are the eight of us sitting here. I had my finger on one facet when I held the gem out to Dead-door, as the girls call him."

"Good name," Haggerwolf said and chuckled. "I'm

guessing your finger was against the facet that displays your image?"

"That's what I think happened," Hillary said. "Then I moved my finger. I knew Windslow's facet was next to mine, but not which direction. I guessed correctly."

""Why not Dead-door make it work?" Molly asked.

Larkstone smiled and patted Molly's hand. "Dear, it is so unusual to hear you asking questions. You three girls have always been at the heart of any mystery on Gabendoor. I know there is still a lot we don't know about you three and probably never will. I've come to learn you're all special, but this is almost amusing. I'd expect you three girls to have the answers."

"I don't know why the stone didn't work for him," Hillary said. "I'm thinking that maybe it would work for any of us eight, but I don't know for sure. Even if that's part of the stone's secret, I don't know how you would use it or make it do something else."

"Now Dreadlore has the clues we have," Windslow said. "I don't know about the stone. But like I said, we need to get you three out of here."

"And like I told you, that's not the best plan," Larkstone said. "Someone always needs to be here to watch Dreadlore. The three of us are better suited to do that than to run around Gabendoor."

"Plan is getting easier," Tillie said. "We only need a do two. Only Windslow and Hillary need a get away."

"An they need a stay away. That why we go too," Nelly said.

Fernbark looked at her.

"Translated," Fernbark said, "she means Windslow and Hillary will need to come back. Whatever needs to be done, needs to be done here at the temple. And the five of us are already here. It makes sense we stay here unless there is something we can do."

"That what she say," Tillie said. "You not need a tell us again."

"Larkstone, we do need your zipper closet," Hillary said. "We met two strange people in a meadow up in the Charm-Mist Mountains. Their names are Faith and Maxwell. They have lots of food and we need to use your closet to move it all to Eldervale."

"Who did you say?" Haggerwolf asked.

"Maxwell and Faith," Hillary said. "They're shepherds and take care of these big rabbit like creatures."

Then the legend is true," Haggerwolf said. "We're close to the end of the paths the legend can take. There are only two branches left."

"What are you talking about?" Hillary asked.

"Well," Haggerwolf said, "there are three types of magic on Gabendoor. There is magic inside Gabendoor. It bubbles up and somber wood absorbs it. It's the kind of magic we and everyone else here in the circle, can use. These funny headbands collect it. Then there is a very special old magic." He looked at the three sisters. "I suspect that's the kind you three have. I'm guessing that's what has made you so special. I think it's the same magic the Secret Library uses."

Windslow looked at Molly, Nelly and Tillie. Molly grinned. Tillie pursed up her lips and whistled a soft tune. "Nope," Nelly said.

"I knew it!" Hillary said. "I just knew it."

"Your mother had it too," Haggerwolf said, looking back at Windslow and Hillary. "If you're ever able to work a spell without somber wood, then you'll know you have it too. I suspect you do, but just don't know how to use it."

"We have it," Hillary said. "We just learned how. Both of us. Watch."

"No, don't." Molly said. "It send out vibrations in air. Dead-door not have special magic, but sometime he feel it, sometime he not. He using circle to try to use regular magic like it special."

"All right, that's two," Hillary said. "What's the third and how do Maxwell and Faith figure in all of this?"

Haggerwolf scratched at his beard. "This is a bit of a guess, and some of it comes from the legend. The third magic is Gabendoor itself. It's like Gabendoor is a living thing. It has its own magic and power. Dream-slipping is from that power. Sometimes Gabendoor needs to take human form to do what it wants to do. When it takes that form, it likes to be a shepherd. In this case, I think it's two shepherds."

"Whoa," Windslow said. "That makes a little bit of sense. At least I think it does. So what about the paths of the legend?"

"I think it means magic is going away," Haggerwolf said. "You can read it one way and Gabendoor is going away. Actually, I think that is one of the paths. The other path is just magic going away. But, on that path, the world of Gabendoor is still here."

"What do you think?" Hillary asked, looking at the three sisters.

"That about right," Molly said. "That part of why we so cranky when all a this begin a go crazy."

"What happens to you three on earth then?" Hillary asked.

The girls shrugged.

"Okay," Windslow said. "Back to the legend. You said you thought there were two branches left."

Haggerwolf nodded. "There are constellations that are missing and some that have stars out of place. In both versions, the stars move. In one outcome, the stars move to where they are supposed to be, magic goes away, and Gabendoor survives. In the other path, the stars move. They move in a way they aren't supposed to move. What's left of the first magic stays for a short time. Wizards fight over it and end up destroying all life on Gabendoor."

Windslow sounded a slow soft whistle. "Wow," he said. "So that kind of means we win and Gabendoor survives. Dreadlore wins and eventually Gabendoor is destroyed."

"And," Hillary added. "What moves the planets are the obelisks and the Star Stone?"

"Yes. That's what we think," Haggerwolf said. "Definitely the Star Stone, or ratStone as it was called. We don't know for certain about the obelisks. They're something that Dreadlore created."

"Great," Windslow said. "Like usual, we don't know what to do, except for a couple things. I never thought I'd wish we had the *Book of Library Secrets* back. I think we could use it about now."

"There is going to be a little problem with my zipper closet," Larkstone said. "But first, let me give it a try and see what happens."

"What do you mean a problem?" Hillary asked and touched the wizard's arm.

"I'll explain," Fernbark said. "These strange somber wood spikes we wear around our heads have points on both ends."

"They're sticking into you?" Hilary asked.

"Not in, but poking hard against," Fernbark answered. "When they absorb magic, there is no inward pressure. To make sure we don't try to use magic on our own or to get away, they can push in. Larkstone will need to use his spell to call up his zipper closet. The somber wood spikes will push in, causing him a little discomfort."

"Discomfort or more than that?" Hillary asked. "Don't sugar coat this for me."

"It could hurt a lot," Larkstone said. "But don't worry. I'll get the zipper closet for you."

"It could kill him," Haggerwolf said.

"No, no we can't then," Hillary said. "We'll try another way. We'll think of something else."

"Molly," Windslow asked. "Is there anything you can do or we can do with our magic?"

"You not have enough experience," Molly said. "We tell Dead-door we not use magic more than one time each day except to help him. I not think this helping him."

"Wait," Windslow said. "You're not supposed to use it more than once. That would mean each of you could use it once if not helping, right?" Windslow asked.

The sisters looked at each other and back to Windslow. "I think that right," Molly said. "I got one an it can be to help Larkstone."

"I got one," Tillie said an I save it to break all a chains."

"And mine not be good to fool guards with and escape," Nelly added.

"Okay," Larkstone said. He gave a sigh. "Either way, let's try it. I don't know what shape I'll be in afterwards. To call up my closet, you need to say the spell, *Mom wants me to clean my room. I won't even need a broom.* The zipper will appear.

You know how to use it after that. To put it away just say, *All done.*"

"Got it," Windslow said. "Molly, are you ready, just in case?"

She nodded.

Larkstone silently said the words to call up his zipper closet. Sweat broke out on his forehead, followed by small dots of blood. The red drops grew larger and merged to form small rivulets that ran down the wizards face and back of his neck.

"Use your magic," Hillary said, grabbing Molly's arm.

"Larkstone shook his head."

"Not yet," Fernbark said.

Something glinted in the air in front of Larkstone. More blood trickled. The shiny brass shape took form.

"He's almost got it," Haggerwolf said.

The image faded and shimmered. Larkstone's eyes opened and rolled back, exposing the whites of his eyes covered with a lace of bright red veins.

"He needs help," Haggerwolf said.

Molly raised her hand and touched it to Larkstone's forehead. His eyes rolled back and shut. The brass form turned solid.

Larkstone's face turned pale and his lips blue.

Windslow grabbed the zipper, and chanted the spell to hide it away.

"He's slipping away," Haggerwolf said. "You're spell wasn't enough, Molly."

Tillie held up her arms. She spread the fingers of one hand and held them over Larkstone's heart. She held the fingers from her other hand to his forehead. She closed her eyes and shivered. Larkstone's lips regained their color and his cheeks flushed. Tillie opened her eyes and took her hands away. "One stick go in too far," she said. "I get it out, but I not fix his head."

"Then it not my turn," Nelly said and scooted in front of the Wizard. She closed her eyes and held her palms up, inches from Larkstone's face. Nelly dropped her hands. Tears formed in her eyes. "I not check a damage. I got plenty of magic to fix it. It way too much."

"You mean you don't have enough?" Hillary asked.

Nelly nodded and wiped her eyes. "I be able make him live."

"No, no, no," Windslow said shaking his head. "There must be a way. Wait," he said and grabbed his sister's hand. He reached out to Nelly and took her hand. "If they can link up, then so can we. Use our magic with yours."

"We never use a linking afore," Molly said. "We not know how it works."

"Well that doesn't matter, does it," Windslow said. "I guess I'm learning about hope. If there is a chance it will work, then we've got to try it. Okay, Hillary. Let's close our eyes and focus on Nelly."

Windslow waited until his sister closed her eyes and then closed his. In his mind, he tried to form an image of Nelly. He didn't form the image he had hoped. Other images flashed in his mind, each one lasting only seconds before another replaced it. Each image was of Larkstone. Windslow watched images from the first adventure he and his sister had on Gabendoor. He saw images of Larkstone at Abbadread. Windslow felt dizzy as the images flashed by too fast for him to focus on. Someone shook him and the images went dark. He tried to bring them back. He felt a slap on the side of his face and opened his eyes. Hillary leaned over him. "What happened?" Windslow asked.

"Larkstone is fine. You saved him. Nelly said we filled her with so much magic she felt like a balloon. I didn't feel much; just some tingling. You passed out."

"Aw, man," Windslow said and sat up. He rubbed his head. "I have a headache."

"All three of you were glowing," Haggerwolf said. "Windslow, you were the brightest. I've never seen such powerful magic. You let Nelly use it for some very delicate healing. But the enormity of what you three held, could have moved this temple if you had let it free."

"I don't know about all that," Windslow said. "The question is, does one of us have enough to get these shackles off. And," he said and yawned. "If that works, how are we going to get out of here?"

"Let's find out," Hillary said. She touched her fingers to the metal cuff around her ankle. "Well, that didn't work," she said.

Windslow gave it a try, with the same lack of success. "So much for having the power to move the universe."

"I not have any left," Nelly said. "You give me such a little bit, I use it all up." She touched her fingers to the shackle on Windslow's leg. The metal clicked and the cuff opened. She touched Hillary's ankle. Another click sounded. Nelly touched her own shackle. Nothing happened. "I guess I got lots left," she said.

Molly scooted up close to her sisters. "This not what we used to," she said. "Most a time we a ones who know what to do. This time it up to you, Windso. That's what a legend and a book say."

"Any ideas on how to sneak out of here?" Windslow asked. How are we going to get past those guards.

"Ha!" Haggerwolf said. "What's the phrase you use on Earth. I believe it is *doof.* What makes you think you need to use the steps where the guards sit. Climb down the blocks. They're just bigger steps. Lots of people go up and down that way." Haggerwolf folded his arms. "I gave you the first part. You figure out the rest."

Hillary leaned forward and kissed the wizard on the cheek. "That means you don't have a clue, but thanks for getting us started. And the word is *dah,* not *doof.*"

Windslow waited while Hillary kissed the other two wizards and gave hugs to the Triplets. He and Hillary slipped over the temple edge. "Thanks," Windslow said and lowered himself down to the next level of stones.

ᘓᘐ

Climbing down the stones was easier than Windslow had thought it would be. As he and his sister climbed down, other people climbed up. One woman, toting a basket of bread on her climb, pointed at Hillary. "You're the maiden in the image."

"No," Hillary said. "But you're not the first to say that."

They both were yawning when they reached the bottom. They hurried through the mass of tents and people to the exit trail from Aberratia. When they reached the path, the same guard who had greeted them stopped them. He held his pike at ready.

Windslow stood as straight-backed as he could and walked up to the guard until the pike pressed against Windslow's shirt. Windslow gave the same salute he had before.

"Oh, sorry," the guard said. "I didn't recognize you at first. I see so many people come past here. Tonight I'm not supposed to let anyone out."

"That's what we were checking on," Windslow said. "I told Dreadlore you were doing a fine job but could use some help. Did anyone else show up to give you a break?"

"Um, no," the guard said.

"I'll make sure that gets taken care of," Windslow said. "The two of us are going to check the trail. Have you heard any strange howling noises or screams coming from the woods?"

"Ah, no," the guard said. He turned around and looked down the trail. "Is something wrong?"

"We'll let you know after we check things, unless you want to come with us?"

"Oh no, I really don't think so. I'd like to but I need to stay here at my post."

"Good, good," Windslow said and patted him on the shoulder. "If we don't return before dark, it means it's not safe on the trail. In that case, we'll see you tomorrow. Oh, and don't say anything about the howling or screams. We don't want to start a panic."

The guard nodded.

Windslow saluted, grabbed his sister's hand and started walking. When they were out of earshot. Hillary started to giggle. "You need to check into drama club at school," she said. "That was awesome."

"Well," Windslow said, "at least it got us out. It just might help us get back in." Windslow yawned. "Right now we need to get ready to dream-slip. Tomorrow we'll find out if we can work Larkstone's closet. After that, all we need to do is save Gabendoor."

"Yes," Hillary said. "Just another day in Gabendoor." She gave a yawn. "You are the one who has kept everyone's hope alive." She slipped her arm through her brother's and walked beside him. "I can see why Gabendoor has left it up to you. For a brother, even a step-brother, you're pretty cool."

Windslow grinned and turned off the road. Both yawning, Hillary and Windslow headed for the flannel thorn hut.

22: Wake up and Makeup

Hillary woke, stretched and got out of bed. She nearly stumbled when she stepped on her backpack. "Oh, good," she said softly and picked up her pack. She held it out. "I don't know how you got here, but I'm glad you did."

Hillary dusted off the outside and peeked inside. "Well, you can't have everything," she said. She was disappointed none of her makeup or other items were inside but was pleased to find her magic zipper pouch. She tossed the bag on her bed, slipped into her bathrobe and headed for Windslow's room.

At his door, she gave a soft knock, but didn't bother to wait for an answer. She pushed the door open a few inches and peeked her head around. Her brother had his robe on and sat in his wheelchair. His backpack lay in his lap.

Hillary slipped inside his room. "I got mine too," She said. "It would have been a little difficult to explain to dad how both of us lost our bags. I got my zipper pouch. Did you get your magic book bag?"

"That's what I was just checking," Windslow said. "Um... I think I got more than the bag." Windslow held out his magic book bag. From the book bag, he pulled the *Book of Library Secrets*.

"Dreadlore's not going to be very happy about that," Hillary said.

Windslow grinned at her. "Yah, and I hope he had it in his hands and was reading it when, *poof*, it just disappeared.

I'm so glad we have the book. I really want to go over all its riddles again."

"You two up?" Bill called from the living room.

"We are," Hillary called back. She turned back to her brother. "When are we going to have time? There's soccer practice, and then a visit to the hospital."

"We better get ready for school," Windslow said. "We'll look at it tonight." He put the book back in the magic bag and the bag back in his pack. "What are you going to do about your stuff?"

"Stuff?" Hillary said.

"Like makeup stuff. The girl junk you lost."

Hillary put her hands on her hips and made a "*Tisk*," sound. "It's not stuff and it's not junk. Call it feminine essentials. And, a smart girl always has a backup set. Besides," she said and smiled, "That's why they invented stores and shopping."

ꕥ

As usual, Windslow got to science class before Molly. When she took her seat next to him, he told her how the *Book of Library Secrets* had reappeared along with his and Hillary's backpacks. Molly told him the magic of the book and the library determined when and where any book would be. She agreed with Windslow that Dreadlore must be furious. She asked Windslow if he had tried Larkstone's magic zipper closet yet. Windslow said he hadn't but would as soon as he returned to Gabendoor.

Windslow asked if any of the guards had discovered that he and Hillary were missing. Molly said no one had and when she and her sisters dream-slipped back, they planned to bring sandwiches and water for the wizards.

Class started. Molly asked Mrs. DiMarco if she could take a couple extra science books home. Mrs. DiMarco was pleased and said yes. Windslow wondered what Molly wanted the books for but didn't have time to ask. When the bell rang, Molly told him to be careful and hurried out of class.

During soccer practice, Windslow was surprised when "the pie guy," as Windslow had been calling him, walked over and sat down.

"Hi," Hunter said and reached out to shake hands. "I don't know if you remember. My name's Hunter."

Windslow shook his hand. "Hey, thanks for the pies. They were great. I'm guessing you didn't come here to talk with me. She's out on the field."

"I figured I had better get along with the brother. I know how I am with my sisters. So are you older or is Hillary?"

"She is," Windslow said and quickly added, but by days, not years.

Hunter waved toward the field.

Windslow turned to look. Hillary waved back, tripped and slid across the grass. She got up, put her hands up to her face and ran to the other side of the field.

"Oops," Hunter said. "I didn't mean to make her trip."

"Ha!" Windslow said. "You didn't do it. She's supposed to be concentrating on the ball, not on guys."

"Um..." Hunter said. "Would you have a problem if I asked her out? And if I did, do you think she'd say yes? Does she have a boyfriend?"

"No," Windslow said and flipped through the papers on his clipboard. "I mean, no I don't have a problem. My dad might though. As for Hillary, she doesn't have a boyfriend and she'd probably fall over again if you asked her out. You know how weird girls are."

"Yah," Hunter said. "Is it okay if I hang around until she's done with practice?"

Windslow shrugged. "Doesn't bother me."

For the rest of practice, when Windslow wasn't doing anything for the players or coach, he talked with Hunter. Windslow had to admit he liked Hunter. Windslow also felt a little jealous. He thought it would be great to have a girlfriend waiting for him to be done with practice. More than usual, Hillary came running over for water. Each time she took a bottle, she barely looked at Windslow. She'd say hi to Hunter and head back out to the field.

After practice, Windslow wheeled out to the parking lot. Hillary was already there. His sister stood on the curb and waved at an older gray car with a crinkled trunk that drove out of the lot.

"Hunter?" Windslow asked when he wheeled up to her.

"Yes, and crisis time," Hillary said. She spun around, leaned down, and gave Windslow a kiss on the cheek. "First, thanks for telling him, it was okay with you if he asked me out. That's another cool thing about having a brother. Next, my backup makeup is totally worthless. And the biggest crisis is dad. Do you think he'll let me go out?"

"Beats me," Windslow said. "He'd probably need to go buy a shotgun first. Do they sell them in makeup stores by any chance?"

Hillary punched him on the arm. "Very funny."

"Here he comes," Windslow said. "Want me to ask him for you?"

Windslow grinned when Hillary punched his arm again. "Keep quiet or you'll be in more trouble than you can handle."

In the van, Bill updated them about Trish. There still wasn't much change. The extra tests didn't reveal anything.

The doctor did ask Bill what he thought about exploratory brain surgery. The specialist thought there might be something that wasn't showing up on the scans.

Both Hillary and Windslow protested about the surgery. Windslow wished he could tell his dad all about Gabendoor but figured that would just earn him a spot in the loony bin.

Hillary did ask about going on a date. She started the conversation by saying that if hypothetically, a boy were to ask her out, what the conditions would be.

Windslow laughed aloud about the way his dad answered.

"Well hypothetically," Bill said. "Why don't you tell Hunter it would be fine if he came over and watched a movie or something with you Friday night? We'll see what happens with that and then talk about an out of the house date. I really wish your mother were here. We're getting into her department."

"Yes!" Hillary said. She thrust both arms up, holding her fists closed as if she had just won the playoffs. "Thanks dad!" She slumped back in her seat. "Then I have another problem. I need some new makeup. I mean... mom would understand. It's crucial."

"Hey," Bill said. He flipped on the turn signal. "Just because I'm the dad it doesn't mean I don't know about some of these things. In case you didn't notice, we just turned into the Mall. I figure we can let you get some makeup. After that, we'll get some dinner. The last stop will be the gun shop. I'll need to start looking at shotguns."

Both Windslow and Bill laughed.

Hillary sat back in her seat. She folded her arms tightly across her chest. She had to turn her head and pretend to look out the window so her brother and father wouldn't see her big smile.

ᘓᘐ

At home, Windslow had gone into Hillary's room to see if she wanted to work on the riddles in the *Book of Library Secrets* with him. She was too busy sorting out her new collection of cosmetics and talking on the phone at the same time. Bill had added another rule; a phone call limit of 45 minutes. Hillary was already half way through her time for that night. She had called Hunter soon after they got home.

Windslow went back to his room, and studied the book at his desk. He took out some paper to scribble notes on, just in case Dreadlore somehow got the book back. Windslow studied the lines:

A special stone moves time and space.
Each of eight must find their place.
Three will go and three will stay.
The other two will find the way.

He was certain the special stone was the Star Stone. Hillary had seen eight faces in the stone, so that made sense too. After scratching his head, he wrote down the names.

"Hm," he muttered. "Three go and three stay. There are two groups of three." He drew a circle around the names, Molly, Nelly and Tillie. He drew another circle around Larkstone, Haggerwolf and Fernbark. "The other two find the way." He drew a third circle around his and his sister's name.

"That fits," he said, "But it doesn't tell me much." He flipped to a page in the book.

Giving up's the easy way
What words did Windslow's mother say?

Hope is hard to understand.
It's fleeting in another land.

"I don't remember what mom said that would fit here, but hope is hard to understand and there's not much of it in Gabendoor. So let's go to the next page."

Aberratia plays a part,
A temple where the stone will start.
ratStone brings them home again.
The future is where it began.

"Well, this makes a little sense. The Star Stone is tied into Aberratia. We figured that out. But who is going home again?" Windslow chewed on the eraser end of his pencil. "Ah," he said. "Maybe it's about getting the people to go back to Eldervale and the other villages. I bet that's it. So let's see what's next."

Hope will never work alone.
You won't find it in the stone.
Hope depends on what you do.
Finding hope is up to you.

"Duh, that's obvious," Windslow said and flipped a page.

Hope begins

With a cheer that wins.

Windslow chuckled. "Is there anything this book doesn't know? That had to be the Sallyforth sisters at the soccer game. So one more I think," he said.

Strength from a sister and love from a brother,
Should they survive could bring hope for a mother.
ratStone begins where will it end?

Windslow puffed his cheeks and blew out the air. "This is the one I don't know if I like or not. It isn't going to be the doctors who make mom well. It's up to me and Hillary." Windslow was about to shut the book, but turned the next page. "Hey," he said. "This is new."

The towers are pretty
But they're just for show.
For using the stone
Only one person knows.

"That's interesting," Windslow said. "The towers must be the ones at Aberratia. And I bet this is talking about Hillary. At least I hope it is. Dreadlore doesn't know how to use the stone. Molly and her sisters don't and neither do the wizards. Hey, book," Windslow said after closing the cover. "For once you were almost useful." He slipped the book back into his magic book bag.

ꕥ

When Windslow woke in Gabendoor, he sat up to see his sister holding her small mirror and new lipstick.

"I don't think we'll run into Hunter here," Windslow said.

Hillary stuck out her tongue at him. "So right now, the only plan we have is to get the food moved to Eldervale. After that, what?"

"I don't know. We have to go back to Aberratia and get rid of Dreadlore, but I don't have any ideas how to do that. So let's get started for Eldervale. Maybe we can figure out something on the way."

Out on the road, they were by themselves. It seemed strange to Windslow not to see the long lines of people heading for Aberratia. When they reached Eldervale, they both stood at the edge of where the village had been and stared.

The only thing left that they recognized was the fountain that had marked the center of town. The stones were still there, but no water. All the homes were gone. Some of the trees had marks from the fire that had destroyed the village. The soot and ash was gone, but so were the fresh green lawns. The whole place looked trampled.

"Now what," Hillary said. "There's nobody here."

"There is someplace," Windslow said. "There's a big cook kettle over there behind the fountain."

"Ho! Windslow, Hillary!" a voice called from the trees off to their left. They turned to see Grandpa Dimbleshoot walking toward them. Behind him walked five other men.

"Not a very pretty sight is it," he said as he approached. "The whole place burned."

"We heard what happened," Hillary said. "We talked to Gilderbun."

"Is she all right?" he asked. "Where did you see her?"

"It was on the trail to Aberratia. She looked fine. There are tents there, and food and water, though not much. How are you and your friends?"

"We're a little better today," Dimbleshoot said. "Last night we decided it was hopeless. Today we were going to head for Aberratia. But things have changed."

"How?" Windslow asked.

"Well, it's like a miracle," Dimbleshoot said. "The rain had washed away a lot of the soot. We cleared up the mess from the fire, the best we could, but there's no hope for the fountain. Without water we figured trying to do anything more was pointless."

"So what changed," Hillary asked.

"This funny looking beast showed up that looked like an overgrown dog with big white teeth. At first, we thought it was some forest creature and was dangerous. When it got close, we saw the strangest thing. It had a book in its mouth. It dropped the book and ran back into the woods."

"A book?" Windslow said.

"Yes, a book. Most interesting book I ever saw. Not that I've ever seen that many. Usually, only wizards have books."

"What kind of book?" Hillary asked.

"It's all about how things work. There were lots of pictures and diagrams. And there was a note too."

"Did it say who the book was from?"

"It didn't say. The note told us to look at the book and then give it to the Forge Twiddlers. It said we should check the forest just east of town. That's all it said. But there was one page folded over, right where the note was stuck."

"What was on the page?" Windslow asked. "Did you find anything in the forest?"

"We just fit the two together," Dimbleshoot said. "The page marked a thing called a sawmill. A sawmill has this great big blade and you build it over a fast running stream. It's hard to explain, but there is this waterwheel that turns the saw."

"We know what a sawmill is," Windslow said. "What was in the woods and what did you fit together?"

"I guess all the rain and the earthquakes caused it. It's in a perfect location."

Hillary threw up her hands. "What is? What did you find?"

"There's a new stream, just right for a sawmill. And we think we could make a grain mill too, if we had any grain, that is. There might be some hope for the future."

"Show us the book," Windslow said. "Did it look anything like this one?" He pulled the *Book of Library Secrets* from his bag and held it out.

"Nope," Dimbleshoot said. "The cover was like thick paper and stiff. It had pictures that looked so real you swore you could hear the sounds of things moving. We didn't wait. One of my friends left straight away to find the Forge Twiddlers. We're going to have them build that mill. Now all we need to figure out is how to eat. We did salvage a few pumpkins from the fields. We made soup. There's still some left. Are you two hungry?"

"No, we're fine," Windslow said. "We brought something that I think you'll like. Let's go sit by the fountain and I'll show it to you."

At the fountain, Windslow looked over the edge. Dimbleshoot and his friends had cleaned out all the soot and sludge. The stone blocks that formed the basin and wall had been recently patched.

Windslow turned around and sat on the low wall. To himself, he said the spell to reveal the closet.

Mom wants me to clean my room. I won't even need a broom.

Two feet in front of Windslow's face, a foot-long shiny brass zipper appeared. Windslow rubbed his palms together and leaned forward. "Hm..," he said. "Maybe we should do this over there." He stood and grabbed the zipper, pulling it slowly through the air until it was ten feet from the fountain. "This will be good," he said.

Windslow grabbed the bottom of the zipper and pulled. The brass stretched, making the zipper longer. When the bottom of the zipper touched the hard packed ground, Windslow released it.

Hillary elbowed him aside, "Just do it. Stop being dramatic." She grabbed the zipper pull. As she drew it down, the two sides of brass teeth, parted. "Okay," she said and reached in up to her elbows.

Dimbleshoot and his friends gasped.

From the motion of her shoulders, Windslow could tell Hillary was moving her arm around inside the magic closet.

"Where did her arm go?" Dimbleshoot asked. He walked all the way around Hillary and the long brass zipper.

"She's reaching into some other place," Windslow said. "If you were at that place now, all you'd see is her arm waving around, sticking out in the middle of the air. Hey, sis, having trouble?"

Hillary pulled her arm out. "I can't feel anything. Maybe it's not working."

"Did you hold an image of all those baskets in your mind or an image of a shelterhund?"

"I like the hounds, but I don't know that I want to be sticking my hand into one of their mouths or something."

"Let me try." Windslow reached in. "Got something," he said. Windslow had to twist so he could fit both arms in the opening. He grunted and lifted out a large reed basket filled with carrots. It dumped on its side. Windslow wobbled back to the fountain and sat down. "Sorry," he said. "With my back the way it is, it's hard enough to walk. I can't lift those."

"Let me give it a try," Dimbleshoot said. Two of his friends picked up the spilled carrots.

"Hey," one of them said and held up three large carrots. "Someone carved some words on these. Look. They say 'Think,' 'Basket' and 'Just.' "

"I bet that would be, just think basket," Hillary said. "Dimbleshoot, just look at that basket. In your mind, think of how it looks and reach into the zipper closet."

Dimbleshoot nodded and reached in. "Hey, I got one," he said and pulled out a basket filled with potatoes. "This is amazing. With this zipper thing, we wouldn't even need to plant any more."

"That's not quite right," Hillary told him as Dimbleshoot pulled out a basket of squash. "Someone else is giving you their harvest just to help out. It's not a replacement for growing your own."

"At least this adds to our hope," one of Dimbleshoot's friends said.

"I'm beginning to see that's what this is all about," Windslow said. "Hey, I can't help with the baskets," he called to the others. "If someone will lend me a knife, I can start cutting some of this up to put in the pumpkin soup."

For the rest of the morning and most of the afternoon, Hillary and the men transferred baskets of food, piling them inside the old fountain.

Hillary took a break and sat by her brother. "Should we head for Aberratia? We could just leave the zipper here."

"I don't think we should do that," Windslow said. "When they've finished with all the baskets they might try to grab a sawmill from someplace."

Hillary smiled and wiped her forehead. "Good thought, brother. Any idea how we'll know when we've got everything?"

"Hey," Dimbleshoot called. "There are more words. They're carved on a pumpkin this time."

Both Hillary and Windslow looked at the pumpkin. The words read;

Enough for winter. More in spring by the spider-vulture.

"I think that's all there is for now," Windslow said. "There is a place up in the mountains by a spider-vulture's tree. I think you find more food there this spring if you need it."

Windslow drew Dimbleshoot a map to the vulture's tree while the men all talked to Hillary, telling her how grateful they were. Windslow said his goodbyes and with his sister headed back for Aberratia. Both yawning, they walked fast to reach the flannel hut before they dream-slipped.

23: Maiden, Daughter, Child

Windslow was first up in the morning. He was disappointed they hadn't made much progress in Gabendoor that night. *I guess at least we did something,* he thought to himself. *For a while, the people won't need to rely on Dreadlore to eat.*

He got ready for school. When it was time to leave, he hurried back to his room to get his backpack. He had packed it earlier, but now the *Book of Library Secrets* lay out and open. Windslow quickly read the new words.

More than wizards give him power.
Destroy the symbols of the towers.
Find the answers, change the game.
Things will never be the same.

"Just what I needed he said, slammed the book shut, shoved it back into his backpack and headed out to the van.

Conversation on the ride to school was all about Hunter. Hillary asked if he could come over again tonight and stay a little longer. Bill said he thought it would be fine.

It worried Windslow that Molly wasn't in science class. He asked Mrs. DiMarco. She said she didn't know anything.

Near the end of soccer practice, Hunter showed up and chatted with Windslow. They hadn't been sitting long when Marcy came over.

"Windslow, I have a question for you," Marcy said. She flashed Hunter her biggest smile. "Oh, hi. I didn't know

Windslow was busy. My name is Marcy. Are you new at our school? I hope so."

Yah, right, Windslow muttered under his breath.

"I'm Hunter." He stood and shook Marcy's hand. When the handshake ended, Marcy hung on. Hunter had to pull his hand away.

"No, I go to Rutherford. I stopped by on my way home to watch Hillary play and hang out with Windslow a little."

"I'm captain of the cheerleader squad," Marcy said. She slipped her arm through Hunters arm. "We could use someone to critique some new cheers we have. Can you come over and help? You won't mind if I borrow him for awhile, Windslow, will you?"

Before Windslow could answer, Hunter pulled his arm free. He stepped back and sat down. "Sorry," he said. "I came here for a reason and that reason is out on the field."

"Oh, I see," Marcy said. She sucked in her lower lip, scowled at Windslow, turned and marched back down the sidelines.

Hunter started laughing. "She's pretty full of herself. Is she a friend of yours?"

Windslow shook his head. 'Not really." He looked at his watch. "I need to get busy. It's time for me to start putting equipment away."

"Okay, I'll help. Tell me what to do"

"Grab that big net over by my backpack," Windslow said. "You can help me round up the extra soccer balls." To himself Windslow said, *I think I could like this guy.*

"Hey," Hunter hollered. "Want me to stick your book inside your backpack?"

"What book?" Windslow asked and spun his wheelchair around. Hunter held Windslow's backpack in one hand and the *Book of Library Secrets* in the other.

"Here, I'll take them," Windslow said and wheeled his chair toward Hunter.

Hunter handed them both to Windslow. "Very cool looking book. It looks old. Interesting title too."

"Yah, I kind of collect them. Ah, by any chance was it open?"

"It was. I shut it. I hope that's all right. I didn't loose your spot or something, did I?"

"No," Windslow said, "Never mind. Can you grab those balls down field for me?"

"Sure," Hunter said.

As soon as Hunter turned around, Windslow checked the book. He sighed when he read the new words.

One is later than the other.
Who will come to help the brother?
The spell can't wait. It's needed now.
Will the one alone know how?

ꕥ

The hospital visit bothered Windslow. Trish woke for a few minutes and asked Hillary about Hunter. For the few minutes Trish was awake, Hillary did most of the talking. She dozed off, then opened her eyes and looked at Windslow. "I'm counting on you, kiddo," she said, her voice soft.

Windslow nodded. When Trish closed her eyes, he closed his, fighting back the tears that were trying to push out.

Trish looked pale, and wore a scarf around her head with wires running out from under the cloth. The nurse had said they were monitoring Trish's brain waves. It was all related to the operation they might do on Monday.

On the ride home, Windslow asked about the operation. Bill simply said there was a lot to consider. Monday they would make a decision. Bill said there was no use talking about it until the decision had been made.

Dinner was tacos at a drive through. At home Hillary rushed around dusting for about the fifth time. Bill kept telling her everything looked fine. When Hunter came, Bill invited Windslow to watch a movie with him in the basement. Windslow told him it was too hard getting up and down the steps and beside, he was tired and wanted to go to bed.

Windslow sat outside his bedroom door and listened. He could hear the faint sounds of a movie coming from the basement. From the kitchen he could hear Hunter and his sister laughing, mixed with the sound of popcorn popping. All that was missing, he thought, was his step-mom checking in with everyone to see if they needed anything. "I'm doing the best I can, Mom," he said softly and wheeled himself into his room.

He dug in his closet for a few extra things to take to Gabendoor. He had rummaged for them in the garage and put them in his room. He grabbed a black hooded sweatshirt that his dad didn't wear anymore. He shoved it in his pack. Beside it, he stuffed in a long wool skirt that Hillary had tried to sell in a garage sale.

He wasn't sure how he was going to fit the dark gray blanket into his backpack. He used scissors to cut a slot in the middle so he could wear it over his head like a poncho. After trying to fold it, and then roll it, he had a thought. He grabbed his magic book bag, and stuffed it in. *I'm so smart*, he said to himself.

"Shoot. I forgot the cutters and I bet they're in dads shop in the basement. I wonder..."

Windslow chanted the spell to call up Larkstone's zipper closet. He rubbed his hands together before pulling it open. "This is so cool," He said. "I wish I had one of these for myself." In his mind he framed an image of what he wanted and reached through the zipper.

Windslow yanked his arm out when he heard his dad yell; almost scream. Shoving hard on his chair wheels, he let his footrests slam open his bedroom door. By the time he got to the top of the basement steps, Hillary, Hunter and his dad were on their way up. Hunter and Hillary were laughing.

Bill grinned and ran his hands through his hair. "Hey, Windslow," he said. "Sorry to startle everybody."

"What's going on?" Windslow asked.

"It was so funny, Windslow," Hillary said as they all headed for the kitchen. "Dad freaked himself out."

Bill opened a can of soda, turned around and leaned against the kitchen counter. "I picked an old horror movie to watch. I was kind of getting into it. Then out of the corner of my eye, I swore I saw an arm sticking out of thin air. It was right over my workbench."

"That's when he screamed," Hillary said.

"Did not," Bill said and took a sip of soda. "It was a manly yell of surprise."

Hillary put another bag of popcorn in the microwave. Over her shoulder she said, "Sounded like a scream to me, Dad."

"I think I was nodding off," Bill said. "Anyway, that's enough of that movie for me. I'm switching to a comedy."

"And I'm going back to bed," Windslow said. He smiled at his dad. "And could you keep it down this time?"

"Good night, Windslow," Bill said. Then he added, "Manly yell."

Windslow hurried back to his room. He knew whose arm it was his dad saw. The zipper still floated in mid air. Windslow formed the vision again, reached in, and pulled out what he needed. He checked the hallway. He could still hear his dad talking with Hillary and Hunter in the kitchen.

"Okay, I think that's it," Windslow said and pushed his backpack under his bed. He took off his tennis shoes and pulled on his hiking boots. He hadn't worn them for two years. He was glad they still fit. Slipping under the covers, he closed his eyes ready for his dream-slip.

ꕥ

Windslow woke in the flannel hut. He looked where his sister would dream-slip back to. As he expected, she wasn't there. After sitting up, he took out the *Book of Library Secrets* and examined the latest riddles.

The towers are pretty
But they're just for show.
For using the stone
Only one person knows.

More than wizards give him power.
Destroy the symbols of the towers.
Find the answers, change the game
Things will never be the same.

One is later than the other.
Who will come to help the brother?
The spell can't wait. It's needed now.
Will the one alone know how?

"Well," Windslow said, still looking at the pages. "Hillary's going to be late. She'd stay up all night with Hunter if dad let her. So that's got to be what the last one is about. But

I can't figure out the spell part. I guess it just means I'll be on my own this time."

Windslow flipped back a page. "Okay, I need to do something with the towers. But, what? Oh well," he said. "I'll just have to go find out."

Windslow closed the book. After a second thought, he opened it back up to the first new page. He shoved it over where Hillary would see it when she came. *If she came*, he thought.

Before heading to the road, he sealed the opening to the hut. On the road, he was surprised to see people again, this time walking away from Aberratia.

As he walked against the flow, several people told him he was going the wrong way. They told him food was scarce in Aberratia. They told him there was no future there. They said there were rumors there was food in Eldervale.

When Windslow got close to Aberratia, he ducked into the woods. He pulled on the long black hooded sweatshirt he had packed. After slipping his head through the slit he had cut in the blanket and pulling on the gray skirt, he looked down at himself. "I wish I had Hillary's mirror." "Wait," he said, grinned and called up Larkstone's zipper closet. After checking himself in the hand mirror, he put it back in the closet. "I kind of look like a cross between the grim reaper and a hunchback." Pleased with his disguise, he headed into Aberratia.

As Windslow hoped, the guard didn't pay any attention to him. Instead of pointing to the stack of tents, he simply told Windslow there were many empty ones.

Windslow mumbled, "Thanks," and headed for the section of temple wall below where the wizards and the Sallyforth sisters were chained.

Not as many of the tents were empty as he had hoped. People still sat at small fires and just stared ahead looking at nothing. Even the children weren't running around. In some of the tents he could see them sleeping or they sat by their parents. He heard one child say she was thirsty. Her mother told her to hush, and that water rations weren't until noon. The air seemed gray, a mixture of smoke and dust.

When Windslow reached the temple, he started climbing. At the third tier, he sat and rested. Because of his legs, going up was a lot harder than climbing down. From his vantage point, he looked around, trying to spot Dreadlore. Windslow didn't see him, an elaborate tent, or other structures. He wondered where Dreadlore stayed, and didn't think it was up on the plaza. Other than the obelisks, and the chained circle of wizards and magic users, there was nothing up there; at least nothing he had seen.

At the second level from the top, Windslow could look over the stones that formed the plaza. Where he stood, he was right below Molly.

"Molly," Windslow said as loud as he dared. "Molly, it's me, Windslow." He reached up and pulled at her chain.

Molly spun around and looked over the edge. "Hi, Windso. Where Hillre?"

"She's not here right now. Maybe later," he said. "I was worried when you didn't show up for school today. I'm here to rescue you."

"Dreadlore put spell on a shackles. It keep us here so we don't dream-slip."

"Hey, could we use a spell like that on my mom?"

"It only work here," Molly said.

"Wow, your mom has got to be really worried."

Molly shook her head. "Mommy Christensen know all about us. We even bring her here to Gabendoor. She faint a lot the first time. I think she still worried though. How you plan a get us free?"

"With this," Windslow said and held up the bolt cutters he had taken from his dad's tools. "Scoot around and stick your foot out."

When Molly held her foot out, Windslow positioned the cutter jaws and squeezed hard on the two handles. They moved slowly. Windslow stopped, took a breath and tried again. A small *clink* sounded. The shackle separated enough for Molly to slip it off her ankle.

"Hi, Windso."

Windslow looked up. Tillie gave him a small wave.

He heard Haggerwolf say, "Shush. Move back so you don't raise suspicion."

Windslow peeked up over the top of the stones. Five faces and one foot greeted him. Windslow quickly snapped the metal cuff from Haggerwolf's leg.

After handing the bolt cutters to Larkstone, Windslow pulled himself up onto the plaza. Sitting between Haggerwolf and Molly, he turned around and faced outward like the others.

'Do you have a plan?" Haggerwolf asked.

"Well not really. I mean kind of, but not much. I want to take a close look at those obelisks."

"That be really, really easy," Nelly said and rubbed her ankle where the shackle had been.

"Nelly right," Tillie said. "Dreadlore put big spell all around it. It keep everything outside out and everything inside in."

"Why do you need to get so close? Maybe we can come up with a sly spell to let you see them without Dreadlore finding out?"

"No," Windslow said. "I want to do it up close. The *Book of Library Secrets* hints that there might be something on them I need to know about."

"Well," Larkstone said and scratched his head. "There might be a way. If this works, I'll go in with you."

"No," Windslow said. "All of you need to stay here. I don't want a guard to notice one of you gone. What's your idea?"

Larkstone snapped off one of the somber wood spikes from the band around his forehead. "Get ready to slide back down that wall if this doesn't work." Larkstone used an underarm throw to send the piece of wood sliding across the plaza. It stopped near the center of the four towers.

"Well that part worked," he said. "The wood is filled with the same magic that forms the barrier. The spell may have hiccupped, but no more than if the wind bounced something off of Dreadlore's barrier. Dreadlore wouldn't build in an alert that would go off for small things like that."

"Okay, there's a piece of wand in there," Windslow said. "How will that help me get in?"

"Call up my zipper closet," Larkstone said.

When the brass zipper hovered in front of Windslow, Larkstone told him to open it, think about the wand, and try to grab it.

Windslow took a sharp breath when he saw his own arm sticking out of the air inside the barrier. He smiled when he felt the wood inside the closet and saw his fingers touch it by the towers. His grin widened when he realized what his dad must have seen in the basement.

"Got it," Windslow said.

"I see that," Larkstone said.

"So now what? Why throw it in there if we were just going to take it back out."

"You're not taking it out," Larkstone said. "This is the tricky part. If you have your eyes open and you climb inside the closet, you'll just be in the closet. If you close your eyes, step through and turn around, you'll be on the other side of the closet."

"I'll be in there," Windslow said. "Cool. Can I open my eyes then?"

"Yes, once you're over there. But there's one small problem. You won't be able to come back the same way. You'll be there, not here and here is where the closet really is."

"Well, that's better than sitting here," Windslow said. Closing his eyes, he stepped into the closet. With his eyes still shut, he squatted down next to the stick and used his other hand to feel for the plaza stones. Carefully he turned and opened his eyes. From the edge of the plaza, Larkstone gave him a "thumbs up" before turning to face outward. Windslow looked for the zipper closet and saw the brass zipper still floating in the air. Larkstone shrunk it and hid it under his arm.

Staying on his hands and knees, Windslow twisted around and crawled to the obelisk that held the bloodstone. The red flecks in dark stone glowed. Windslow checked all four sides of the stone spire holding it. Letters chiseled into the front surface spelled out, "The Beguiler."

"That means this one matches up with Dreadlore," Windslow said softly. He scooted over to the other three pillars and looked for words. The one with the orange stone had the words, "Daughter of Secrets." The obelisk holding the green stone read, "Maiden of Truth." Words in the fourth pillar, which held the black stone, spelled out, "Child of Intuition."

"Okay," Windslow said and sat back on his heels. "They're all constellations. What else do I know? They're in the legend. They're in the book. Each has a different color."

He turned his head to look back at the wizards and Sallyforth triplets. "Green, orange, black," Windslow said. He looked at the three stones and back to the sisters. "Na," he said and looked again. "Green is the Maiden of Truth. Tillie always tells the truth and has green hair. Nelly has orange hair. Orange is the Daughter of Secrets. Nelly always says things backwards, kind of like a secret. And Molly; black hair, black stone. That would make her the Child of Intuition. Molly always seems to know what's going to happen next."

Windslow put one hand on his head. "Geeze, it kind of fits. It fits too good. I don't like how I think it fits together, but it does."

"Hey, you. What are you doing!" someone shouted.

Windslow stood.

A guard with a purple hood and long pike pole stood slightly back from the obelisks.

"Get over here," the guard yelled.

"You come in here," Windslow said.

The guard took a step forward, bumped into the magic barrier and stepped back.

"You can't, can you." Windslow said. "Dreadlore sent me in here to polish the towers. If I wasn't supposed to be in here, then how would I have got past the magic?"

The guard fidgeted with the bottom of his hood. "So where are your cleaning supplies?"

"You know, you don't just use soap and water on these," Windslow said. "That's what the blanket is for. I keep it over my shoulders so it won't drag on the ground." Windslow picked up a corner of his makeshift poncho and used it to wipe the face of an obelisk. "Don't you have work you're supposed to be doing? Hey, what's your name? Maybe I should talk to Dreadlore about you."

The guard let go of his hood, nodded and briskly walked away.

"Oh, I am so good," Windslow said.

"And just how good would that be?" someone asked.

Windslow spun around.

Five feet away, Dreadlore leaned against his obelisk, his arms folded, and his eyes locked on Windslow.

24: Late

Dreadlore unfolded his arms but stayed leaning against his obelisk. "I'm surprised you came back and I'm surprised you got past my barrier. What are you looking for? By your comment, and the way you dealt with my guard, I assume you found something. What was it?"

Windslow moved backward until the magic barrier stopped him. "I figured out that you're the Beguiler. The tower you're leaning against represents you. Having a bloodstone for a symbol is appropriate."

"What else?"

"That's it," Windslow said.

"What about the other three?"

"Nope," Windslow said. "I can't figure them out."

"I'll help you then," Dreadlore said. "They represent the Sallyforth Sisters."

"Oh. Yah. That would make sense," Windslow said and nodded.

"You're not as good an actor as you think. I didn't see a sincere look of surprise."

"Um... That's because it all kind of fits what I'd been thinking."

Dreadlore walked to Tillie's obelisk and ran his hand along the smooth stone. He turned back to Windslow. "So tell me, how does the Star Stone work with the stones on the pillars?"

"I figured you'd know that," Windslow said. "It beats me how they all tie together."

Dreadlore swung his arm through the air.

Even though Windslow was twenty steps away, the blow, transmitted by magic, twisted Windslow's head to the side and nearly knocked him over. The skin on his face stung. His jaw throbbed. He tasted blood.

Dreadlore held up his arm and twirled his hand, as if spinning an invisible lasso.

A force twisted Windslow around. The same force yanked him back two paces and slammed him forward into the magic barrier.

Windslow groaned and tried to push away. The force pulled him back and slammed him a second time. The force released him. Windslow slid to the ground. His face and chest hurt.

"Oh, it looks like you have a rescue party," Dreadlore said. "Let's see what they're up to."

Windslow raised his head. On the other side of the Barrier stood the Sallyforth triplets and behind them, Haggerwolf and Fernbark.

"Here my one magic use for today," Molly said and held up her hand.

Blue light danced off her fingertips. The magic bounced off the barrier in a shower of blue sparks.

Dreadlore blew out a breath, as if blowing out a candle. Molly stumbled and fell, nearly doing a backward somersault.

Nelly and Tillie stepped to the wall and stood shoulder to shoulder. They raised their hands together.

Windslow cast his own spell, directed at Dreadlore's boots.

The spell kicked Dreadlore's feet from under him. He landed hard on his side.

Windslow took a quick glance over his shoulder. Nelly lay on her back. The two wizards dragged her away by the arms. Tillie walked backward holding her left hand in her right.

Dreadlore's magic lifted Windslow and slammed him into Molly's obelisk. The blow hurt. Windslow wrapped his arms around the smooth stone to keep from falling down. He felt the obelisk move, teetering a fraction of an inch.

Dreadlore pointed.

The blow doubled Windslow over and threw him in the air. His back slammed against the barrier and he dropped to the ground. Holding his arms across his stomach, he couldn't get a breath. He tried to relax and slowly drew in air. Dreadlore rolled to his stomach and put his hands on the ground to push himself up.

Windslow had to force out the two words of the spell he cast. "Greased pig."

Dreadlore's hands slipped on the greasy surface. He tried to stand and slipped again.

"Ball bearings," Windslow said after drawing in his first full breath.

Tiny silver balls littered the plaza stones around Dreadlore. Twice he made it to his feet. Both times he slipped on the grease and metal bearings and fell. Back on his stomach, Dreadlore stretched out one hand. A small ball of fire floated just above his palm. The ball grew. Windslow could begin to feel the heat.

Something jerked at his belt. Windslow wiggled, but whatever it was pulled harder.

"Slide back," Windslow heard Larkstone say.

Windslow twisted his head. Behind him he saw an arm sticking through a shiny zipper. Windslow shoved with his feet, closed his eyes and ducked his head.

"You're out," Larkstone shouted.

Windslow opened his eyes. He sat off to one side of the wizards. The obelisks blocked his view of Dreadlore. Where Windslow had been, the air lit up with the flash of a fireball striking the inside of the barrier. Windslow pointed his hand and cast a spell.

Upside down, inside out, double layer with no way out.

"What did you just do?" Larkstone asked.

"Hopefully I just screwed up his barrier."

"Get up," Larkstone said. "We need to get away from here as quickly as possible."

Windslow stood. Every part of his body hurt. He put his arm around Larkstone's shoulders to keep from falling. "Is everybody all right?" he asked as they headed for the edge of the plaza. The people who had formed the circle were gone. Only the chains that had held them remained.

As they climbed down the blocks, Larkstone answered Windslow's question. "Molly got the wind knocked out of her. Tillie has a broken arm or bad sprain. Nelly blacked out a few minutes. I think they're all okay."

They were halfway down when they heard Dreadlore scream in rage.

"I think your trick with his barrier worked," Larkstone said. "We still better hurry. It won't hold him."

When they reached the ground, Windslow noticed only tents and unattended fires. Dust filled the air. "Did everybody leave?" Windslow asked as he and Larkstone moved across the packed earth.

"I'd say there was a bit of panic that started," Larkstone said.

Windslow stumbled. Larkstone couldn't hold him. "My legs are giving out," he said supporting himself on his hands and knees.

A loud clap of thunder sounded. They both looked back at the temple. Dark clouds formed above it. Lightning licked down in small bolts. A second louder peal sounded, making the ground shake. The clouds thinned quickly. Dreadlore appeared at edge of the plaza.

"This won't be good," Windslow said. "Let's go." With Larkstone's help, he struggled to his feet.

A wall of flame formed at the base of the temple. Spanning the clearing, the flames reached halfway up the stones. Dreadlore held up both arms. The wall of flame rolled forward.

"It's faster than we are," Windslow yelled. His legs gave out and he fell again. The flames crackled and sucked in air that kicked up dust. Tents burst into flames as the wall neared them.

"Windslow felt light headed. He slumped in Larkstone's arms. "I think I'm going to pass out," he said, his head spinning. "Use your magic."

"I'm sorry, son. I don't have the power to stop that."

The wind's speed sharply increased and blew cold. Low hanging, silver gray clouds formed. A drizzle began that quickly turned to a wall of sleet and rain. It moved toward the flames. When the two met, thunder shook the air. Lightning flashed first blue, then green. Two magics battled. Steam rose from the ground and mixed with the clouds. When the steam, the clouds, and the dust cleared. Windslow could still see Dreadlore at the top of the temple. "What do you think he'll try next?" Windslow asked.

"I wouldn't wait to find out," a familiar voice said up ahead. "Hey, slowpoke, sorry I'm late. How'd you like my magic?"

"Hillary," Windslow hollered.

His sister ran to Windslow and helped him on his feet. "You really made a mess," she said. "Come on. I don't think this is over."

They were nearly to the trees when Larkstone shouted. Trees in front of them snapped. As they crashed to the ground, limbs and leaves ripped themselves away. The trunks split and shattered into thousands of long, pointed wooden shards.

"Lay down flat!" Hillary yelled.

Larkstone and Windslow dove for the ground. Hillary plopped down next to them on her knees. She held up her hands. "Boomerang!" she yelled.

Dreadlore released his magic. Aimed well, the wooden spears arched high in the air.

"Crud-o," Hillary shouted. "It's not strong enough."

The projectiles completed their arch and pointed downward.

"Link!" Larkstone yelled.

Windslow grabbed his sister's hand.

"Boomerang!" Hillary screamed.

The sticks bent and flattened. They rose, spinning rapidly. At the top of their flight, they flew back toward the tree line and descended. When they neared their starting point, they turned to spears and launched themselves back toward their targets.

"Dreadlore did that, I bet," Windslow said. He gripped Hillary's hand tighter. "Cast your boomerang spell again."

"Dreadlore will do the same thing again," Hillary said.

"That's what I'm counting on. Do it."

"Boomerang," Hillary shouted.

"Touched by magic, turn to dust," Windslow said, casting his own spell.

He rolled to his back so he could see Dreadlore. "Dust seeks where magic begins," he said, adding to his spell.

The sticks turned to boomerangs, and the boomerangs back to sticks. From sticks, they turned to a cloud of sawdust.

Windslow watched Dreadlore raise his hands again. The sawdust swirled in a cloud that raced to the temple obscuring it from view.

"Nice touch," Hillary said. She helped Windslow up. He put one arm around his sister's shoulders and the other around Larkstone.

"Teamwork," Windslow said. He looked over his shoulder. The cloud of sawdust pushed back, swirled and reformed. "Ha!" Windslow shouted. "How do you like that, Dreadlore? I told you I was good. Together, my sister and I are awesome. You'll have to stop using magic to get rid of the dust. How long will it take you to figure that one out!"

Hillary laughed. "He can't hear you from here."

"I know," Windslow said as they hurried down the road, "But it felt good to say it."

"What next" Hillary asked.

"I don't know," Windslow said, but I have figured a couple more things out. He looked at Larkstone. "Where is everyone else?"

"They're waiting for us in that little hut you made."

When they got to the hut, two things surprised Windslow. The first was how well camouflaged it was. The second was how large it was.

"Is everyone all right?" Windslow asked and then yawned.

"I fixed everyone's cuts and bruises," Haggerwolf said. "No one was seriously hurt. What did we miss?"

Windslow yawned again. His sister yawned too. Her eyes fluttered.

"Larkstone will have to fill you in," Windslow said. He flopped on his back, closed his eyes and settled into his dream-slip.

ꙮ

Windslow woke. When he turned his head, it hurt. When he moved his arms, they hurt. When he used the trapeze over his bed to move into his wheelchair, everything hurt. He didn't see any light coming from under his sister's bedroom door or shining down the steps from his dad's bedroom upstairs.

"I'm taking a bath. A long bath," Windslow said and wheeled into the bathroom. The mirror over the sink fogged with steam from the hot water. Windslow leaned back and soaked. He had light purple bruises on both legs, an ugly dark purple bruise that spread across his chest and around his side. Both arms had dark spots. What worried him most was his face. You could hardly see the small cut on his lip. You couldn't miss the purple spot high on his cheek, just under his eye. He twisted the faucet handle and let the hot water warm up his bath even more.

A soft knock sounded at the door.

"I'm taking a bath," Windslow called, assuming it was his sister.

"How long?" Hillary called back.

"Five minutes." Windslow sighed and pulled the plug.

When he was out of the tub, he toweled off, put on his robe, and glanced in the mirror again before opening the door. Hillary stood in the hallway, leaning against the wall.

"Oh my goodness," she said. Hillary wheeled him backward into the bathroom and shut the door.

Windslow tilted his head back as his sister's fingers reached toward his face. She took her other hand and put it on top of his head.

"Hold still," Hillary scolded. Very gently she touched her fingers to his cheek. "This is my fault," she said. "Hunter stayed until midnight. I had such a good time, I sat up and wrote about it in my diary. I didn't mean to have you face Dreadlore alone."

Hillary pulled open a drawer and took out several jars, tubes and plastic cases that held her makeup. "I can make this look a little better, but dad's going to notice it. What are you going to tell him?"

"I don't know." Windslow shrugged. "I'll think up something. So what about tonight?"

Hillary looked at him for a moment before plopping down to sit on the edge of the bathtub. She stared at her hands before looking up. "I don't know. I was planning to have Hunter over again. I really like him, Windslow."

"Well, dah, that's obvious," Windslow said. "Move. You're blocking my way. I want to get dressed. I'll think of something to tell dad about my face. You think about what you want to do tonight. Neither of those are very big problems to solve compared to what's waiting for us in Gabendoor. You know, mom said she was counting on me. That was just a figure of speech. She's counting on both of us."

Hillary didn't say anything. She looked back at her hands. Windslow opened the door and wheeled to his room.

ꙮ

Windslow and Hillary both found solutions. Windslow told Bill that he had dropped something on the floor last night. When he bent over to pick it up, he banged into the corner of his desk. Bill took a close look at Windslow's eye and wanted to take him to see a doctor.

"No way," Windslow protested. He pulled his head away from his dad's hands. "I'm kind of tired of doctors and hospitals. My eye is fine. It just looks bad. Hey, I'll tell everyone at school I got into a fight with Hunter."

"Very funny," Hillary said. "I think they'd notice his face is perfect."

Both Windslow and Bill stared at Hillary before bursting into laughter.

Windslow held both hands up to his cheeks. In a falsetto voice, mimicking his sister, he said, "Oh he is so perfect."

Bill still grinned. He patted Windslow on the shoulder. "That's enough. Hunter's a good looking kid, and I don't think we should be teasing Hillary about him. I'm still not convinced about you not seeing a doctor. Your mother wouldn't even discuss it. She would have you half way to the doctor's office by now."

"Yah," Windslow said. "But that's why we have moms *and* dads. Dads are here for a bit of reality."

Hillary chuckled. "Oh, you think you are so funny. If mom heard you say that, you'd be washing dishes for a week." She looked up at Bill. "Windslow's face is fine. How about my suggestion? Please, dad? Pretty please?"

"I think it would be cool," Windslow said. "It's the kind of compromise mom would figure out."

"Okay," Bill said. "I can't win when you two team up. If it's okay with Hunter's parents, then I suppose it's okay with me. But..." Bill said. "I drive you to the mall. I know Hunter has his license, but he is still a little short on experience. If his parent's can't give you a ride home from the movie, then I'll come and get you."

"Thanks, dad," Hillary said and gave her father a long hug.

"Keep an eye on the time," Bill said. "You need to be home by eight. That should give you plenty of time to see the movie and hang out at the mall." Bill turned to Windslow. "So, you feel like hanging out with your dad today?"

"I don't know," Windslow said. "Doing what?"

"How about a guy flick?" Bill looked at Hillary. "At the theater across town from the mall." He looked back at Windslow. "We can shoot some baskets at the gym and grab a burger."

"Sounds great, but what about visiting mom?" Windslow asked.

Bill pulled out a kitchen chair and sat down. "We'll take a break today and spend more time with her tomorrow. I talked to her doctor. She's not waking up. Not even for a few minutes. She mumbles in her sleep. Something about move the stars, move the stars." Bill gave a heavy sigh. "I agreed to let them operate on Monday. So," Bill said. He clapped his hands together, stood and shoved the chair back. "Hillary, give Hunter a call and see if that's okay with him and his parents. I'm going to get some laundry started."

"Dad!" Windslow said. "Don't let them operate on mom. She's going to be fine."

"I agree with Windslow," Hillary said. "I don't like the idea of someone drilling a hole in her head and poking around in there."

Bill folded his hands behind his neck. "I know, I know. But they don't have anything else to try." He let go of his neck and put both hands on the table. "I just don't know what else to do." Bill lifted one hand, wiped it across his eyes and put it back on the table.

"Come on," Hillary said and stepped behind Windslow. "We both need to get ready. I'll give you a ride to your room."

Bill didn't move or say anything as they left the kitchen.

"This isn't easy for him," Hillary said. "I think dad was going to cry. You were right."

"About what?" Windslow asked.

"About Mom. She's counting on us. We only have two more trips to Gabendoor to fix things. I promise you I won't be late."

ꕥ

Hunter's parents volunteered to drive both ways. After they picked Hillary up, Windslow and Bill went to a movie as planned. They decided to skip the gym, neither of them in the mood. Instead they spent time at a bookstore. Bill looked for books that Trish might like to read when she came home. Windslow hung out in the music department. Instead of burgers they went to a fried chicken place that neither Hillary nor Trish liked because they said it was too greasy. It was Windslow's favorite restaurant. He and his dad talked a little about the movie, but it was more just to keep the silence away. Windslow was glad when Bill said it was time to go home so they would be there when Hillary's date ended. Windslow wanted to use the extra time to try to come up with a plan for Gabendoor. The problem is he had no ideas at all.

25: Crisis

Windslow sat at his desk, going over the clues and riddles in the *Book of Library Secrets.* He played with his new glitter ball he had purchased at the bookstore. Made of rubber, the six-inch clear ball held some sort of thick fluid and purple glitter. It was like the paperweights that would look like they were snowing inside when you shook them up. When Windslow bounced the ball, the motion made the glitter swirl. Catching the ball, Windslow put it on his desk, leaned down and watched the glitter sparkle.

Windslow flipped another page in the book, and gave the ball another bounce. He was starting to have some ideas that he wasn't too happy about. He spun around when he heard the front door slam and his sister calling out, "Dad, Dad!"

Windslow shoved on the wheels of his chair. He rounded the corner to the living room about the same time his dad did. Hillary threw her hands up in the air, marched over to the couch, and sat down. "Dad," she repeated. "We have a major crisis. I have a major crisis. What am I going to do?"

"What? What happened?" Bill asked, his voice loud. He rushed to Hillary and sat on his knees in front of her on the carpet. "Honey, what did he do to you?"

Hillary gave her dad an odd look. "Who?"

"Hunter," Bill said.

Hillary flopped back and threw her arms over the back of the couch. "He wants to take me to the homecoming dance. Dad," Hillary said and leaned forward. "I could really use mom for this, but she's not here. You are. You'll have to do."

"Oh thanks for the vote of confidence," Bill said. "So that's the crisis? Hunter asked you to a dance?"

"Dad, you don't understand," Hillary said. "I need a dress. I need to get my hair done. There are a million things you won't understand."

"Don't worry," Windslow said. "I'll help. Want me to get that box of dresses from the garage. You know, the box marked for a garage sale."

"Argh..." Hillary shouted and threw up her hands.

Bill grinned, got up and sat in the recliner. "Windslow," he asked. "Aren't you going to the dance too? You could use a haircut, maybe a new suit. Have you thought about flowers? See," he said turning back to Hillary. "I'm not a total idiot. I feel another trip to the mall coming up tomorrow."

"Oh, dad. Not a mall dress."

"All right," Bill said. "I'll give Mrs. Christensen a call. Maybe she'll volunteer to be my advisor. So other than that, how was the date?"

"It was really fun. I'd love to talk dad, but I need to go and start making a list. I need to call some of my friends too."

Bill laughed. "Yes, I can see how much you have to do. Hey, Windslow. Would you like to play a board game or watch some TV?"

"Thanks, Dad," Windslow said. "I've got a lot of homework. I want to finish it up tonight because I have a feeling we'll be spending a lot of time shopping tomorrow."

"You're a wise young man," Bill said.

Windslow watched Hillary scowl at Bill's comment. It made him smile until he thought, *Geeze, flowers. I'm going to need three of everything. I didn't think about a suit.* "Hillary," he called and headed for his sister's room.

Hillary sat at her desk and scribbled on a sheet of paper. "Hillary," he said. "I need your help. I haven't thought about the homecoming dance. All I've been thinking about is Dreadlore. I'm going to heed your help with the dance stuff."

"Don't worry," Hillary said. "It's a lot easier for guys." She turned and looked at him. "But you're right. Gabendoor and mom come first. Any ideas for tonight?"

"I've been spending as much time as I can and I have some ideas... Oh crud," He said and leaned back in his chair. "Never mind the dance stuff. For me, I mean. I don't think I'll be going."

"What do you mean?" Hillary said. "You can't let Molly, Tillie and Nelly down. You can't do that."

"I don't think they'll be there. I mean here. I mean... oh crud. Let me tell you what I think I've figured out. This is all such a mess."

Windslow and Hillary spent the next hour going over Windslow's ideas and the passages in the book. Both of them got their packs ready and headed for bed, ready for Gabendoor; ready for Dreadlore.

ꕥ

Hillary and Windslow woke about the same time. Across from them waited Larkstone, Fernbark, and Haggerwolf.

Windslow sat up. "Has anything changed?" He asked. "I suppose we should wait awhile and see if the Sallyforth sisters come."

"They already have," Haggerwolf said. "They got here about half an hour ago. They headed straight for Aberratia."

"To do what?" Hillary asked and got up on her knees.

"I don't think they have a plan," Fernbark said. "They just said to catch up with them. They wanted to keep an eye on Dreadlore and round up some help. "I don't know where they're going to find any. No one wants to go up against Dreadlore. Do either of you have a plan?"

Windslow looked at his sister. She shrugged. "Not really," Windslow said. "We need to get the Star Stone. It's the key, but we kind of knew that. Yesterday I think I figured out the towers. Molly and her sisters are the Maiden, the Child and the Daughter."

The three wizards looked at each other. "Of course," Haggerwolf said. "That makes sense. They've been on Gabendoor as long as anyone can remember. That ties them to the constellations."

"And that ties them to the Stone and the legend," Windslow said. "I'm afraid that if magic is going away, part of all this means they're going away too. Here," Windslow said and opened the *Book of Library Secrets*. He flipped it open and turned it around so the Wizards could read the page.

A special stone moves time and space.
Each of eight must find their place.
Three will go and three will stay.
The other two will find the way.

"This is what I think," Windslow said. "Hillary discovered there are eight segments on the Star Stone. Each of the eight segments relates to one of the *eight who must find their place.* The eight are you three, the triplets, Hillary, and me. Three go and three stay. I'm assuming the three who go are the Sallyforth triplets. You three stay. Hillary and I find the way. I think that means it's up to us two to figure out how and to make the stone work.

"It could be us who go," Larkstone said.

Haggerwolf shook his head. "As much as I don't want the triplets to be the ones who go, I think Windslow is right on this one."

Windslow showed them the other passages. "It looks like the towers aren't important for changing the stars, but still are important for something. I wish I could figure out a way to knock them down. When Dreadlore slammed me against one, I felt it teeter a little."

"Well," Fernbark said. "That can be the start of a plan. Part one is knock down the towers. Part two is to get the stone. What's part three."

"You make it sound so simple," Hillary said and rolled her eyes. "Unless anyone has an idea we need to work out, I think we should go find Molly and her sisters. Then we need to see if we can figure out what Dreadlore has planned for the day."

Everyone agreed. Haggerwolf used magic to create a doorway. When they were out of the hut, he sealed it again.

The road was empty. "Look," Hillary said and pointed to the bushes near where the clearing began. She pointed to a pile of purple hoods. "It looks like some of Dreadlore's followers have changed sides. That's a good sign."

"We'll need more than that," Fernbark said.

The first to enter the clearing, Windslow stopped and looked back over his shoulder. "Fernbark, I think we do have more than a few guards who changed sides."

"Wow," Hillary said. "There must be a thousand people here. Why are they all back?"

"That's why," Windslow said.

Rimming the clearing, the inhabitants of Gabendoor stood five or six people deep. In front of them, Molly, Tillie and Nelly stood, wearing their homemade cheerleader outfits. Spaced fifty feet apart, they led the crowd in a cheer.

Gabendoor our world
It belong a us.
Go back where you belong
An don't make a fuss!

The girls waved their silvery pompoms and jumped up and down.

"Now all a you say it," the three girls yelled to the crowd and repeated the cheer.

The crowd repeated the cheer. Each time it ended, someone else in the crowd started the cheer again.

Molly came running over to Windslow's group. "People need a have hope," she said. "They need a feel like they part of this. This way or that way, it going to be a biggie day for them to remember."

"For all of us," Windslow said. "So what's Dreadlore up to?"

"He getting ready to try stone again," Molly said.

Windslow looked at the temple. He could see people up on top. Chained wrist to wrist, at least fifty people formed a circle around the Obelisks. Each wore a spiked somber wood headband as before. Ten guards with purple hoods, and holding pike's, formed a second ring spaced around the first. In the center of the obelisks Dreadlore stood by something new; a six-foot tall, thick wooden post.

"Well, now what?" Hillary asked.

Windslow chewed on his lip before answering. "Okay, we have the crowd. Dreadlore seems to be ignoring them. That's good. Maybe he won't be watching for us. So here's my plan."

"The one you just made up?" Hillary asked.

Windslow smiled and nodded. He huddled with everyone and told them his thoughts. Hillary was the only one who protested, but no one had any other ideas. Molly reminded Windslow that she and her sisters still only had one magic use apiece. Larkstone offered his magic closet to Windslow, but Windslow declined.

"If we get the stone," Hillary said, "we'll all need to be together to use it I think. Any plans for that?"

Windslow shrugged again. "Nope. *When*, one of us gets the Stone, the rest of us will just have to find a way to get together."

The crowd abruptly stopped their chant. People screamed. Those standing in front pushed back.

A rhythmic humming, thrumming, sound filled the air. Windslow turned and looked at the temple.

Dreadlore stood inside of the ring of chained magic users. With both hands, he gripped the wrists of people forming the link. As before, a stream of magic flowed from each stone fixed to the top of an obelisk. This time the streams didn't meet in the center. They attached to the Star Stone, sitting on the top of the wooden post.

Eight streams of amber colored magic radiated outward, like spokes on a wheel. Continuous yellow lightning crackled. A burnt scent drifted in the air. Slowly the amber rays turned, as if the Star Stone were rotating on its wooden perch. The rays stretched to the trees and beyond, not stopped by simple leaves and branches. People in the crowd ducked or sank to their knees.

In unison, the rays slowly angled upward. They lit up the clouds as they streamed through them. When the rays touched together, the thrumming sound changed to a continuous crackle of energy. As a single beam, the light reached far beyond Gabendoor.

"What's he doing?"" Windslow yelled so the others could hear him over the sound given off by pure magic.

"He's trying to move the stars," Haggerwolf yelled back. "But it isn't working. He's tearing a hole in the fabric of magic. This can't be how it all ends. We haven't had a chance. The legend isn't supposed to work this way."

"And I don't think the stone works that way either," Windslow yelled. "Come on. Let's go."

26: Glitter Ball

Windslow could manage to walk, but not run without using his crutches. He pulled them from his backpack and extended them. Keeping pace with Hillary, Windslow hurried to the bottom row of stone blocks forming the temple of Aberratia.

"I agreed not to try this alone," Windslow yelled to Hillary over the crackling sounds coming from the magic. "But stay here. I'll climb up the back side."

Hillary nodded.

Windslow hurried around the first corner of the temple, climbed up two levels and headed for the second corner. When he rounded it, he climbed again, but stopped short of the top and looked over the row of blocks.

Dark black and tarnished silver clouds filled the sky. Where the beam of magic ripped through them, a hole had opened. Clouds rolled and boiled at the edge of the hole. Yellow lightning flicked out at the beam from the clouds. The beam struck back with its own display of blue lightning. Peals of thunder and long air-splitting cascades of crackling from the thunder and the magic obliterated any other sounds.

The clouds began to rotate, making the sky and the hole look like pictures Windslow had seen showing the eye of a hurricane on Earth. A sudden wind blew against Windslow's back and pushed him against the stones. Over the lip he watched the magic users release the hand grips that formed their link. Those close to an obelisk, wrapped their arms around the stone. Those with nothing to hold, held on to each other and grabbed at the chains that held them together.

Windslow pulled himself up to the plaza, but stayed flat. He realized it wasn't just wind pushing at him. He could feel an unseen force pulling at him, trying to lift him up. He looked for Dreadlore and spotted the wizard at the far edge of the obelisks. Dreadlore used both hands to grip the chains that bound everyone together. His feet pointed toward the wooden post that held the Star Stone. Windslow felt the force of magic try to lift him as he watched the same force lift Dreadlore's legs off the plaza, then release them.

The rhythmic thrumming sound grew louder and its pitch lowered. With each *thrum, thrum, thrum,* Windslow felt the magic pull. In the three seconds between each *thrum,* the pull relaxed. Windslow began counting in his head, repeating over and over, *one, two, three, and thrum. One, two, three, thrum.* He waited, counted and scrambled on hands and knees to the black obelisk. When he said *three,* in his thoughts, the force pulled at him.

Windslow took a breath, counted and stood. He beat the count and wrapped both hands around the obelisk to keep the magic from sucking him in. At the next count, he maneuvered around the obelisk so he could see across the field to the tree line.

A large group of townspeople huddled around each of the three wizards. In each group, anyone who could get a handhold gripped the legs, belts and clothing of two men on their knees. The men on their knees struggled to hold the legs of Larkstone, Haggerwolf and Fernbark. Out in front of them lay the Sallyforth sisters. Larkstone held Nelly's ankles gripped tightly together. Fernbark had a grip on each of Tillie's legs. Haggerwolf struggled to keep his one hand grip on Molly's shoe.

At first, Windslow couldn't understand why the force wasn't pulling at the villagers. He quickly realized the hole Dreadlore had torn was only hungry for people with magic. *The post!* Windslow thought. When the count was right, he twisted around the obelisk so he could see the wooden post holding the Star Stone. The bottom of the post sat like a Christmas tree on two crossed pieces of wood. Windslow chewed on his lip. He hoped his idea would work.

Windslow counted, twisted and glanced back at the tree line. The Sallyforth sisters squirmed and wiggled. With their arms stretched out sideways, they struggled to grab hands. Windslow had no idea what they were trying to do but urged them on in his head. *Come on, come on. Stretch. You're almost there! Stretch Molly!* He cheered aloud when they grabbed hands, but the sounds from the magic storm swallowed up his words. He held tight and watched.

The sisters pulled themselves until all three had their arms wrapped around each other. Windslow's heart pounded hard as he watched them each let go with one hand. Three arms stretched out. Three hands turned to fists. Three small fingers pointed toward the raging column of magic.

Each sister used her last spell to cast out a blue rope of magic. Three ropes extended from three fingers. The far end of each rope coiled around the magic, just above the Star Stone. The ropes spiraled upward. Where blue touched amber, silver sparks leaped outward.

The ropes tightened. The thrumming rose in pitch. More sparks flew. Windslow glanced back at the Sisters. Even from this distance he could see them straining. More townspeople tried to help hold the three wizards in place. Windslow worried abut the three pairs of old and tired hands. The words from the *Book of Library Secrets* shoved into Windslow's thoughts.

Three will go and three will stay.
The other two will find the way.

He hoped this wasn't the time or place for those words to come true.

A loud *crackle* and *boom*, shook the Temple. The sound hurt Windslow's ears. He shook his head before realizing the pull was gone. He looked for the sisters. Their ropes were gone. Haggerwolf, Larkstone and Fernbark scrambled on their hands and knees to where the Sallyforth sisters lay motionless. The townspeople huddled around them, blocking Windslow's view. Releasing his grip on the obelisk, he looked for Dreadlore.

Dreadlore rolled over onto his back. He lay still for a moment, then sat up and held both hands against his forehead. Dreadlore let go with one hand and used it to steady himself. On shaky legs he stood. Still chained together, the magic users squatted down, letting the metal links clatter against the stones.

Windslow moved fast and slammed his shoulder into the wooden post. Twisting, he stretched out both hands. As he fell to the plaza floor, the amber Star Stone landed in his hands. Worried about the stone, Windslow cast a spell. "Glitter ball," he shouted. A rubber ball, filled with fluid and glitter formed around the Star Stone. It matched the ball he had back home, but was larger, nearly the size of a soccer ball. Windslow pulled the ball against his stomach, like a football player clutching a winning pass. Rolling to his side, he pulled up his knees, pushed with one hand and jumped to his feet. Windslow jumped over the chain and was nearly to the edge of the plaza when something bound his feet. Protecting the gem, he twisted and fell hard on his back.

"Stop!" he heard Dreadlore yell.

Windslow tipped his head up and looked at his ankles. There was nothing binding them that he could see. After wiggling his feet, he rolled over and got to his knees. Across from him, Dreadlore pointed and called out a spell.

Death to a heart, which no longer will beat!

Without thinking, Windslow clutched his free hand to his chest. He held his breath and waited. Nothing happened. Windslow cast his own spell.

Knock him down and spin him around.

Nothing happened. Dreadlore stood still and glanced at his hand and then to Windslow. Dreadlore pointed and mumbled. Nothing happened.

Windslow chanced a look up at the sky. The clouds still swirled around the gaping hole. Dreadlore's movement snapped Windslow's attention back to the wizard. He had stepped over the chain and stood in the middle of the obelisks. Dreadlore rushed toward him. Windslow moved from his knees to his feet, but stayed hunched down. When Dreadlore reached for the ball, Windslow sprang up, dove to the left and rolled to his feet. Dreadlore fell and slipped over the edge of the plaza.

Windslow tried another spell. "Crud-o," he cursed. "The magic's gone." Behind him, Dreadlore pulled himself back up onto the plaza. Windslow headed the opposite direction, but stopped in the center of the obelisks. In front of him, just past the chained magic users, stood three of Dreadlore's guards. They held their long pikes up, ready to throw as javelins. Windslow ducked sideways between the three obelisks grouped together. He stayed facing the center of the plaza as he backed up.

To his left, he saw Dreadlore. The guards had him blocked on his right.

"Give me the stone," Dreadlore demanded.

Windslow grinned and gave the ball a single bounce. After catching it, he looked at Dreadlore. "Not a chance." He looked at the chained magic users. "You know, you might want to get out of here. Nobody has any magic left."

The people stayed down. Several of them yanked on the chains before giving up.

Dreadlore took a step closer. "I might not have magic, but I do have them," he said and pointed to his guards. "Thank you for putting something around the Star Stone to protect it. Guards," Dreadlore shouted. "Kill him."

Together, the three guards drew their arms back. Windslow tensed, ready to jump. Something slammed into the back of the guards' legs knocking them down. Two pikes clattered across the floor and off the plaza's edge. The third guard managed to hold his.

"Hey, bro," Hillary said. She stepped into sight holding the long pole that been the pedestal for the Star stone.

Windslow stomped on the wrist of the guard still holding a pike. The guard yelled. The pike rolled away. Hillary dropped the post, snatched the pike and moved up beside her brother.

Dreadlore smiled, and folded his arms. Six of his guards scrambled over the edge of the plaza and stood beside him. "Look down on the field."

Windslow twisted his head. Ten more guards ran toward the temple. "Hey," Windslow said, looking at the magic users closest to him. "The only thing holding you is those towers. I bet you could knock them over. I felt one move once when Dreadlore slammed me into it."

"No! Don't!" Dreadlore yelled.

People stood and used the chains to pull against the obelisks. The tower with the name, *The Beguiler* teetered.

"Stop them!" Dreadlore shouted to his guards.

Hillary swung her pike from side to side at waist level. The guards took nervous steps forward.

With a loud crash, the tower fell. People cheered. They pushed against the broken pieces of stone and freed their chains.

"No!" Dreadlore yelled. He grabbed a pike from one of his men. Wood clacked against wood. His quick move knocked the pike from Hillary's hands. Hillary stumbled backward. Dreadlore drew his pike back, ready to thrust it into Hillary.

"Catch," Windslow yelled. "He gave the glitter ball a bounce that sent it towards Dreadlore. Dreadlore used both hands to catch the ball and let the pike fall. "Get around to the other side," Windslow shouted at his sister and grabbed the pike before it hit the ground.

"You'll need this," Windslow yelled to Dreadlore. Windslow pulled his new Swiss Army knife from his pocket. He pulled open the blade for the corkscrew and held up the knife. "If you had tried to open my glitter globe with magic, the glitter would have destroyed the Stone. Same thing happens if you try to open the globe with anything other than a glitter twister." Windslow folded the blade and shoved the knife back in his pocket.

"A fortune for whoever gets me that twister," Dreadlore said to his men. With their pikes held level, they moved toward Windslow. Clutching the glitter ball, Dreadlore followed.

Windslow swept his pike back and forth, as his sister had done, but faster. When Windslow backed around the standing obelisks. The guards stopped. The obelisk for the Maiden of Truth slammed onto the plaza close to them and shattered. The guards stepped over the pieces.

"Kill him if you have to. Kill him!" Dreadlore yelled.

"I think every one of us needs to worry about staying alive," Windslow said to the guards. He kept moving. The guards matched his slow pace, but with their pikes now pointed toward the magic users. Chunks of broken obelisk had become hammers. Men and women stood with sections of broken chain hanging from their wrists and faced the guards.

"Hillary," Windslow said to his sister without looking at her. "You keep going. When you get to the edge of the plaza, stop. Stand there and pretend you're at the Rutherford scrimmage."

"Are you crazy?" Hillary called from behind him.

"Just do it." Windslow didn't dare take his eyes off the guards. He hoped Hillary was doing what he asked. He looked at the guards. "Hey, guys. Let's stop and think for a minute." Windslow had to take a quick step. The chunk of stone from Daughter of Secrets obelisk skittered past him. Four of the guards lowered their pikes. Behind them, Dreadlore rolled the ball over and over in his hands.

"Look around," Windslow said to the guards. "When the last obelisk falls, the only thing left for the magic users to go after would be you guys." Another crash sounded. No more towers stood. "Gee... sorry," Windslow said. "I think that means they're out of rocks to take out their anger on."

One guard threw down his pike. He ran to the edge of the plaza and began climbing down. Five more pikes clattered as the rest of the guards ran.

Windslow grinned and stepped backward.

"Look out!" Hillary shouted from behind him.

Windslow's heels hit a large chunk from one of the shattered obelisks. He wind-milled his arms, but couldn't regain his balance. In a heartbeat, Windslow lay on his back.

Dreadlore dropped down on one knee beside him.

Windslow saw something metal and silver flash in Dreadlore's hand. Something pointed and sharp pressed at Windslow's neck. He stiffened when he realized it was a knife. "Stay where you are," Windslow yelled at his sister. He held his breath when the knife pushed harder.

"Give me the twister and show me how to use it," Dreadlore commanded.

Windslow moved slowly, carefully pulling the Swiss Army knife from his back pocket. He put it on the hard stones of the plaza and gave it a small shove away from his side. Windslow let out his breath when Dreadlore grabbed the Army knife and stood at Windslow's feet. "If this twister doesn't work on the ball, my knife *will* work on your throat."

"I just have one last thing to tell you," Windslow said.

Holding the glitter ball in one hand and the Swiss Army knife in the other, Dreadlore looked down at Windslow. "Then say it."

"Well, it goes like this," Windslow said.

"If we gonna win," he yelled, "We got-a begin. We want a goal, so kick it through the poles."

Dreadlore gave Windslow a puzzled look.

Windslow kicked with his right leg, his foot connecting squarely with the glitter ball.

"No!" Dreadlore yelled.

Windslow rolled to his side and gave another kick, this one aimed at Dreadlore's legs. The wizard tumbled. As Windslow scrambled to his feet, he looked for the ball. It had sailed high, dropped back to the plaza, bounced and now arched toward Hillary. Windslow hoped she had figured out his hints. "Goal!" Windslow shouted when Hillary adjusted her stance and kicked high.

Still worried about Dreadlore, Windslow ran ahead a couple steps before looking back. Dreadlore held the wooden post he had used for the stone. He used the post to fend off the magic users who were slowly surrounding him.

When Windslow reached the plaza's edge, Hillary had already climbed down one level. She stood against the stone blocks and waited.

"Where'd it land?" Windslow asked his sister as she helped him down.

"Like you said. Call it a goal. Your glitter ball bounced six times, but made it to Haggerwolf."

ജ്ഞ

Windslow and Hillary hurried to the tree line. They had to push through throngs of people who headed toward the temple. At the trees, Haggerwolf greeted them. He held out the glitter ball. "We're not finished," he said. "What are we going to do about that?"

Windslow looked where Haggerwolf pointed. Clouds still boiled and rolled around the opening in the sky.

"How's everyone else?" Hillary asked and took the ball.

"Not well," Haggerwolf said. "Me, Larkstone and Fernbark, we're okay. The Sallyforth sisters aren't doing so well. They're alive and they're not hurt, but something has happened to them."

Hillary grabbed his arm. "What"

"They're changing," Haggerwolf said. "I'll take you to them. I think they might be dying."

27: Star Stone

Haggerwolf led Windslow and Hillary to a spot just inside the tree line. Fernbark and Larkstone sat on the ground. In front of him lay the sisters. Each lay on their right side, cuddled up to each other; Molly first, Tillie in the middle and finally Nelly. All three had their eyes closed.

"Are they--" Hillary asked.

"Sleeping?" Larkstone said, interrupting her. "Yes they are sleeping. They are very tired. To quote Molly, we need-a rest right now. Wake us up when Hillre and Windso come back with Starry Stone."

"They look different," Windslow said.

"Shush!" Hillary scolded. "Don't talk so loud. And don't you dare say anything to them about how they look."

"Their faces look older," Windslow said softly.

Hillary scowled at him. When Windslow shrugged, Hillary poked him.

"Okay," Windslow said. "Haggerwolf, do you have a knife?"

The wizard nodded and handed Windslow a small bone handled knife he took from inside his robe.

Windslow squatted and put the ball on the ground. He used the knife to puncture and then slice half way through the rubber ball. Peeling back the edges, he pulled out the Star Stone and handed it to Larkstone. Larkstone used the corner of his robe to wipe it off, before handing the stone to Hillary.

"It's up to you now, sis," Windslow said. "You're the only one who has the faintest idea what to do with it."

"There isn't much to my ideas," Hillary said. "Something else worries me. What if I need magic? Does anyone have any left?"

"No," Haggerwolf said. "The common magic that we wizards used is gone. The special magic, the kind you and the sisters could use is gone too. I do think that Gabendoor itself has some magic left. It's the magic it uses to change the seasons. It's the magic that gives things life. When that's gone, nothing will be able to live on Gabendoor. And I'm afraid the magic that is left is being sucked out through that hole in the sky."

"I think you had better wake the sisters up," Hillary said.

Fernbark gave the sisters a gentle shake. Molly looked up first. "Hi ever-body," she said after rubbing her eyes.

Tillie sat up and yawned. "I glad that over with. My ankles hurt. Why a magic have a pull so hard?"

Nelly rolled up onto her knees and stretched. "I wide awake an feel wonderful. Where Dead-door. I not want to hurt him for starting all this."

Molly used one hand to push herself up. Her hand slipped on the grass and she fell back down. Haggerwolf moved behind her, slipped his hands under her arms and helped her up. Larkstone and Fernbark did the same for the other sisters.

"You got funny look," Molly said to Windslow.

Windslow glanced at his sister. She scowled at him. Windslow scowled back then tried to put a happy look on his face when he turned back to Molly. "I was worried about you. I saw what you and your sisters went through when you choked off the stream of magic."

"That hardest thing we ever do," Tillie said. "We half a use our last spells."

"It was so easy," Nelly said. "I not worried at all that it might make us go *poof*." When she said the word *poof*, Nelly threw her hands up in the air.

"*Poof*?" Larkstone asked.

"Like thing Hillre make for Nassy Nellie," Molly said. "I feel like I almost turning inside out. Magic pull me this way. I pull that way. Other magic pulling, wizzies pulling, everbody pulling."

"But you're okay, right?" Hillary asked. "I mean, you're just tired and need some rest?"

Molly walked to Hillary and took her hands. "We not okay," Molly said. "All a our magic gone. We very, very, very old. Magic make us look and feel any age we want a be."

"I love a way we look and feel now," Nelly said. "I so glad I have a mirror to look into."

"We have mirrors," Tillie said. "All we have a do is look at each other."

"I like a stand and talk, but Hillre have work for us a do," Molly said. "We need a go back on field and get ready."

"Um... ready for what? I don't know what I'm supposed to do," Hillary said.

"Have we ever known?" Windslow said. "It never stopped us before. We still have hope. That's about all we've ever had on this trip to Gabendoor. Come on. Let's see if we can finish this."

ꕥ

Out on the field, Hillary formed them in a circle. She arranged them in the order the images had shown on the Stone. She and Windslow were about to take their places when they heard a commotion coming from a group of people moving away from the temple.

Townspeople and several of the magic users walked in a group. In front of them, bound in chains, walked Dreadlore. Whenever he slowed, someone from the group gave him a shove. They stopped just short of Windslow and Hillary. "What should we do with him?" one of the people asked.

Windslow looked at his sister. She shrugged. He looked at the three wizards. They shrugged. He looked at the sisters.

"Let Gabendoor decide," Molly said. "I only decide for myself what a do."

"Me too," Tillie said.

"Not me," Nelly added.

All three sisters stuck their thumbs in their ears, wiggled their fingers, and stuck out their tongues.

"There," Molly said and folded her hands. "I done."

"I keep going," Nelly said and dropped her hands.

"I finished too," Tillie said. She folded her arms and looked at Hillary. "Now it Gabendoor's turn," she said. "It time for you to help Gabendoor."

"You'll regret this," Dreadlore said. "You've ruined everything. The magic's gone and you've accomplished nothing. Now the Stone is worthless."

"Let's see if you're right," Hillary said. "Everyone get in their places. You might want to stand back," she said to the crowd, "But, leave Dreadlore there."

The crowd pushed back. Hillary took her place in the circle formed by her brother, the wizards and the triplets.

"Look," Windslow said. The *Book of Library Secrets* lay open in the center of the group.

They all watched as words appeared, one letter at a time.

Three will stay; Haggerwolf the Elder, Fernbark the Benevolent and Larkstone the Compassionate.

"Hey, cool titles," Windslow said.

Hillary hushed him.

More words appeared.

Three will go; Nelly the Daughter of Secrets, Tillie, the Maiden of Truth and Molly the Child of Intuition.

"No," Hillary said. "No, that can't be. That can't be right." She held her hand up across her eyes. "No," she said again softly. Her hand couldn't stop the tears.

Water welled up in Windslow's eyes. "I was worried..." Windslow stopped and swallowed hard to get rid of the lump in his throat. He tried again. "I was worried it would be you three. Does it have to be that way? Maybe there's some.... Some... I mean maybe..." The words wouldn't come out. Windslow stopped trying. Both he and Hillary put their arms around the triplets. The wizards added their bodies to the group hug. Every face had tears.

"Heart breaking," Dreadlore said.

A woman from the crowd rushed forward and slapped Dreadlore on the back of the head.

Molly pushed all the huggers way. "That not a way to do things," she called to the crowd. "Me an my sisers all done with our work. Now it your turn. You need a take care of Gabendoor. Hurting people not a good way to get hope back. It time a start helping people. It time a use a Star Stone."

Windslow held Molly's hand as he watched Hillary wipe her face and check everyone's position. Her space, between him and Haggerwolf, was open. Next to the elder wizard stood Fernbark, then Larkstone. After the wizards were the Sallyforth sisters, first Nelly, then Tillie and Molly last. Holding the stone, Hillary stepped into place.

"It's pointless," Dreadlore called. "You don't have any magic to channel."

Everyone ignored him. Murmurs rose from the crowd. A few people standing in the front row tried to step back.

"All right," Hillary said. "All I know is when you touch a facet on the stone, a different one of us shows up on the face. The only idea I have is for each of us to touch their finger to their facet. We're all in order. I'll start."

Hillary held the top edges of the stone with one hand. Using her other hand, she touched one finger to her facet.

Gasps from the crowd mixed with their murmurs when a soft column of light rose from the center of the stone. An image of Hillary floated in its center. Haggerwolf reached out and placed his finger next to Hillary's.

Sounds from the crowd grew louder. The light broadened and the image showed Hillary standing next to the wizard. The image changed. The crowd grew silent as everyone watched Hillary and Haggerwolf enter the Gorlon's lair, part of Hillary's first adventure in Gabendoor.

Fernbark touched his finger next. The image changed again. Murmurs and gasps changed to cheers and handclaps as the crowd watched the new scene. Fernbark, Windslow and Hillary struggled against a time mist from their second adventure.

Larkstone's hand shook as he added his touch. The blue image showed him battling thinkabees during Windslow's third adventure in Gabendoor.

The three sisters reached out their fingers together. The image showed them laughing, giggling and making funny faces.

As everyone watched the images, Windslow felt Molly's hand change. Held in his, her hand grew. Her skin softened. Windslow looked away from the images and looked at Molly. Windslow blinked. It wasn't Molly who stood next to him. He held the hand of a girl his own age. She was as tall as he was. Her sleek black hair reached to her shoulders. She looked at him and smiled. Windslow thought she was the most beautiful girl he had ever seen. He stared into her eyes. He blinked again. Molly's face, looked back at him. "You missing all a good parts. Now it your turn," she said and looked away.

Windslow looked at the stone. When he touched his finger to the amber gem, it felt warm. Now balanced by eight fingers, Hillary no longer needed to hold the edges. The crowd cheered as they watched a new scene from past adventures of the Children of the Wind.

The image blinked out. The beam of blue light narrowed and soared to the clouds. The beam didn't slice through the clouds as Windslow thought it might. The top of the beam spread, bathing the dark and angry clouds in silvery blue.

The ground shook. People screamed. The sounds of stone clattering against stone drew everyone's attention to the temple. Remnants of the obelisks swirled in a tight spiral of stone and dust. The top of the spiral twisted to the hole in the sky. When it touched the blackness the bottom drew up, sucked into the void.

The temple shook again. The top layer of stones separated and moved. They tipped on edge and rolled down one level.

In the sky, blue lightning crackled across the hole, from one side to another. After each flash, the strands of lightning stayed, as if stitching up the hole. Again the ground shook. More blocks tumbled. Blocks that reached the ground, moved themselves, lining up against the others, as if moved by master stonecutters. When the stones stopped moving, Aberratia no longer stood as a stepped pyramid. The stones formed a new plaza, one layer of stones high. Around the outer edge, other stones formed a wall, to border the flat expanse. A small section of the wall broke into smaller stones. They moved to form an opening and set of steps.

Overhead, the strands of blue, drew themselves in, closing the gap Dreadlore had opened. The clouds settled and thinned, turning shades of silver white and faint gray. Sunshine lit them from above.

The blue light from the Star Stone spread farther bathing every thing and everyone in its glow. The air in the center of the plaza shimmered. A solid form emerged.

"It can't be," Dreadlore said. "It's the Secret Library."

Someone in the crowd shouted out, "The Library!"

Other voices joined in. "The Library. The Secret Library. It's here."

Windslow looked at Molly. "Is it really?"

"Yes," she said.

Her look, and the way she answered, worried Windslow. Her head slowly moved up and down with each breath. Each breath seemed long and drawn out. Each blink of her eyes, made him worry she might not open them again.

People screamed again. The grass drew back forming a clear path made of flagstones that began at the plaza steps. More grass pulled away. The path grew in length, extending itself straight toward the crowd. Bodies pushed and shoved as they quickly made room. When the path reached Dreadlore, it stopped.

"Get these chains off me!" Dreadlore yelled at the crowd. "I need to go in the Library. There are books in there. There might still be magic in there. I can still save everyone!"

The crowd pushed back even farther.

The blue glow shrank back into the Star Stone. Windslow looked at his friends, not sure what to do. He jumped like everyone else when the doors to the Secret Library slammed open. Not coming from the stone, a new light formed at the doorway. The blue changed to multi-colored hues.

Dreadlore screamed. An aura formed around him, its colors and hues matching the light from the Library's door. The aura changed to wisps of colored magic that circled around Dreadlore's body. He stood stiff and silent, frozen in time. His clothes turned to cream colored parchment with text in black ink. The wisps swirled again. Hands, feet, face and hair, everything that was the man Dreadlore, was now paper.

A leather book cover appeared at Dreadlore's feet. A sheet of parchment peeled itself from Dreadlore's sleeve. The page floated to the book to form its first page. Another sheet pulled away, then another. The flurry of parchment sheets, churned and tumbled, mixing in the air like a swirl of leaves in a fall wind. Pages left the swirl and added themselves to the book. In moments, the air was empty. The book was filled. Dreadlore was gone.

The cover slowly closed and the book rose, hovering over the path. It began to spin, slowly at first, and then so rapid it became a blur. The spinning book floated up and over Windslow's head. Moving slowly, it entered the blue light from the Star Stone and disappeared.

"I not be first," Nelly said. She removed her finger from the Stone and stepped back. "You all my worst friends."

"I always a middle one," Tillie said. Her hand dropped and she moved beside Nelly. "I almost going to cry."

Windslow had to let go of Molly's hand to wipe his face. Tears ran down his face and dripped off his chin. Before he reached for Molly's hand, he wiped his own hand dry on his shirt. When he put his hand back down, Molly wouldn't hold it. She stood up on her tiptoes and gave him a kiss on the cheek.

"Molly, I... I..."

"Shush," she said. "You still my best-ist boyfriend. You always be that."

Windslow put his arm around her, pulled her tight and kissed the top of her head.

Molly eased herself from his hold and moved to Hillary. They managed a one arm hug that included sobs and tears from both of them.

"Why?" Hillary asked.

"It always supposed to be this way," Molly answered. "We come here a long time a go to help all a people with magic. That job done. Now either we go *poof* or we go home. You and Windso make everything right so we get a go home, not *poof*. It very nice gift you give to us."

Molly moved to the wizards, giving each a kiss. All eyes were wet from tears. People in the crowd wiped at faces or openly cried.

The three girls stood side by side, with arms around each other's shoulders. The blue light from the Stone winked out. New, soft silver light spread around the three Sallyforth sisters. The aged look from their encounter with Dreadlore's magic faded. The girls stood straight, their faces youthful, their eyes bright and sparkling. All three smiled.

Molly pointed her fingers at the doors to the Secret Library. The doors shut.

Tillie stretched out her hand and wiggled her fingers. Bright colored flowers sprang up, bordering the path. More flowers appeared in gardens around the plaza.

"I not doing nothing," Nelly said and pointed. Deep green shrubs, clipped and trimmed to resemble animals, dotted the lawn. A small stone fountain appeared. Carved from cream-colored stone, a sculpture of three wizards stood in the crystal water.

Hillary sniffed and wiped her nose. "It's you three," she said to her wizard friends.

Windslow blinked several times, both because of his tears and because the three triplets looked out of focus. Specks of silver mixed into the light, and sparkled as the clouds moved away from the sun. The sparkling increased, making it harder to see the sisters. The flecks of glitter joined together, forming marble-sized, silver spheres. Drawing from the sun, the silver spheres grew so bright, Windslow had to squint his eyes to keep watching them. He drew in a sharp breath when the tiny stars launched skyward. Behind them trailed streaks of silver.

When they moved out of sight, Windslow realized he had been holding his breath. He let it out with a heavy sigh, looked down at the grass and wiped his sleeve across his face. He could hear Hillary and Fernbark crying. Haggerwolf had the hiccups, and repeatedly blew his nose. Windslow didn't want to look at any of them. He knew if he did, he'd start crying again himself.

Larkstone was the first to speak. "How long do we need to hold the stone?" he asked.

Windslow squeezed his eyes tight to push out tears. He looked at his sister when he opened them.

"I don't know," she said.

"Without the sisters' fingers, it should fall over," Windslow said. He cautiously drew his hand back. Nothing happened.

Hillary and the wizards did the same. The Star Stone did not fall, but did move, slowly rotating. Its polished surface dulled. Its color seemed to fade. As they all watched, the faceted gem called the Star Stone turned to amber sand. And like grains in an hourglass, a ribbon of sand fell from its bottom. When the last grain of sand fell, the small mound of amber vanished.

"Is it over?" Hillary asked, looking at Haggerwolf.

The elder wizard nodded. "It is. Gabendoor is safe. But it seems we paid a heavy price."

"The doors won't open. They're locked," someone yelled.

Windslow, his sister and the wizards moved to the path and walked toward the library.

"It's beautiful here," Hillary said. "The flowers smell wonderful. It's so different now."

"They might want to change the name," Windslow said. "I don't think Heart-Thorn forest fits anymore."

"In a way it does fit," Fernbark said as they neared the doors to the library. "The heart represents the love we have for those sisters and the time they spent with us. The thorn represents the pain of having to say goodbye."

"The doors *are* locked," Windslow said as he pulled on the handles of the large wooden doors. "And I don't see a key hole or any kind of a latch."

"That is because you are not the one to open it," a voice said from behind them.

"Maxwell and Faith," Hillary called out.

"Hi, there," Windslow said. He bent down and petted the shelterhund. Windslow looked up and saw that the wizards had backed away. "Don't worry," Windslow said. "They're really gentle." Windslow smiled and let the beast take his whole hand in its mouth.

"Larkstone, Haggerwolf, Fernbark, come here," Hillary

said. “I would like you to meet our friends, Maxwell and Faith. They live in the Charm Mist Mountains. Maxwell and Faith gave us all that food for Eldervale.”

Windslow didn’t know what to think when the three wizards bowed down and kept their heads lowered.

“Oh, stand up,” Faith said. “That tradition went away a thousand years ago.”

“What tradition?” Windslow asked. “Do you all know each other or something?”

“None of that is important,” Maxwell said. “It’s time for the people to discover the joys of their library.”

“The doors are locked,” Windslow said.

Hillary looked at Faith. “You said we weren’t the ones to open it? Who is?”

Faith answered. “It shall be a child.” She turned around and looked at the crowd of people.

A young girl stood pressed against her mother. Her face smudged and hair pulled into a ponytail, she held her arms around her mother’s hips and rested the side of her head on her mother’s waist. The girl smiled.

“Would you like to open it?” Faith asked.

The girls face brightened. Her smile changed to a grin and she nodded her head.

“All you need to do is pull on the handle,” Maxwell said.

Windslow, Hillary and the wizards stepped back. The girl walked past them, grabbed the handle and pulled. The wooden doors opened.

Gasps filled the air as people from the crowd moved forward. Faith took her brother’s hand and motioned to the girl’s mother.

Hand in hand, the girl and her mother entered the library.

Faith motioned again. Windslow grabbed his sister's hand and followed. Behind them came the wizards.

Maxwell turned to the crowd. "You are all welcome. It belongs to you." He and his sister entered the library.

ᘐᘑ

Everyone marveled at the rows and shelves of books. Windslow had expected books about magic and spells. Instead, he found sections on science, history, mathematics. There were sections for children, sections marked adventure. He showed Hillary the small section he found labeled "The Children of the Wind." He was about to look at one of the books when he yawned and his vision blurred for an instant. When he looked at Hillary, she yawned too.

"You'll be dream-slipping very soon," Faith told them. "You need to say your goodbyes."

"We won't be dream-slipping anymore, will we?" Hillary asked.

Faith shook her head.

Windslow and Hillary rushed to find the wizards. Their goodbye was filled with more tears, hugs and promises to never forget one another. Windslow yawned in the middle of thanking Maxwell. Maxwell blurred. Windslow turned to look at the wizards. As he turned his head, books, bookcases and people faded, replaced by the black of space, planets and stars.

He flew toward Cassiopeia. To the left of the constellation he saw three formations of stars brighter than any others around them. Somehow, he knew the three constellations were the Maiden, the Daughter and the Child. Ahead of him, a blue green planet welcomed him. Windslow's eyes grew heavy and he closed them to finish his last dream-slip.

28: Homecoming

It was Bill's shouting that woke them both up.

Hillary shouted back when she heard knocking on her bedroom door "It's okay. Open it!"

Bill poked his head into her room. "The hospital just called. Your mom's awake. She's asking for us. Hurry up and get ready."

Before Hillary could ask any questions, the door shut. She tossed back her covers, grabbed her robe and headed for the bathroom.

She skipped taking a shower, did the best she could with her makeup, and hurried back to her room to dress. When she passed Windslow in the hallway, she asked him what was going on. He said he didn't know and told her he had to get to the bathroom.

*ഇ൬

Bill drove a little fast on the way to the hospital, but Windslow didn't say anything. He and his sister both asked their dad more questions. The answer was always the same. He didn't know.

Hillary pushed Windslow's chair when they got to the hospital. Bill held the doors open and walked quickly ahead to catch an elevator for them.

Outside Trish's room, they all stopped and tried to calm their nerves. Bill walked in first.

"Finally!" Trish called. "I thought you'd never get here." She sat up in bed and held her arms out. "I have missed you guys so much."

Hillary tapped her foot as she waited for her dad to finish his hug. Windslow pushed his wheelchair as close as he could to his mother's bed.

"Come on, Dad," Windslow finally said.

Bill gave Trish another kiss before standing up. Hillary bounced on the bed and wrapped her arms around her mom.

"I have room for more," Trish said and slid her feet over the edge of the bed so she could hug Windslow too.

"Aren't you supposed to stay lying down?" Windslow asked.

"Oh, I'm supposed to do a lot of things. But you know your mother," she said and winked. "You two did it," Trish said. She grabbed both their arms and gave them a little shake. "I knew you could."

"Did what?" Bill asked.

"They won their soccer game," Trish said and gave both Windslow and Hillary another wink. "Hillary made a great kick and Windslow took care of strategy. This is my winning team."

"So your memory is back? Bill asked. "What do you remember?"

"Oh," Trish said and pushed herself back against her pillows. "The accident. I remember that. I remember being worried about Windslow and Hillary. Bill, I remember you visiting me almost every day, even when you needed a shower."

Both Hillary and Windslow laughed.

I remember Mrs. Follen coming to talk with me and I remember her son is very cute. So, how's that going?" Trish asked looking at Hillary.

"He asked me to the homecoming dance," Hillary said. "That's how it's going."

"Oh, oh," Trish said. "That means I need to get out of here. We have shopping to do, appointments to make."

"Oh, Mom," Hillary said and gave her mother another hug. "It's so good to have you back."

"And you, young man," Trish said, turning to Windslow. "You'll need a new suit. We'll look at some corsages. Hm... what else. Bill, do you have a piece of paper and a pen. We should start a list."

"I might need shoes too," Windslow said. "And I want a really cool tie. Maybe... maybe..." Windslow lowered his head. "Oh, I forgot. I'm not going to the dance."

"Why not?" Bill asked.

Windslow didn't look up. "I think the Sallyforth sisters moved out of town or something."

"What?" Bill said. "I just talked to their mother yesterday. She didn't say anything."

"Um..." Hillary stammered. "I only think a few people know." She glanced at her brother.

"Yah," Windslow said. "They're keeping it quiet."

"Oh that's nonsense," Trish said. "Bill, I could really use a cup of real coffee. All they let me have was decaf. Would you be a dear and go get me a cup of regular coffee?"

"You got it," Bill said and headed out the door.

Trish sighed and looked at Windslow and Hillary. "I know it's hard," she said. "When I was your age and left Gabendoor for the last time, I was devastated. That's why I had Haggerwolf cast a memory block. That was one of the dumbest things I ever did. I'm so glad you two helped me break it. My memories are bitter-sweet, but I cherish them."

"You know what happened?" Hillary asked.

Trish nodded. "I was trapped in a dream-slip because Dreadlore moved the stars. I could catch little bits of what was happening in both worlds. Last night I had two visitors. They pulled some strings so I could see everything that happened on Gabendoor."

"Two visitors?" Hillary asked. "Who?"

"Maxwell and Faith," Trish answered.

Hillary and Windslow stared at each other.

"Your mouths are open," Trish said and laughed. "Windslow, honey, your dance date may still be on."

"But the sisters are gone. I think they turned back into constellations," Windslow said.

Trish leaned over and patted his knee. "They aren't gone. They went home. They were overdue. It was supposed to happen. They aren't dead or anything. Maybe they can take a short vacation."

"Oh, I'm so glad I thought they were..." Hillary didn't finish her sentence. "But still," she said, "things just won't be the same."

"No they won't," Trish said. "But, most things change. That's part of life."

"Here's your coffee." Holding a cup out in front of him, Bill stepped in the room. "Hillary and Windslow, I think maybe you need a cup too. I think you're both still half-asleep. Look who I found waiting for you in the cafeteria."

Windslow's jaw dropped. He took a quick look at his sister. Her mouth was open too.

"Molly," Trish said, breaking the silence. "You changed your hair. It makes you look so *different*. I love the *new look*."

"Oh, yah," Windslow said. "You look great."

Windslow couldn't stop staring. Molly looked like she had for that one instant when he held her hand back on Gabendoor. Her hair, no longer black and spiky, framed her face. She stood as tall as Hillary and her simple dress didn't hide a figure that made his heart beat faster.

"Ouch," he said when Hillary jabbed him with her elbow

"Word choice," little brother.

"Oh," Windslow said. "I mean you look cool."

Hillary elbowed him again.

"Um... really great. Fantastic and... and... really good."

"I think you look fabulous," Trish said and patted the bed. "Come sit."

Windslow pulled his head away when Hillary reached out and used her hand to gently push up on his chin. Windslow scowled at his sister, but closed his mouth.

"We are moving," Molly said after she sat down. "But not until after the dance. Nothing would stop my sisters and me from our first date, with our *best-ist* boyfriend."

She reached over and put her hand on Windslow's shoulder. When her fingers stroked along the skin on his neck it made him shiver.

"All three of you are here?" Windslow asked.

"Of course," a voice said from the doorway.

Everyone but Molly turned to look.

"Wow," Windslow said, louder than he intended. "Hi, Tillie."

"You're blocking the door," another voice said.

Tillie moved aside to make room for Nelly.

"Whoa," Windslow said.

Hillary elbowed him again.

"I mean, cool. I mean... I mean..." Windslow stammered. "You're all... You're all really... I mean..."

The sisters laughed.

Molly looked up at Hillary. "Will you help him with his vocabulary?"

"I will," Hillary said. "I have the feeling he will need more than a couple lessons before the dance."

From behind her back, Nelly held out a package wrapped in brown paper and tied with a simple white string. She passed it to Tillie.

"It's time for us to go," Molly said and stood. "We won't be seeing you at school, but we can talk on the phone and we could get together next weekend, if you like."

"Yah," Windslow said nodding his head. "I'll call. I'll call you later today and uh... Friday? Saturday? We have a date?"

Molly leaned over and kissed Windslow on the cheek. Windslow felt his face flush. He was too embarrassed to look at his Mom or Dad.

"This is for both of you," Molly said. She took the package from Tillie and handed it to Windslow. "We need to go. Mom is waiting for us in the car."

"Wait," Hillary said when Molly stood in the doorway. "What's in the package?"

Without turning, Molly answered from the hallway. "It's a book. I thought you and Windslow might enjoy it."

꧁ The End ꧂

The Secret Books of Gabendoor.

Book 1, *The Book of Second Chances*

If you were twelve years old, in a wheelchair, and found a magic Book of Second Chances what would you do? Would you use it to walk again or to save a distant world? That's the choice Windslow and Hillary face when they dream-slip to the world of Gabendoor each night and battle the evil wizard Fistlock and his shadow beasties --like the Trundle-wraith that lurks under beds or the Tellagain, that makes old men repeat the same story over and over.With an odd assortment of companions and three colorful wizards, Hillary and Windslow struggle to solve the book's mysteries that face them on Earth every day and on Gabendoor every night.

Book 2, The Book of Broken Promises

Hillary and Windslow return to Gabendoor to save it from the wizard Gristle-tooth and his time-mists.

His spirit is free and his time-mists will end all life. Magic helps Hillary and Windslow dream-slip back to Gabendoor to battle the wizard Gristle-tooth and his assistant, Aghasta, for *The Book of Broken Promises.* No one understands the secrets in the book or which promised to keep and which to break. One wrong choice and the Book will grant Gristle-tooth's promise to destroy everything.

Join the Children of the Summer Wind on their second adventure in Gabendoor along with their three wizard friends and the Sallyforth triplets. Dream-slip across time and space to the world of Gabendoor.

Continue the incredible saga that began in *The Book of Second Chances.*

Book 4, The Book of Library Secrets

Just who are the Sallyforth triplets? In their most dangerous adventure yet, Windslow and Hillary must stop the wizard, Dreadlore, before someone dies.

Whoever solves the ancient riddle of Gabendoor will learn the location of the Secret Library and its magic

books. Whoever learns the secret of the mysterious ratStone will control the stars. The books and the magic stone, both hold the power to destroy Gabendoor and to save Gabendoor. Using either one will mean death for Hillary, Windslow, or one of their companions. In their most dangerous adventure yet, the Children of the Wind race against time and the evil wizard Dreadlore. They must succeed. Back on Earth, their mother's life depends on what they do in Gabendooor.

www.gabendoor.com

Amarath, The Birth of Magic

The Ghost of the Keepers Monk is part legend, part mystery. It holds two of three mysterious stones that control all magic. The war lord, Califae, controls the third and most powerful stone. He's using it to help him conquer all of Amarath.

Daran, a teenager who calls himself Rat Boy to shield his real identity, unravels the ghost's secrets, and is "adopted" by intelligence in the Monk's two stones. The stones control events and pit an unwilling Daran against Califae. The stones' first task for Daran's alternate identity is a rescue, but there's a problem. The princess he's sent to rescue, despises Rat Boy but dreams of a romance with Daran, not knowing they're the same person.

When Daran tries to sort things out, the magic further complicates his life, manipulating him into a third identity and deeper into the politics of the growing war. Daran wants to resume his quiet life as Rat Boy, but the magic stones of Amarath have other plans.

Biography

J. Michael Blumer is a long time storyteller who finally found time to become a writer thanks to encouragement from his family. Long ago, his children dubbed him an "alternative life form" because of his "creative" parenting techniques, such as making them sing their arguments. He's married to a second grade school teacher which explains why his marriage has lasted so long. His wife knows just how to handle him. Mike lives in Stillwater, Minnesota with his wife Jane, and the wildlife that wanders through their backyard. Read more about the world of Gabendoor at www.gabendoor.com. :)